THE FALL

Anna Kronberg Book 3

ANNELIE WENDEBERG

Cover: Nuno Moreira

Editing: Tom Welch

Bonus material at the end of this book:
Preview of *The Journey* - Anna Kronberg Book 4

The World of Anna Kronberg

Get pre-publication access to the

newest Anna Kronberg books:

THE FALL

Anna Kronberg Book 3

Two Men

❧

And soon the rotting corpses tainted the air and poisoned the water supply, and the stench was so overwhelming that hardly one in several thousand was in a position to flee the remains of the Tartar army.

Gabrielle De' Mussi, 1348, on the Siege of Caffa

For this moment, this one moment, we are together. I press you to me. Come, pain, feed on me. Bury your fangs in my flesh. Tear me asunder. I sob, I sob.

Virginia Woolf

Wednesday Night, October 22nd, 1890

Cold metal pressed my head hard against the mattress. Two sharp clicks and the scents of gun oil sent my heart jumping out my throat. The muzzle was flush against my temple. If fired, the bullet would rip straight through my brain, driving blood and nerve tissue through the mattress and down onto the floor. If the gun were tilted just a little, the bullet would circle inside my skull, leaving a furrow in the bone and pulp in its wake.

I don't know why those were my first thoughts. What does one normally think when faced with imminent death?

'Get up,' a male voice cut through the dark. 'Slowly.'

I opened my eyes.

'Sit over there,' he rasped, waving a bullseye lantern toward the table. I rose and shuffled over to a chair. My knees felt like water. I sat and the backrest squeaked in protest.

A match was struck, illuminating a face chiselled in hardwood, cracked by tension and age. Sulphur hung in the air. A man of approximately fifty years sat across from me. He held the match to a candle, and cast the room into unsteady light.

He sat back and stared at me, waiting. Waves of goosebumps rolled over my skin. He seemed to be waiting for me to speak, to ask what he was doing here, and why he was holding me at gunpoint. But I had no words.

'You are good at hiding,' he said.

Not good enough, though. I swallowed. Would I beg at some point? Should I, even? Probably not. It was more likely that a word — a wrong word — would end my life in an instant.

Suddenly, my ears picked up a sound. Nearly inaudible. I tried to analyse it, play it back in my head to understand what had caused it, what it meant. It wasn't one of the noises an old house made when the wind leant into it.

The man interrupted my thoughts. 'Last spring, a group of physicians was captured by the police and led to trial. Only two months later, they found their end at the gallows.'

I remembered that day. I'd sat on this very same chair and read about the hanging of sixteen medical men along with the superintendent of Broadmoor Lunatic Asylum and four of his guards. All convicted of murder and manslaughter. And I still remember the fear that had crept in when I realised that not one of the articles reported on the experiments these men have performed on abducted paupers. That same fear raised its head, and I knew what the noise behind me meant: the floorboards had produced a lone pop. The tiny hairs on my neck rose in response. As though to assess the danger lurking there.

'All but one,' the man interrupted.

My neck had begun to ache. There was another noise, behind me and very close: the soft hiss of air through nostrils.

Shock widened my senses with a snap. Was the man behind me a backup? Someone to break my neck, if needed? I coughed, flicked my gaze toward the window and back again. For a short moment, I shut my eyes, examining the reflection burned into my mind: the small prick of candlelight, the table, the man sitting, myself in a nightgown, and a tall, slender figure behind me. I opened my eyes, hoping the behaviour of the man facing me would tell me more about the other.

'Only Dr Anton Kronberg made his escape. He even overpowered Mr Sherlock Holmes. Odd, isn't it.'

My fingertips grew ice cold. The Club! Holmes had given this dubious title to the group of physicians that tested deadly bacteria on workhouse inmates. It had taken us months to round them up. Yet we were unable to identify the head of the organisation who had caused so much suffering and death. Ever since my escape to the Downs, I feared he would find me and take revenge. I eyed the man in front of me, wondering why he talked to me at all, and what he planned to do to me before pulling the trigger.

'Imagine my surprise when I finally found Anton Kronberg. He lives in a small village in Germany. Scrapes by as a carpenter.' A smile tugged at the man's face.

I couldn't breathe.

'The man has a single child. A daughter. But you know

that of course.' Again that half smile. 'Tell me, *Doctor* Anna Kronberg, what shall I do with you now?'

'What have you done to my father?'

He flashed a row of yellowed teeth. I made an effort to slow my frantic heart, and stop my imagination from showing me the corpse of my father. I forced my senses outward, to the man behind me. He seemed calm. No hitch in his breathing, no quickening. All was according to plan, it appeared.

'You do say rather little,' the man in front of me said.

'You have not asked a single question,' I croaked.

No audible reaction from the man behind. The man facing me smiled a thin line and fingered his gun. His eyes were glued to my face, as mine flicked between his and the weapon's hammer. He repeatedly pulled and released it. *Click-click. Click-click.*

'Will you admit to these accusations?' *Click-click.*

'Your accusations must have escaped my notice.'

The clicking stopped. His eyes flicked sideways and back at me again, as though he wanted to check with the other man, but could not reveal that man's presence by looking at him directly. Behind me, I heard a faint smack. It made me think of wet lips being pulled apart. Was he smiling? For a heartbeat, I had the insane thought it was Holmes.

'Do I amuse you?' asked the man in front of me. *Click-click. Click-click.* He had both elbows leisurely propped on his thighs, his weapon held loosely in his right hand. The lantern at his feet seemed to illuminate only the triangle of knees, hands, and gun. The light reflecting off the hammer's silvery tip — polished by repeated toying — stung my eyes.

'I find you remarkable unfunny,' I answered.

He waited. We both did. And then I made a mistake. 'What does a man from the military want from me?' It was only a guess based on the few things I had seen: how he moved, how he expected instant obedience, how he held the revolver, his physique.

'What do you know?' he snapped, just before noticing that he, too, had made a mistake.

'You broke into my cottage to press a gun to my head and tell me things I already know. There is a man behind me who is very calm, approximately six feet tall, and rather lean. I'm guessing that he is the brain of this operation, while you are merely the brute.'

There was no time to flinch before his fist hit my temple.

~

WHISPERS TICKLED MY CONSCIOUSNESS. I heard a groan; it came from inside my chest. My head thrummed, and blue flashes of light flickered across the inside of my eyelids. I found myself on my mattress, my hands bound across my stomach. I inhaled a slow breath, and the whispering stopped. Blinking, I turned my head. Two men sat at the table, and looked at me as though expecting to be served tea and biscuits, plus the latest gossip.

'Funny,' I said.

The taller of the two pulled up his eyebrows. 'You do realise that having seen my face diminishes your chances of survival?'

I said nothing.

'Shall we continue, then? How did you escape? And how the deuce did *you* overpower Mr Holmes?'

Oh, well. How indeed could a woman of my statue knock out a man who was said to never have lost a fist fight? I almost laughed. My throat tightened as I thought back to the day Holmes and I went separate ways. I certainly wouldn't explain the details to those two men. Or anyone for that matter. I cleared my sticky that and said, 'It was rather simple. I kissed him.'

The tall man's nostrils flared. He threw back his head and barked a laugh. A heartbeat later, he recovered from the emotional outbreak. Turning to the other man he said, 'Colonel, what about a drop of tea?'

At once, the Colonel stood and made for my kitchen. I heard a match being struck, the soft hiss of the oil lamp followed by the clonking of earthenware. The hearth was still hot. I used it to get a little warmth into the cottage during chilly autumn nights. In winter, I would have used the fireplace, too. But it seemed that there wouldn't be a winter for me here.

More wood was thrown onto the embers. The tall man observed me silently, and I realised he had come to decide whether I should be shot immediately or maybe a little later.

While we waited for the tea, he said, 'We learned a few things about you, Dr Kronberg. But there are gaps I'd like filled.' He approached, bent over me, grabbed my neck, and pulled me up into a sitting position. Casually, he sat on the mattress next to me. 'You lived in London disguised as a male medical doctor for four years. You must have met Mr Holmes over the course of summer or autumn 1889, is that correct?'

I nodded, knowing my trembling chin betrayed my shock.

'A little more information would help extend your lifespan.'

I felt the blood drain from my face and drop to my toes. 'I met Mr Holmes at Hampton Water Treatment Works in the summer of last year. A cholera victim had been found floating in the water and Scotland Yard wanted us to provide expert opinions. Mr Holmes saw through my disguise, but decided not to report me to the police. The corpse bore signs of abduction and maltreatment, but the evidence was weak and the Yard did not think it worth investigating.'

I looked up at him. He was waiting for me to continue. And so I did, weaving lies and facts into one, 'There was very little to go on, and Mr Holmes soon lost interest in the case. Or so I believed. Meanwhile, I did research on tetanus at Guy's and later visited Robert Koch's laboratory in Berlin. I was able to obtain tetanus germs in pure culture; it was a sensation, and the papers reported it widely. You are aware of this, of course.'

He dipped his head and fraction, and I continued. 'Only a few days later, Dr Gregory Stark invited me to give a presentation at Cambridge Medical School and I came into contact with all members of what Mr Holmes later called the *Club*.'

'How charming.'

'I knew it couldn't have been Bowden,' I said. 'You were the man at the centre.' Holmes and I had believed that Dr Bowden was the head of the Club. Doubts about the importance of his role surfaced only at the very end of our investigation. But we could prove nothing and had no clue who the leader might've been.

'I am merely a bystander,' the man said with a wink.

My skin crawled. 'The bystander who pulls the strings?'

He said nothing for a long moment. Just looked at me as though he wasn't quite sure what to ask next. I jumped when he leant closer. He pulled a blanket over my shoulders and smiled. It made me think of how I killed my hens: I calmed them, caressed their heads and backs until they were entirely unsuspecting. And then I cut their head off.

'You infiltrated the Club and brought them down with the help of Mr Holmes,' he said.

I forced my eyes to look into his and remain steady. 'Not quite, although in hindsight, even I could possibly interpret it as such.'

He leant back a little, cocked his head, and nodded at me to continue.

And so I did. 'Just after I returned from Berlin I was mugged and badly injured. I needed a surgeon, but whom could I have asked? Certainly not my colleagues. So I told a friend to find Dr Watson, who — like Holmes — knew my secret. That is how I met Holmes again, and only two days later he told me about his suspicions — that someone had been conducting medical experiments on paupers in Broadmoor Lunatic Asylum. I thought he was out of his mind.'

The man turned to his companion, and I got the impression that he grew impatient. My time was running out.

'I started working at London Medical School, developing vaccines against tetanus. We also had the prospect of a cholera vaccine. But we knew that wouldn't come without sacrifices.' Images of a dying woman invaded my mind. I shoved them away. 'Holmes kept insisting that what I was doing was wrong and I should instead help him arrest my colleagues.'

'Mr Holmes would never have asked you for your assistance. You are a liar, my dear,' he declared.

For once a reaction I had anticipated. 'You are correct. He would have never asked such a thing from just anyone.' I paused. It sickened me what I had to say next. 'But Holmes and I are made of the same material. He was fascinated by a woman as intelligent as he and equally strong-willed. And I fell for him because I had never met such an observant and sharp man in my life. That is the reason I saved his life in Broadmoor and the reason he set me free.' And I remembered the kiss, that singular kiss, and turned my gaze away to look out of the small window where night slowly retreated and the sky paled to greet the new day. Would I see the sun? Maybe it did not matter much. I had seen it many times already.

I gazed back at the man and said, 'I know you want something from me, or you would not have given me the time to utter a single word. If you allow me to make a guess — you need a bacteriologist to continue your work. I am your first choice, but you do not trust me. Naturally.'

He smiled again. It was worse than a gun pressed to my head. 'No, I do not trust you in the least. And yes, I require the services of a bacteriologist. Although you are the best to be found in England, you are also the one bearing the greatest risk. I need to be certain I have your loyalty.'

What could I possibly offer? My life? He already had it in his hands.

'Of course, you could choose to be shot right away. But decide quickly now, or I will do it for you.'

I gazed down at my hands, anticipating the moment I would drive a blade into the man's throat. Slowly, I let go of all the air in my lungs. 'Am I to isolate pathogens for warfare?'

Another warm smile.

'You remind me of him,' I whispered. His stunned expression opened a wide spectrum of possibilities for me. He blinked the shock away so quickly, that I wasn't sure I had even seen it.

'You have my loyalty,' I answered.

All I got as a response was a scant nod. 'Drink your tea,' he said, and filled my cup.

Finally I noticed the peculiar situation — the brute had made tea, the brain served it. I gazed at the two men. 'What did you put in it?'

'Chloral,' the taller answered lightly.

'Ah,' I exhaled. 'How much?'

'A few drops.'

I nodded and took the cup. The harmless-looking tea produced circular ripples just before I tipped it into my mouth. The brew carried a peculiar sting. 'You never introduced yourself,' I noted.

'My apologies. This is my friend and trustworthy

companion Colonel Sebastian Moran, and I am Professor James Moriarty.'

Slowly, my surroundings unhinged. I looked at the window which seemed unnaturally far off. Had it not been rectangular a few minutes ago?

'I forgot to mention a small detail,' said Professor Moriarty, his voice reverberating in my skull, words melting into one another. 'By the time you regain consciousness, your father will be my hostage. Should you do anything that could jeopardise our work or my safety, he will die immediately and, I must say, rather painfully.'

The world tipped and the table approached with shocking speed.

Day 1

✥✥✥

Nausea hit as I opened my eyes. The ceiling wafted from left to right. The taste of vomit bit my tongue. I touched my face that felt like ants had built a nest under my skin. Blinking, I looked around. The nightgown I wore was unfamiliar, as was the room and the bed I was in. I had no recollection of how I had got here.

My throat tightened. I couldn't breathe.

I slapped my cheeks, rubbed my eyes, and slowly, memories trickled back. I remembered two names. Professor James Moriarty, Colonel Sebastian Moran. I had never heard of them before...was it...yesterday?

The last words Moriarty said — before the poison swallowed me — hit me like a hammer. My father was a hostage! My breath came in bursts. I pushed myself upright, fighting to stay conscious. Bile welled up, and I forced it back down. Reality seemed to crack. I could almost see fissures forming around me. Shaking, I sank back onto the bed.

I threw an arm over my face and squeezed a sob into my sleeve. Part of my mind began puzzling over a way to fix this. Fix everything. But most of me was frozen in shock.

This won't do. Pull yourself together! I sat up, and found a glass on the nightstand. A cautious sniff told me it was probably only water. I drank it all and it helped clear my head a bit. I took deep breaths. In and out. My heart wouldn't calm, but my mind slowly did. My goals were clear: save my father, foil Moriarty's plans. But how would I get there? Could I even? Yes. I would and I could, because there was no other way.

Although I wanted all this to happen at once, I knew I needed patience. Patience to find my father and free him. And then I would find the weakness in Moriarty's plan. The keystone that, once extracted, would make the vault crumple.

Good. A plan always made me feel better. I let my eyes sweep the room. There was only one word to describe this place: luxurious. Oddly, the two windows lacked bars. I rose and took a few steps toward the nearest one. A timid knock stopped me.

Hastily, I sat back down and pulled the blanket over my legs. 'Yes?'

A short woman stepped in, curtsied, and said, 'Are you feeling a little better, Miss?'

'Yes, thank you. Who are you?'

'I am Gooding. Your personal maid, Miss.'

'You are jesting,' I blurted out. She blushed, and took a step back. 'My apologies, I'm not used to...all this. Can you tell me what time it is, Miss Gooding?'

'It is quarter past five in the evening. May I help you get ready for supper, Miss?'

'I'm not sure I can eat yet.'

'Would you like to wash?'

I nodded.

'Very good. I will bring warm water and towels in a moment.' She curtsied again, and shut the door. I waited for the sound of a key in a lock, but it didn't come.

Had I dreamt my own abduction? What a stupid thought. I shook my head and instantly regretted it. My brain was sloshing around in my skull. I doubled over, gulped air until I felt better, and walked back to the window.

There was a large, well-tended garden two storeys down. Maple trees waved red and golden foliage at the evening sun. Old ivy scaled the wall of this side of the house. An escape route, easily laid out. I began to doubt my sanity.

The maid returned, carrying an ewer, a towel, and a small package. She placed everything next to the washstand and looked at me inquiringly. Did I need anything else? I searched my sluggish mind. 'Can you tell me where I am?'

'Why Miss, this is Professor Moriarty's house,' she answered, rather puzzled.

I nodded, instantly feeling sicker. 'Could you show me where my clothes are?'

She rushed to a wardrobe that had escaped my notice, despite its size. She opened both doors, revealing several dresses. None of them were mine.

After she'd left I tottered around in the room, trying to make sense of what I saw. The only thing there that belonged to me was myself. Even my clothes had been taken away. No doubt this had been done on purpose. But why? To leave me feeling even more vulnerable?

My bare feet sank deep into the heavy rug, the soft wool snug between my toes. Beneath it, the floorboards creaked. The bed was large, and its cherry wood frame supported an embroidered cotton canopy. My gilded cage.

Then I discovered the letter. Night-blue handwriting rolled over the heavy paper.

DEAR DR KRONBERG.

I hope you are feeling better. My apologies for the inconvenience of the chloral. I trust you have noticed the comforts offered you, but I do hope these will not lead you to incorrect assumptions. Any attempt you should make to leave the premises would be futile. The dogs know your scent and would tear you to pieces. My steward will accompany you everywhere, except of course into your private room. He reports to me immediately and has my full trust. Should you disappear for but a moment, your father will lose his left hand. A second disappearance will result in the loss of his right hand. A third will cost him his head. I sincerely hope this will not spoil your stay in my humble home.

Yours,

Professor James Moriarty.

PS: I shall be delighted to meet with you tomorrow at supper time.

THE LETTER SAILED BACK onto the mattress. I pressed my knuckles to my mouth to stop the cry that wanted to tear my throat wide open. My poor father...

My cheeks felt wet. I dashed at them, irritated. Not a single clear thought was to be found in my mind. My heart was hammering. *Find something to do. Don't fall apart.*

I made for the wardrobe. The fancy silk dresses were all too large for me. I stepped back and spotted a small wooden box on a chest of drawers. I turned the key, and blinked at a collection of earrings, necklaces and rings adorned with pearls, amethysts, and other gems I'd never seen before.

All of this had once belonged to someone. Was she dead? I couldn't help but look for bloodstains on the walls and furniture, for any sign of the identities and number of Moriarty's victims, or how they might have met their ends.

I caught my foot on the rug. My head hit the bedpost, and I finally came to my senses.

Sitting on the floor, I rubbed my aching forehead and analysed the few things that I had seen today.

The yellow-haired, doe-eyed maid. The cap she wore made me think of an embroidered mushroom. Comical. If her naiveté was genuine, I might be able to extract information without her noticing.

I looked up. The lamp hanging from the ceiling looked entirely different from any gas lamp I'd seen. I pulled up a chair and investigated the contraption. Inside it was a glass bulb shaped like a pear, with a cable leading from the device to a switch next to the door. Electricity! The house had to be in a city. Maybe even London? Hopeful, I rushed back to the window, trying to find something familiar. I saw only trees, bushes, lawn, fencing, and more trees and lawn. I tried the window. It opened easily and I leant out. Far to the right, I spotted the bluish roof of a large house with a small tower in the middle. It, too, was obscured by trees, but looked faintly familiar.

There were no other houses on the premises, which was good — no one could easily watch me through the window. But there were no other houses or streets within view. Sending light signals would make little sense. And would be too dangerous.

The water in the jug was still warm. I opened the package, revealing a small can of tooth powder, a toothbrush, a hairbrush, and a bar of soap. The scent of patchouli curled up, contrasting with the stench of vomit stuck in my hair. I washed thoroughly. My temple was still sore from Moran's punch, but I found no blood on it.

I rubbed my skin and hair dry with what must have been the softest towel in the world, thinking that whatever I would find would be either important — or irrelevant — to my father's survival.

Whatever might come at me, I would greet it without emotion.

And yet... My heart seemed unable to listen to my cold mind. It was still trying to crack my ribs.

~

WITH NOTHING ELSE TO WEAR, I dressed in the nightgown again and pulled the bell rope. The maid arrived a few moments later.

'Miss Gooding, might I ask you to lend me a dress? These here,' I waved at the wardrobe, 'are too large.' The maid was slender and small, her clothes should fit. But my enquiry seemed to shock her.

'Oh, but Miss, the tailor should arrive any minute now.'

'The tailor?' I was stunned. 'Miss Gooding, can you tell me whose room this is?'

'Why, it's yours.'

I wanted to jump at her. 'Who lived here before me?'

She shrugged. 'No one.'

'Whose dresses are these in the wardrobe?' I was getting desperate.

The door flung open. Miss Gooding clapped a hand to her mouth.

'Gooding, go back to where you came from. Dr Kronberg, questioning the maid is useless, for she knows nothing.' The man's skull shone through sparse hair. With his jacket tails, and the impeccable shirt stretched over his barrel chest, he looked like an austere house martin in black and white. His stance and expression, though, were those of a bully with experience.

The maid used the moment of distraction to slip out the door.

'Durham, the steward.' He managed to dip his chin ever so slightly. 'The tailor will arrive in a minute. Supper will be served in an hour. That is all you need to know for now.' He turned on his heel, shoes squeaking, tails flying. The door snapped shut, and I relaxed my fists.

A knock announced the tailor. He was a small man with mouse-like features. He rushed in, closed the door with a jerk of his arm, and scurried toward me. His small hand took mine gingerly and he bent down to breathe on my knuckles. He introduced himself as Mr Nicolas Smith, of Smith and Associates. He pulled out a measuring tape, flicked it here and there, scribbled numbers onto his notepad, and was finished within seconds. 'What materials and colours do you prefer, Miss?'

'Dark, please. Simple cuts without buffs or laces, as they would hinder my work. I prefer front-buttoned dresses.'

His pointy face collapsed. Women of the upper class expected to dress elaborately, with useless appendages that made it impossible to even lace one's own shoes. God forbid they should dress or undress without the help of a maid! But I had no claim to a social status whatsoever — for years I had masqueraded as a man. The results were an obscene urge for independence and an education that far exceeded that of most women. I had always observed such social categorisation from a safe distance. But now I would have to pay attention, as I was being placed in the same cage as all the other pretty birds — wives, sisters, and daughters of men with more money than they had need for.

I dropped my gaze to the hems of my nightgown, already missing the freedom that trousers provided.

The tailor fidgeted, and lowered his head in sad acknowledgement.

'Thank you, Mr Smith.' I said softly, upon which he blushed. 'Can you tell me how long it would take you to finish one dress? Mine were destroyed, and now all I have is this.' I picked at my nightgown.

'Oh, I'm so sorry.' He pushed his glasses up his nose.

'Well, I think under these circumstances I could finish the first dress in two days. Would that be acceptable?'

Two days in a nightgown? 'Mr Smith, do you think you could make one of these fit by tomorrow morning?' I showed him the contents of the wardrobe.

He inspected each dress and chose one made of dark green silk. 'This one should be fairly easy to resize. I could deliver it tomorrow morning.'

'I am deeply indebted to you, Mr Smith.' I produced a tiny curtsy.

He chuckled, red-cheeked, then left with a bow and a muttered 'Farewell'.

I stared at the closed door, as though it were his back. The man had seemed friendly and caring, but blushed so easily that I did not think him fit to lie for me without being discovered. I pressed my ear to the door. Footfall. No conversation.

Durham must have been puzzled by Mr Smith's state. But then, I was in a nightgown. For a man to blush and be nervous around a scantily clad woman would be considered normal. And perhaps I was giving Durham too much credit.

My fear was giving him too much credit. And the sluggishness of my mind was making me even more fearful.

I drank all the water from the ewer to wash out the remaining poison. Then I inspected the room again, starting with the area around the bed. There were no doors to neighbouring rooms. Good. I wasn't certain whether or not I tended to talk in my sleep.

But something essential was missing. I rang for the maid.

'Miss Gooding, I could not find the chamber pot....' Her lopsided smile stopped me.

'We have water closets, Miss.'

'Oh.' The rich all had plumbing and hot water. Of course.

'May I show you to it, Miss?'

'Where is Mr Durham?' I had barely finished speaking when his heels came clacking over floorboards, were briefly dulled by carpet, and then his head showed in the door frame.

'Miss Kronberg wants to see the water closet,' the maid explained, her head bowed.

'I will take it from here,' Durham said. 'Follow me, please.'

We walked through a corridor and turned to the right. He opened the door to a small room with wood-panelled walls and a flowery porcelain bowl with a wooden seat.

Without a word, I entered and shut the door.

I had never seen a water closet in a private home. Its drain looked different from the ones I had seen at Guy's and the medical school — it appeared...S-shaped? Definitely not straight. The nonexistent stink was puzzling. I almost thrust my hand into the drain to investigate.

Was it possible that the water standing in the bend of the drain prevented foul odours from rising up through the plumbing? If every Londoner had a water closet installed, would it prevent the spreading of disease? We could possibly even get cholera epidemics under control. How would London change if people no longer dug cesspits? I stood back, wondering whether the problem of disease transmission would truly be reduced, or only relocated, together with the waste.

My chest froze. Water exited this house unsupervised. The question was, how I could use this to my advantage.

Durham stood at attention only inches from the door when I emerged.

'How can I reach the water closet when you are not available?' I asked, cringing at the thought of being at his mercy for such private matters.

'Gooding will bring you a chamber pot.'

Back in my room, supper waited on a small table. The smell of cabbage was sickening.

~

It was past eleven o'clock at night. An oval moon peeked through the window, casting silver onto the floor. My bare feet walked irregular helices, in and out of the moonlight, from the rug to the naked floorboards and back again, gradually covering the entire area. By the end of my third round, I could recall every one of the sixteen places that produced a squeal when stepped upon.

I took a break and drank cold tea, forced the patterns from my mind and watched the yard below. The moonlight had painted the maples' foliage silvery blue. Fog rose and swirled up where the dogs ran. Four large, broad-chested animals with short coats and flapping ears — mastiffs, perhaps? I had never been afraid of dogs, but I knew well enough that they are predators. In that, they did not differ much from mankind.

I shut my eyes, turned from the window, and walked blindly to the door and back to my bed without producing the slightest noise. Satisfied, I went back to the door and placed the empty teacup like a stethoscope to the wall.

Shuffling. Quiet breathing. Durham must have been leaning against the wall precisely where my head was. I pushed away and went all around the room, listening at every wall, but could hear nothing. The wall facing the corridor was the thinnest. The others were all weight-bearing and fairly massive. Durham could easily listen to all my movements in the room. It felt like being displayed in a fishbowl. Was Moriarty aware it worked both ways?

I took the small clock off the sideboard, placed it in the sheet of light that pushed through the gap beneath the door, and listened. Durham didn't seem to move much. I sat down and wrapped a blanket around myself. It would be a long night.

Despite the exhaustion, worries about my father kept me awake. I tried to push my imagination aside. It only served to terrify me. I replaced it with old memories, closed my eyes, and smiled at the small horse he had made for my tenth birthday. Its mane and tail were bits of rabbit fur, its glass eyes had tiny lids made of thin black leather. A little worn, with eyes not as shiny as eighteen years earlier...it now stood in the window of my old room gazing out into my father's garden.

I pressed my face into my sleeve, and swallowed tears. I shifted my weight, focusing my attention on noise outside the room. Nothing happened for a long time. Until, close to one o'clock, sharp footfalls echoed in the entrance hall. Then someone climbed the stairs, and passed through the corridor below. The stairs creaked again, this time closer, and feet approached to stop at my door.

'Professor,' Durham said.

My heart galloped. I pressed a fist against my breastbone.

'Is she inside?' asked Moriarty.

That confused me. Certainly, he would know I was here with Durham guarding my door?

'As you wished,' was Durham's answer.

'Bolt the door. And then you may retire.'

'Of course, Professor.'

A key was turned, a bolt slid into place. Two pairs of feet walked off in two directions. Durham's softer footfalls left for the stairs, while Moriarty's sharper heels went only a few steps further. A door was being unlocked, then it snapped shut.

He couldn't be sleeping in the room next to mine!

Gooseflesh prickled on my neck. I crept to my bed and pushed my ear against the wall. I heard him kick off his shoes and walk about softly. An occasional rustle, a *clonk* — perhaps from his watch being placed on a table or dresser. I thought I heard him go to bed with a growl. But he was tossing and turning, not finding rest. I kept listening until a sharp noise cut through the wall. I jerked my head away. My blood turned to ice.

In Moriarty's room, a woman cried out.

Day 2

❦

The maid woke me before sunrise. I had been restless most of the night, listening for noises outside my enclosure, fighting the temptation to climb out the window and race until my lungs burned. But I couldn't outrun the dogs. Nor did I know where to find my father, or how to save him. The night had been an excruciating exercise in patience.

Miss Gooding brought my new clothing. As she strung up a corset that was slightly too large, her gaze swept over my face, neck and arms. Her lips tightened. Fine ladies didn't have tanned skin, god forbid discernible musculature. Impossible to get those from sitting in pretty parlours, doing needlework, and sipping tea all day long. In Gooding's eyes, I must have looked a savage. *Yes,* I thought, *wonder why I am here. In a house like this. Begin to ask questions.*

But she did not dare ask. It would have been unsuitable.

To need a servant to get dressed was highly embarrassing for me, though a normal routine for women of social standing. Disgusting. I'd use this quiet time with my maid to get to know her better. To prod and probe. Everyone has a weakness.

Even my captor.

I followed her with my gaze, until she disappeared behind me to button the back of the dress the tailor had resized for me. We did not speak, and I let the silence grow heavy. She knelt and laced my boots. She cleared her throat as she stood, but didn't look me in the eye. Her lids fluttered and her breath hitched.

She picked up a brush from the vanity, and began pulling it through my black curls. Each stroke reached down to my neck only. The bristles tickled my skin and raised gooseflesh. She must wonder about the shortness of my hair. Perhaps she thought I had sold it.

'Thank you, Miss Gooding,' I said as she stepped aside. 'Do you think I might take a walk through the house and perhaps go outside?'

'Why would you not, Miss?'

'I was told not to leave the room.'

She blinked.

'Is Mr Durham available?'

'I will call for him, Miss.' She curtsied and left.

I made for the vanity, but changed my mind and sat on the bed. I did not dare look at myself and wasn't sure why.

Durham arrived eventually. As we walked, I listened to the noise his shoes made on the various surfaces. The hard carpet of the corridors on the second floor, the creaking of the stairs. The first floor with carpeting identical to the second, and the steps down to the ground floor, creaking louder.

At the end of the stairwell, we took a sharp right turn and our heels produced four clacks on the stone tiles in the hall before we entered the dining room. It was a beautiful mixture of elegant and rustic features, with a white lime plaster ceiling, and smoked oak beams stretching the length of the room.

A row of neatly dressed servants lowered their heads in

unison, were introduced by Durham, and swarmed back to their respective tasks. I was amazed. As far as I had learnt, Moriarty lived without wife and children. Yet he employed a scullery maid, a kitchen maid, a parlour-maid, a chamber-maid, a laundry maid, an in-between maid, two cooks, a lady's maid, a page, and a manservant. Whatever for?

Durham bade me sit at the massive oak table in the centre of the room. He cleared his throat, took up a position beside the door and stared at me until my breakfast was served. With a clipped voice and an air that tasted of bleach, the housekeeper introduced herself as Mrs Austine Hingston. Her movements were precise and swift. Her rank below Durham did not allow her the freedom to show any of the disrespect she clearly felt for me. Only her eyes betrayed her. Whenever her gaze slid over to me, the hint of warmth that seemed reserved for Durham only, vanished.

I wondered what Moriarty had told his servants about the new guest.

Certainly not the truth.

'What's on the program?' I asked Durham after Hingston had left.

He lifted his eyebrows. 'You think I am to entertain you?'

'You have a peculiar sense of humour,' I mumbled.

There was not the slightest change in his expression. Very appropriate for a servant. Today, he wore a slight sneer. I wondered what it would be tomorrow. Most likely the same.

'Shall we go for a walk, Mr Durham? The sun is shining, the day is mild, the geese are calling to go south,' I babbled, knowing that he did not care in the least. He shook his head.

'Well, I think I shall go by myself, then. After all, one could easily get sick without regular exposure to fresh air.' Shock touched his face as I rose to my feet.

'I will accompany you,' he announced.

Good, a little leverage over the manservant could prove

useful one day. Especially if he daresn't tell his master about this small slip in controlling the captive.

∾

LATER THAT DAY, I lay on my bed staring at the ceiling as impressions of the morning flitted through my mind.

Durham and Hingston appeared to have some kind of comradeship, and both seemed to agree I was a thorn under their fingernails. Clearly, neither of them would help me willingly. But if they had a secret romantic relationship, I might be able to put them under pressure. Yet somehow, I found it hard to imagine that either of those two would embrace anything but a cold pillow.

I pushed the issue aside. More pressing was the meeting with Moriarty. He would want to discuss the isolation of bacteria, and probably the laboratory setup as well. All I wanted was to discuss the well-being of my father or, rather, to beg for him to be released. What a waste of time this would be! I had to control myself and I needed help — someone who could take my father to safety while I acted against Moriarty. There was only one man I knew, but how could I possibly contact him? Simply walking into the post office and sending Holmes a letter was out of the question.

I sat up. I could use the name I had given him last spring! *'Promise me that you'll place an advertisement in* The Times*, asking for Caitrin Mae, when this case is either solved or threatens your life. I'll find you then.'*

Would I ever have an opportunity to send a message? How much time would I have? It would take months to isolate bacteria, test their virulence, and produce a large enough amount to be used as a weapon. My stomach clenched at the memory of my human test subjects — paupers who'd been abducted from workhouses the previous winter. Men and women who had happily accepted two sovereigns in exchange for their lives. They would have sold their children to us, too, if I had allowed it.

~

EVENING ARRIVED and Durham led me to the dining room. The table was set with porcelain and silver. Several candles were lit. The door closed behind me. Swallowing a breath, I stepped forward.

The professor sat in an armchair, bent over a book. The lit fireplace behind him made his silhouette flicker.

'Good evening,' he said, shutting the volume with a soft thud. He rose to his feet and walked to the table like a large cat, gleaming eyes focused on his prey. His voice carried a low purr beneath the hardness. A tall, gaunt figure with a high forehead and greying temples — an *ageing* cat — possibly in his forties. His long hands closed around the back of a chair. He pulled it out and gave me a nod.

I approached and sat. Turning my back to him felt very wrong. My neck ached in anticipation of a blow.

'You may breathe now,' he said, moved to my side, and lifted the silver top off a casserole. 'Allow me to be your servant tonight.'

I wondered if Durham were guarding the door.

A bird sat in the casserole, carved, vegetables decorating its outlines. Moriarty arranged parts of the animal on my plate, peas rolling about until they drowned in gravy.

'Thank you,' I squeezed out.

'My pleasure.'

We ate in silence, each assessing the other. I could not recall the taste of anything I'd eaten.

'May I ask how you found me?'

He seemed amused by my attempt to control my burning interest. The corners of his mouth twitched a little.

'An acquaintance stumbled upon an article in the *Brighton Gazette*. Apparently, a simple woman had performed a Cesarean section with great skill. I took a chance and sent Colonel Moran to investigate. When he returned, he described you to me. You seemed to look like Dr Anton Kronberg's sister. Oh, he did not make much of it. But I wondered who this woman could be. Naturally, I paid a visit. It was unmistakable.'

I dropped my gaze to my plate, silencing a groan. Such a small gesture had betrayed my father and me. After having ignored it for months, I had finally been forced to pick up my doctor's bag and run to a neighbour's aid. Mary had been on her bed, moaning, rolled up protectively around her enormous stomach, blood seeping through her skirt. Her uterus had been hard as a rock, trying to push out the infant that refused to emerge. John's pale face, sweat glistening on his forehead, his trembling hands helping with the ether and stroking his wife's hair as I slit her open. I had peeled the child out of its enclosure, the shimmering water bag covered with a spider's web of blood. A boy with skin so blue I thought he was dead. I sucked the mucous from his mouth and nose, massaged his tiny chest, and blew air into his small lungs. After only a minute, he'd begun to squirm. And then holler.

But something about Moriarty's explanation rang false. I wasn't sure what it was precisely. I looked up. 'Can we take our discussion outside? I'd prefer a walk.'

'But of course. The sunset will be likeable.' The word *likeable* sounded ridiculous coming from his unforgiving mouth.

Once outside, I started toward the large maple trees at the far side of the premises.

'Tomorrow you will be inspecting your laboratory. Or

what remains of it.' Seeing my surprise he added, 'You'll be working at the medical school.'

Good. That would make things easier.

'My coachman will take you there and back. The same rules apply at the school as do here at my home. Your assistant will keep you under surveillance.'

I clasped my hands behind my back. My fingers grew cold. The evening breeze brought a promise of winter. 'I need to know what germs you want me to isolate and how you are planning to use them.'

'We will be discussing that in a minute, my dear. Germany and France are considering chemical warfare. So far, their attempts have been...shall we say, premature? The incentive is not great enough, I suppose. A war seems too distant.'

'What is *your* incentive?' I wondered aloud. He ignored me and kept walking. 'Money? Ah, power. You don't necessarily want to end or win a war? A man like you can live anywhere, sell his *services* to anyone?'

'I see.' He stopped in his tracks, took my hand, and kissed my trembling fingers. 'I am very pleased to have made your acquaintance, my dear.' His voice crackled with mockery.

The cat was playing with its food. I yanked my hand from his grip, unable to silence a growl. And slapped his face. 'I am *not* your dear. I used to be England's best bacteriologist until I ran into that incapable group of doctors *you* employed! If Bowden had had a brain, he would have trusted me earlier, and the whole operation would not have come to its sorry end.'

He lunged and wrapped his hand around my throat. 'I am aware that using Bowden was a mistake. But trusting *you* would be outright foolish. Although I am glad you don't attempt to flirt with me, you are already insulting my intelligence with your lies!' His face and mine were only an inch apart. I saw the brown specks scattered along the rims of his grey irises, large pupils that were bottomless pits, incisors shown in a sneer.

My stomach roiled. Sweat itched in my armpits.

'Whatever you choose to you do,' I croaked through my constricted windpipe, 'I need to know how you plan to deliver the fatal germs. How will the enemy be infected? Will other weapons be used? The vector and the pathogen have to be a perfect match. Else you will fail.'

He released me, his expression empty. 'We will begin with the obvious: soldiers and horses.'

'How specific do you want me to target?'

He looked at me quizzically and I explained, 'Disease does not know friend from foe.'

'You are a poet.' He chuckled. I looked away from him, holding onto my hands. 'You wish to know how important it is to prevent collateral damage?'

'Yes.' I guessed the answer from his tone.

'There are soldiers on both sides. Men march into battle and die. Collateral damage is acceptable as long as significantly more losses occur on the enemy side.'

'That makes things easier,' I said. We had now reached the maple trees and I picked up a leaf. Blood red flowed into orange and into gold. I curled my fingers around it. A souvenir from the outside world. 'What diseases were you thinking of?'

'The Plague,' he answered.

'The...*Black Death?* You are out of your mind!'

'You may choose to abandon our agreement at any time,' he said coolly.

'The wolf does not make an agreement with the rabbit, Professor. A predator may play with its prey. Ultimately, the prey always ends up the same way.'

'It is a pity you see it that way, Dr Kronberg.'

'How else could anyone see it? My father and I are your

prisoners, and you seem to plan to wipe out the whole of London, because that's precisely what will happen should we dare play with bubonic plague.'

Without reply, he turned and walked away.

'I know nothing of warfare,' I continued, catching up with him, 'but I assume that whatever weapon you hold in your hand should be controllable. At least to some degree.'

'And you claim to be unable to control the Plague? Well, perhaps I erred,' he muttered. 'I will find one of your students. Someone should be willing to do what I ask.'

'You can choose to walk through life and pay people for the opinion you want to hear. Truth exists nonetheless.'

'Interesting theory,' he answered, now walking faster.

He began to hunch. Just a little. His left shoulder was pulled up more than his right. Interesting. When we had supper together, he had held the fork in his right hand. His handwriting also looked right-handed, but I had seen him using his left hand for most other tasks. He must have been born left-handed. I wondered whether little James Moriarty had complied quietly, or if they'd to break the boy to make him behave "normally".

I scrunched along the walkway and did not see it coming. He wheeled around. His pupils were pinpricks, and spittle sprayed onto my cheeks as he hissed, 'Be very careful. Your choice of words may one day cost you your life.'

He turned and walked stiffly back toward the house. I noticed how much more crooked he suddenly appeared.

Walking up the stairs to the entrance, I considered what I had witnessed. He was a controlling and possessive man. Curiously, though, a sign of opposition appeared to cause his muscles to clench, as though his mind were bending his body. Wondering whether I had found his weak spot already, I stepped into the house.

'Come here!' his voice shot through the hall. I saw him

walk through a door opposite the dining room, and followed. The room was large, its walls covered with bookshelves. The massive desk bore piles of books and papers. He sat down, rubbing his neck, blinking often. A headache, perhaps? I wondered how severe it was.

He did not invite me to sit, so I remained standing, feeling the rage ooze off him like a rabid dog's saliva.

'Is it not true that the Black Death would be the most dangerous weapon to hold in one's hand?' he asked, his half-closed eyes directed at the desk.

'Yes.'

'So why do you think you know better? Or is it that you as a woman are by your nature incapable of murder? The weaker sex that faints when an inappropriate word is uttered?'

'Interesting. You know nothing about me after all.'

Harsh silence fell. I waited for him to speak, or to do any other thing but stare at his desk. He didn't, and so I continued. 'In the 14th century, the Tartars catapulted thousands of corpses — their own soldiers — over the walls of Caffa. The bodies carried the bubonic plague. Imagine mountains of plague-infested flesh enclosed by a city wall, Professor. It was the stench of rotting cadavers and the fear of the disease that drove the people out of Caffa. They took the Black Death with them. Onto trading routes and into Mediterranean ports. This is the first historical account of using the bubonic plague as a weapon, and it resulted in the greatest health disaster in the history of mankind. Twenty-five million victims. Half the European population.'

Silence fell again. The tension was sharply visible, straining the space between him and me, driving itself into the flesh between his shoulder blades.

'You chose me because I am a skilled bacteriologist and a thinking one. Developing germ warfare is a creative process. You don't want a soldier-type who indiscriminately does what you command. You want a scientist who has her own mind, and uses it.' He did not move, but his rage and resistance seemed to dampen a little. 'I need access to a library, to study historical accounts of germ warfare. I haven't been reading any scientific publications for several months now. There must be an alternative.'

Irritated, he jerked his chin down and waved me away.

I found Durham in the hall. He led me to my chamber, where, exhausted, I undressed and got ready for the night. I took my pillow and blanket and sat next to the door with the cup to my ear, and my eyes shut. For a long time, I heard nothing. The cup sank to my lap as I drifted off to sleep.

Footfalls awoke me. I glanced at the clock. Past midnight. And just like the night before, Durham locked my door and Moriarty went into the room next to mine. Weary, I rose and listened at the wall to his room.

The rustle of him undressing, the clonk of his watch on the dresser, followed by a female, 'Oh!'

The bed creaked and I heard him grunt. My ear wanted to rot off my head, but I kept listening. I needed to know whether the woman was there of her own free will, but she made no other sound. Then, I heard him climax.

I pushed away to sit by the door again.

Not long afterwards, the door to the room next to mine closed with a snap. Moriarty reached my room. Two black shadows cut through the sheet of light beneath the door. I felt as though I were drowning. After a too-long moment, he finally left. I sprang to my feet, opened the window and sucked in the cold night air.

The moon gazed down upon me. *La Luna*. I'd always liked that name more than *The Moon*, or *Der Mond*.

My thoughts drifted back to the Sussex Downs, to the day I had remembered my true calling. All because little Peter had needed help hatching from his mother's womb. I thought of softly rolling hills and a sunset that was so much more beautiful than any before. My hands had seemed different, too. I'd realised then that they weren't the hands of a farmer, but the hands of a woman who practised medicine. As the sun had dipped into the horizon, wisps of clouds had been splashed with orange, pink, and violent purple. The sky had darkened and stars began to pinprick the black velvet cloth that stretched above. And as on every night in the Downs, my thoughts had wandered to the men I'd loved. And still did.

Day 3

The maid was clacking up the stairwell. I snatched up my blanket and pillow, rushed to bed, and pretended to sleep.

The sliding of the bolt, a quiet knock, footsteps approaching my bed. I wondered if she ever questioned the bolt. Or did she find it perfectly normal that I was locked in my room? Perhaps so, if the woman next door were imprisoned, too.

I opened my eyes and yawned. We exchanged pleasantries. She left me an ewer of warm water and announced that my new clothes had been delivered.

I thanked her, and just before she left, I said timidly, 'Miss Gooding, I wonder if you could tell me...'

She smiled.

I smiled back. 'Last night I thought I heard a woman cry in the room next to mine.'

Her face snapped shut.

'It might have been a bad dream,' I added, and saw her relax a little. Did she think Moriarty mounted me, too? The thought that he could expect that of me stopped my heart. I forced my gaze and thoughts out through the window.

Miss Gooding left without a word. Her knees crackled a little as she curtsied.

She returned with a pile of clothes, placed them on my bed, and invited me to inspect them. I noticed the quizzical look she tried to hide.

There were silk and wool walking dresses, wool skirts, lightly laced cotton and silk shirts, and a collection of under-garments and accessories. The pants, shirts, the coat, and cravats must have caused the confusion.

At the bottom of the pile, I found a cloak. I knew very little about fashion, but this one must have cost a fortune. It was made of the finest black wool, richly trimmed with a silvery fur I could not identify. It looked like fox, but I had never seen one in that shade of grey. Was it Moriarty's wish to turn me into a lady?

I almost laughed at the thought. It appeared that he planned to have me masquerade as a male medical doctor during the daytime and act the decorative female in the evening. I shot a glance at Gooding, wondering whether she shared his bed, too. If so, she probably believed he loved her.

I dismissed her and picked a dress, feeling very revolu-tionary. I had lived as a man for so many years within an exclusively male medical establishment. But women were now allowed to enrol at British universities. That suited me well, because there was no urgent need to hide my sex any longer. But most importantly, I could visit the lady's lavatories at the medical school without my assistant's company. That gave me the much needed space for planning an escape. I did wonder, though, how many female medical doctors had found employ-ment at the London Medical School.

Possibly none other than myself.

~

AFTER A TOO-RICH BREAKFAST and a surprising lack of comments on my outfit, Durham led me to the waiting brougham. The driver greeted us with a nod, his face hidden behind the collar of his cloak. A stiff wind fingered my ankles and blew cold drizzle down my neck. With a shiver, I climbed into the carriage and Durham shut the door.

How curious! No one had blindfolded me or permanently darkened the brougham's windows. As we left the premises, I understood why. The roof visible from my window now came into full view: the All Saints Church of Kensington Palace. I should have recognised it earlier. Moriarty had his home on the most expensive street in the British Empire — Kensington Palace Gardens. I thought of Garret then, and wondered whether he had ever dreamt of burgling this area. I shut my eyes and leant back, losing myself in memories of a man with flaming orange hair and calloused hands. And of his gentle lovemaking.

We arrived at London Medical School after a two-mile ride. The driver jumped off and opened the door, offering a helping hand. I took it and gazed up at him. His muffler was pulled up over his mouth, his brown eyes slightly bloodshot. Black hair stuck out from beneath a wool hat that was hiding his brow. All I could see was a strip of face that was mostly hair, eyes, and nose.

I thanked him and the wrinkles around his eyes suggested a smile. Then he turned and waved to a man across the street, who was just starting toward us.

He stubbed his toe on a cobblestone, and narrowed his eyes at the coachman. 'Where is Dr Kronberg?'

'I am right here.'

His eyes snapped to me, went up and down my body, and then he huffed. 'I have no time for such foolishness.'

'Nor I. Would you be so forthcoming as to show me to my laboratory?'

He threw another glance at the coachman, who observed our exchange with some amusement. 'You better do what she says, my friend,' he said through his muffler.

The man blinked twice, as though to wipe away the picture of a female medical doctor that didn't fit his reality. He pulled himself together soon enough, nodded once and held out his hand. 'Dylan Goff is the name. If you would follow me.'

I turned to the driver. 'Thank you, Mister...'

'Garrow,' he offered, then flung himself back onto the carriage, and flicked the horses. Steam rose where the whip bit the animals' skin.

Mr Goff started across the street, then turned and looked back at me with impatience. Wary, I gazed up at the five storey building that contained nothing but dreadful memories, knowing I should expect many more to come.

Despite knowing our destination, I let Goff lead the way while I considered whether to adopt behaviours that he might be expecting of me: to speak little and only if asked, to never show emotion, to pretend to faint once or twice a day, and to seek his company for safety's sake. Act as though unable to think or decide for myself. As though I could not detect or use any slip in his guard to my advantage.

We reached the laboratory. It was clean and empty, save for shelves and workbenches.

Goff spoke with determination. 'Before...*we* begin, we need to procure a rather large amount of equipment. Glassware, an incubator, Bunsen burners, an autoclave.'

I nodded, slightly amused. He did know he was my assistant? Or did he not? Was the simple fact that I was a woman and he a man enough for him to believe he could reverse the hierarchy?

'We'll also be needing gelatin, at least ten pounds of it, mineral salts, beef broth, and swine blood once we prepare the media. You are not writing this down?' His gaze dashed toward me, a little annoyed, a little puzzled.

I smiled innocently, indicating that I had neither pen nor paper.

'Professor Moriarty would like us to isolate the bubonic plague,' he said.

'I see.' I put a hint of consideration into my voice. Goff seemed to have no idea where to place me. I decided to let him roast a little longer. Soon, uncertainty drove blood to his cheeks.

'Hum. I wonder how we can obtain the germs...' He scratched his chin

He probably hoped I would answer his question. For a moment, I imagined him sitting through an exam, eyes darting left and right, trying to catch a clue from his fellow students but never acknowledging them once they'd provided the much-needed help. What a twisted situation: I was to be his superior in profession, but supposedly his inferior in sex, character, and intellect. The prospect of letting him clean up after me was very appealing.

'What, in your opinion, are we to do with bubonic plague germs, Mr Goff?'

The man froze. 'We are not to talk about such details without the professor present.'

So he knew that whatever Moriarty was up to wasn't purely charitable. 'What is Professor Moriarty's field?' I asked.

'Mathematics, but he is retired now.'

Why would he retire so early? I wondered. 'Where did you study bacteriology, Mr Goff?'

'Cambridge.'

'An excellent school. How did you obtain this post?'

'Erm…,' he said, absentmindedly scribbling on a notepad. It must be the list he'd intended me to write. That he needed to write down those few things was…a good thing, I supposed.

Goff had his back to me, and I used the moment to inspect the room. The place felt like it had a year ago. I nearly expected to find remnants of cholera-contaminated faeces on the floor, a heap of dirty blankets, a dying woman within.

As Goff turned, I looked up at him, signalling that I was waiting for an answer.

'I am not allowed to talk about it.'

Ah, how interesting. The man was all enveloped in secrecy and seemed to love it. I wondered whether his ties to Moriarty went deeper than the mere connection of an assistant.

'You have worked here before, I understand?' Goff asked without looking at me.

'Yes.'

'I never heard of a female medical doctor working here. Or anywhere else in London, for that matter.'

'I have not either.'

Exasperated, he turned toward me. How could he be so dense to believe that the Dr Kronberg sitting in front of him now, and the Dr Kronberg he'd read and heard about, were two different people?

'So how could you possibly be a medical doctor?'

'What do you think?' I gifted him a smile.

His gaze flickered, as though he suspected something behind my facade. Then, it finally hit him. 'You…you masqueraded as Anton Kronberg.'

Such a bright boy. I lifted a shoulder, took off my hat, and stroked any disorderly strands of hair back into place. Then I sighed and folded my hands in my lap.

Goff relaxed back into superiority.

The man was a gift. He would not see the truth even if I were to shove it up his nose. As long as he believed me naive and stupid, he would be more prone to slips. And I would have a little more space to plan my escape.

After an hour of merely sitting and occasionally agreeing to Goff's suggestions, I feigned boredom and asked to be shown to the library. After all, I had some reading to do.

In addition to an exploration for potential loopholes.

I felt as though I were trying to hide in two shadows at once — two shadows that weren't even in close proximity to one another. I had to plot my escape, and that of my father. And I didn't even know where he was.

It was maddening.

∾

MORIARTY WAS NOT at home when I returned. That postponed the inevitable confrontation over my choice of clothing. A female medical doctor might produce publicity if I were to be introduced as one. However, using my male disguise would probably make matters worse. Dr Anton Kronberg might draw the attention of the police, or get himself arrested for medical malpractice, murder, abduction, and hitting Sherlock Holmes over the head.

Although...the prospect was rather enticing.

Durham led me up to my room where my supper was served minutes later. I ate without appetite, thinking of Goff and his list of equipment and reagents. He could have assembled it without my help. My sole role was to isolate and test deadly bacteria. My assistant was too young and inexperienced for such dangerous work, but he would surely learn from me. And one day I would be replaced, rendering both my father and me disposable.

I did not plan to stay that long.

Goff's relationship with Moriarty made me curious. Had the two men known each other before my assistant's employment? He seemed to have information Moriarty would not likely have shared with a mere footman. I had to assume the two talked regularly, and that soon my charade of being a submissive female would raise suspicion.

Perhaps I could disguise the charade by officially playing Goff's assistant? That would make my presence at the medical school more acceptable, and my submissiveness would also suit Moriarty's purpose. On the other hand, Moriarty would warn Goff not to trust my fake tameness.

I rubbed my tired eyes, pushing one problem away to deal with the next. My head was still spinning with the scientific publications I had just read in the library — mostly from the *Proceedings of the Royal Society of London* and *The Lancet,* as well as historical reports on germ warfare.

Germ warfare was far from a new invention. On the contrary, mankind's history of using disease as an offensive weapon was long and diverse. Emperor Barbarossa had poisoned wells with human bodies in Italy. The Spanish mixed wine with the blood of leprosy patients to sell to their French foes, the Polish fired saliva from rabid dogs into the faces of their enemies, and the British distributed blankets from smallpox patients to American Indians. Napoleon flooded the plains around Mantua in Italy to enhance the spread of Malaria, and the Confederate army sold clothing from yellow fever and smallpox patients to Union troops in America. The list was long and there appeared to be no limits to our resourcefulness. Mankind had invented endless methodologies for murder. The almost parallel advancement of science and weaponry indicated a dark future for countries that were too poor to afford such research. The thought of poisoning them all with a deadly disease might appear to be a good solution. At least for someone who hated mankind. Was hate Moriarty's motivation?

I had my own ambivalence toward my fellow humans. Often, I felt far away from the mass of men, women, and children. Why was that? Was I arrogant? Did I believe I had a superior mind? I was not sure, not today, and not here. Moriarty had thrown me off balance.

Or had he? Had this non-balance begun long ago? Meeting Holmes, I discovered my cool distance from people had, in fact, changed. I noticed that I was no longer standing with both feet firmly on the ground, and that, perhaps, for years, I had not been feeling as comfortable as I'd imagined. Gradually, but inevitably, I came to realise that I wanted to be a woman — a woman allowed to practise medicine without having to masquerade as a man. Without having to cut my hair, bind my breasts. Ha! And without having to wear a fake cock.

I rose and walked to the door, sat on my pillow and listened to the movements of the house. The room was dark, save for the little light seeping through the gap beneath the door. I closed my eyes and let my mind wander back into the labyrinth of possibilities and impossibilities. With my father held hostage, my alternatives were painfully limited. In fact, I could see none. I kept running into walls, and no matter how often I turned, I collided with yet another barrier. But there must be cracks in the structure. I would have to steadily enlarge them until Moriarty's fortress fell.

Day 10

***

'The master wishes to see you,' Durham announced as I sat down for breakfast.

'Now?'

'After you have eaten.' He took his usual position next to the door, eyes directed at an imaginary spot above my head. He was vacant so long as I busied myself with my food. As soon as my gaze strayed beyond the tablecloth, he glared at me as though he wanted to chase my thoughts back into a dark cave.

I chewed demonstratively. He put his vacant mask back on. What a well-trained servant he was.

That Moriarty wished to speak to me only a day after the laboratory had been set up, and with Goff and me ready to isolate germs, was no coincidence. But I wondered how and when he had exchanged information with my assistant. In my ten days of capture, I had not seen or heard a single guest in the house. Moriarty himself was out frequently, and I'd so wished to follow him.

And find out where he kept my father.

The breakfast turned foul in my mouth. Did my father

even have enough to eat? I squeezed my eyes shut, but images of the lovely old man being mistreated, starved, and chained were impossible to get rid of.

With a heavy sigh, I pushed away from the table, and made for the study with Durham following me like a duck its flock. The steward shut the door behind me. Moriarty sat at his desk, poring over a pile of papers. He did not bother to look up as I sat on a chair, bolt upright, hands curled in my lap.

'Good morning,' he said, gathering up the papers and placing them into a drawer. 'I would like you to assume that everything might be possible.' He looked up. First at the door, considering, then he turned his gaze on me. His pupils dilated. 'Controlling the spreading of the plague, for example. I want us to theorise about possibilities, and how these might be brought to fruition.' The low rasp of his voice contrasted each sharp "s" that felt like a claw puncturing my skin.

I inclined my head to signal agreement, knowing that I would not give in. Never.

'Very well. I believe you may require a little background on strategics and warfare in general.'

'How can I be certain my father is being treated well?' I interrupted.

'I give you my word that he is.'

My short laugh brought the rage back into his face. 'You question the word of a gentleman?' he asked.

'You must be jesting. Of course, I do!'

'I do not care in the least whether you believe me or not.'

'I think you do,' I said.

'You give yourself too much credit.'

'If I had reason to believe that you are torturing, or have even killed, my father, I would do the same to you.'

'I would not give you the opportunity.'

'There is no need to give me one. I would simply take it.'

His eyes darkened. 'You would die trying.'

'And you believe that I would care?'

'You have just told me that you lied.'

I pulled up my eyebrows.

'A few days ago you tried to make me believe that you wanted to cooperate with me, and now you tell me you want to put an end to me.'

'Can you not comprehend that my family is more precious to me than my life and my career?'

Coldness spread over his expression like a November frost.

'It puzzles me,' I added. 'That a man of your intelligence cannot fathom that the men funding your research into germ warfare would be keen to employ me, once you are dead.'

At the time of the Club, Moriarty's research had been financed by several wealthy men. Holmes had arrested them, together with all the physicians who had experimented with dangerous diseases on paupers. It was only logical that, now as then, Moriarty had access to more than just his private funds to pay for bacterial weapons.

'You are playing a dangerous game, my dear—'

I smacked my armrest. '*You* started this game! I would happily do what you ask if you were not treating me like your prisoner. As if you *own* me. By holding my father hostage, you are *making* me your enemy. This isn't necessary! You could have simply come to the Downs and asked me.'

'You are lying. You were hiding from me.'

'I was hiding from the police and from the man who rejected me. I felt unable to live in London with Sherlock Holmes all over the papers and the police searching for Anton Kronberg. Is that so hard to understand? How could I have possibly known you even existed?' I was amazed at how easily I threw such private matters at him. My heart didn't even give an extra twitch. It felt as if one part of me stood right next to me and watched with a mix of shock and wonder. And disgust. I would have to deal with the latter once I was free.

'So you ask me to trust you?' His voice was brittle with irony.

'I ask you to put yourself in my position. Besides, what kind of trust could you possibly mean? You trust I am skilled enough to control the plague for you. A *dangerously* misplaced trust. At the same, time you don't trust me to work with you of my own free will, which ultimately leads you to take drastic measures. Holding my father and me hostage only damages what would be a fruitful cooperation.' *And, you pig, will one day die for this.*

For a moment, he considered what I'd said. Brushed the tips of his fingers across the polished surface of his desk. Cleared his throat once. 'He shall write a letter to you. I do hope he can write?'

'I want to see him.'

'Impossible.'

'How am I to know you will not make him write a letter, and then kill him?'

'Enough!' he growled, pressing his knuckles on the desk. 'You write a letter to your father, and in it, you will ask him questions, the answers to which only he and you would know. Once you receive his reply, you will cease this circus!'

'You have someone who speaks German,' I said.

He inclined his head.

I gestured agreement, and the end of the discussion. How interesting that he had made an effort. Finding someone he could trust, and who was able to communicate with the hostage, that could not have been easy. I had expected him to engage a translator only after my first letter was written. After all, neither of his prisoners could be allowed to communicate without interception. That he already had someone...

Was that a good thing or a bad thing? What did he have planned?

Moriarty splayed his fingers on the desk, gazed at them for a moment, then pushed away and stood. He folded his hands behind his back and began pacing the room. 'Very well, then. You wish to know which weaponry might be used in a future war. Needless to say that whatever we discuss here is not to leave this room.' He threw me a sideways glance.

As if he feared I might leave. The man was mocking me.

'Naturally,' I replied.

'Britain is developing a motorised war car — a machine-driven carriage. It is bulletproof, and has articulated tracks that enable it to run on any ground, no matter how muddy or irregular. It has three main disadvantages, however: It is exceedingly expensive, transporting it is bothersome, and it is very hard to manoeuvre.' He had circled the room twice. Stretching his neck, he came to a halt by the fireplace. 'Another weapon of great interest is poison gas. You have probably heard of the 1874 Brussels Convention on the Law and Customs of War prohibiting the use of poison bullets. And this is where it gets rather amusing. France, Germany, and Britain are actively involved in the development of xylyl bromide grenades.' He lifted an eyebrow at my somewhat bland expression. 'Tear-gas grenades,' he explained.

'Ah,' I said, wary of the direction this was taking. And he seemed to be far from finished.

'The art of war is changing, Dr Kronberg. Where men once slaughtered one another with swords and bayonets, now countless more will be killed with weapons of unimaginably broad impact. Gas will crawl over battlefields to bring terror to man and beast. The Kaiser has been stirring up conflict for months now.' Here he paused. It was done for effect. I sat more erect. And then, Moriarty said with an unnaturally soft voice, 'The Kaiser might be pushing for war. We need to be prepared, else we will be overrun.'

For a second I had a ridiculous vision of children playing war in the slums, where the one with the biggest stick or the burliest friend was king. 'I see,' I said, leaning back in the chair and staring at the ceiling. The ensuing silence was heavy. He neither moved nor spoke. I pictured him staring at me, unsure whether I was contemplating the discussion or ignoring him.

'I think you are looking at the problem from the wrong angle,' I said, focusing back on him. 'You see how big the threat is, and naturally, you want your threat to be even bigger. The most terrible weapon would certainly be the bubonic plague, and so this is what you choose. However, I believe we must select what is most useful. And that is not necessarily the most threatening weapon we can think of, but rather the one we can wield without killing ourselves.'

'I will not tolerate your subversive attitude much longer—'

Impatient with his rapid onsets of rage, I snarled, 'How do you plan to tell millions of fleas and rats to go one way only, and not the other? Both are vectors of the plague. Do you intend to *train* them?'

This was obviously more resistance then he had expected. His face grew pale. His jaws worked.

'Let me finish, please,' I said, and he jerked his chin down once. 'Correct me if I'm mistaken. Despite the technological advancements you mention, and the novel machinery that could possibly be used to deploy germs, a potential war would still be fought by thousands of soldiers, horses, and mules, all of which represent targets for the weapons we will develop.' He nodded and stiffly sat back down.

'Are we talking about a specific war, Professor? What I

mean is, do you know for certain that there will be a war in the very near future?'

'As I've already said, the German Empire seeks conflict. As do others — Transvaal and the Orange Free State, for instance. The beginning of a war is like tipping a scale. One can predict the collapse of the balance when precisely one grain too many has hit the bowl. Which might just be the instant the first shot is fired.'

I sucked in a breath. 'Very well. I will speak in purely hypothetical terms. What we want, then, are two diseases.'

That caught his attention. He cocked his head. I continued, 'The first to bring down equines, and the second to kill men. Both diseases have to spread among the enemy quickly, fast enough to give us a chance to win a battle, but slow enough to allow the disease to spread between groups of soldiers and horses without burning itself out.'

His back stiffened. *So much impatience.* I had no idea how to use that against him, but I knew I would find a way. Or...I hoped I would. Had to.

I wiped my sweaty palms on my skirts. 'What if, after great effort, we managed to bring one man behind enemy lines to infiltrate and infect a battalion, but the disease proved so extremely aggressive that the entire unit died before the germs had sufficient time to spread to neighbouring units?'

Slowly, he leant back, and motioned for me to go on.

And so I did. 'In warfare, gas seems a wonderful idea at first. But what if the wind turns? In germ warfare, we face the same problem. What if infected rats, fleas, people, horses, wind, or water do not behave as we've planned? This is a serious issue we have to consider.' I kept saying *we,* in hopes he would notice and get used to it. Let it be a fact that this was cooperation and not slavery.

He searched my face. The silence between us felt very

loud. A screaming void that made the ears wilt. My heart kicked my ribs as his gaze drifted between sharp and clouded. Observant and inward cast.

'What do you recommend?' His voice carried a warning. I had to be convincing.

'I will learn all there is to learn about the history of germ warfare — what succeeded, and what turned into a disaster. Spreading the plague would certainly fall into the latter category.'

His expression hardened. I jumped up from my seat. 'I would *never* use the plague, Professor Moriarty. I don't believe my father would want to live if, for his sake, millions of innocent people must needs die because his daughter has spread the Black Death across Europe.'

I tried to soften my expression. There was no need to augment the impression that he would lose this debate. I paced the room, hands on my back, mirroring his earlier posture. 'It *has* to be a germ that can be handled by untrained men,' I said. 'Something that is safe enough in a small container, even if the container breaks. We need a germ which, in its transportable form, must be injected, ingested, or inhaled in large amounts to cause an infection. But as soon as there is a diseased individual harbouring the active form of this germ, the disease must be highly contagious. Yet, it should not be too aggressive. It must not kill before it can spread.'

I turned and looked at him. A face that was open with interest snapped shut as soon as our eyes met. I walked over to my chair, sat down, and waited for a response.

'You have a particular germ in mind.'

'P...perhaps.'

He was seething with impatience, so I quickly added, 'Glanders and anthrax.'

'Why those two?'

'Glanders germs are fairly easy to isolate and can be added to fodder. Infected animals usually die within two weeks. The disease is transmitted by physical contact, and can infect men also. It is a nasty enough disease, and under unhygienic conditions, it spreads like fire. Anthrax is a bacillus I studied in Robert Koch's laboratory in Berlin. It has one great advantage: It produces spores.'

He frowned at that, so I explained, 'It is a very recent discovery. Spores are like eggs that hardly ever lose their ability to hatch. These spores can be stored as a powder for many years. When inhaled, the lungs will be infected after a day or two. Another week and the man will most likely be dead. One can add anthrax spores to food, clothing, air, or water. This germ is much more dangerous than glanders and nearly as terrible as the plague. But it's relatively easy to control.'

Again, the silence. Only the crackling fire filled the void. A thing to hold on to. For me, at least.

'Very well.' He drummed his fingertips on the desk. 'Very well.'

~

WRAPPED in my blanket I cowered near the door, head leant against the wall, one ear listening to Durham. My mind was racing. The bubonic plague would have been an uncontrollable and immediate danger if I had agreed to isolate its germs. The thought of growing large batches of these organisms right there in London — with millions of people around me — was utterly terrifying. The risk of transmission was high, if not guaranteed. Especially in a hospital with all the comings and goings, and the prolific rat and flea populations... It wouldn't take long for the plague to sneak out of our laboratory. Suggesting glanders and anthrax was a foul compromise, but I could see no alternative. He wanted a deadly disease, and I had to supply him one if I wanted my father to live. The only improvement was that these germs could be controlled and would not accidentally slip out to kill hospital staff, patients, and...well, half of London.

At least not so long as I was the bacteriologist, and had any say in the matter of conducting isolation and growth experiments.

I wondered whether France and Germany were considering bacterial weapons. After all, Louis Pasteur and Robert Koch had been working with deadly diseases for years. With tear-gas and modern war machinery to deploy grenades, germ warfare would be but a small step further. It was only a question of who would be the first to lift a foot and dare to stick it into the dangerous soup of pathogens.

It was clear that Moriarty kept the flow of information to a minimum. And I found that highly annoying. Why did he want these weapons? What war did he fear?

The thought of the woman next door diverted my focus. Who was she and why did she remain in her room all day? Was she a prisoner, too?

My heart ached as my mind steered back to my imprisoned father.

It took a long time to push the swarm of fears aside.

My mind crawled slower and slower, until I finally closed my eyes and let my thoughts escape to the Sussex Downs. *I opened the door to my cottage, changed my dress for trousers and a shirt, picked up my old crossbow and ventured out into the dark to hunt rabbits.* Gently, the kernel of my mental exercise, the one thing that truly mattered sank in: All that I created, I could destroy.

Of that, I was certain.

Day 14

✣✣✣

Goff would lead me to the library and hang on me like a tick for the remainder of the day. In the laboratory, he allowed me room to move about, but whenever we ventured into a populated area, he would turn into my personal parasite. I suspected that this was Moriarty's main reason for choosing him as my assistant and gaoler: Goff would do anything to please his master. His eyes were sharp enough to spot deceit, and his legs and mouth quick enough to report it before I might be able to utter a word of protest. But he had no grasp of abstract concepts and lacked any desire for creative play. Most of all, he lacked imagination. He'd never be a great scientist. Or a great watchdog.

I pushed the heavy oak door open. The old wood was cracked and slightly worm-eaten, its width embraced by black iron bands. The hinges creaked invitingly and the smell of aged leather, old paper, and oiled wood shelves pulled me inside.

The librarian spotted us instantly. Without moving his head, his eyes darted over his spectacles and quickly back to his book. His hair was black, and sleek from the Macassar oil that held his few remaining strands tightly to his skull — a shiny, well-polished sphere striped black and white. Beneath that were scrubby mutton chops in a silvery shade, and farther down, a lean frame hugged by tailored jacket and trousers.

I had observed him for several days now and believed him to be a sensitive, intelligent and observant man. Others might think him slow of intellect, because he read with his index finger tracing down the page, while his lips moved quietly, as though his eyes and brain needed a crutch. He was slow in responding to requests, and when he spoke, he used words sparingly.

To me, though, he was like a lynx, with ears constantly pricked to detect the slightest disturbance in his kingdom. As I walked along the shelves, picking out medical journals and history books, I noticed that the librarian was observing me, too. I was the only woman there, and thus a curiosity. And I was absolutely certain he had also noticed the strangeness of my companion. But what would the man decide? Judging from my selections, he must conclude I have a medical education, but Goff's disinterest in everything on the shelves was certainly leaving him the oddest of impressions. What man visits a library only to hang onto a skirt?

For the past two days I had been gauging the man's reactions. Each time Goff got too close to me, I would flinch or edge away. And the librarian's eyes would shoot up for a moment. He would furrow his brow, then look back at whatever it was he was reading. He was observant and discreet. But before I should act, I needed to know...if the man had courage.

≈

AFTER SUPPER, Moriarty awaited me in his study. I was

nervous, to put it mildly. My father's answer was overdue. I had not even tried to sneak a secret message into my letter to him. The two pages I had written could have essentially been shortened to two lines: *How are you? I am well.* And yet, not a word from him. My wariness was growing into dread.

'Have you got a letter for me?' I asked Moriarty, as soon as I entered the room.

He raised his head. His empty expression flickered briefly with a cold smile. His hand slid beneath a pile of papers to pull out an envelope. I stepped forward and took it from his hand.

'Sit and read it now,' he said.

I paused. He wished to observe me. I should have expected it, of course. I swallowed, and unfolded the paper. Seeing my father's childlike scrawl softened the rock in my stomach and tightened my throat. With a sigh, I sank into a chair and read his words, written in German:

MY DEAR CHILD,

I would like to put more into this letter than I am allowed to. I am told to answer your question, so you know I am alive. Let me tell you first that I am being treated well. Please don't worry about me and do what you must. You asked what you dreamed of when you were a little girl. You dreamed of many things, but most of all, you wanted to understand the language of the trees. I think you did, in a way. You understood our cherry tree.

I hope you are well.

Love, Papa.

TWO DROPS SLID down the sides of my nose, landed on the blue ink, and smudged my father's words. I turned away and covered my eyes with my hand.

'Are we settled now?' Moriarty said.

I nodded, and inhaled. 'I will write him each week and ask him a personal question in each letter. If I don't get an answer within ten days, I will assume he is dead. Can we agree on that?'

'Certainly,' he said with a smirk. He had anticipated my request.

~

I SAT ON MY BED, bending close to the candle on the night-stand, and unfolded my father's letter again. I let my fingers trail over the lines he had written, imagining I could feel his hands. I held the paper close to my nose and inhaled, but the aroma of fresh wood shavings that followed him wherever he went was missing.

He'd been away in his workshop for weeks.

"...*do what you must.* ... *You understood our cherry tree.*" The essential information. Our cherry tree... My mother died soon after giving birth to me. It had been a cold winter with a great amount of snow, as my father had told me so often. When she ran a high fever, no one but my father was there to help. And when she was dead, no one came to bury her. My father covered her body in the snow beneath our cherry tree. And there she remained for weeks before she was properly buried. As a child, I believed her soul lived in that tree. A small part of me was still believing it.

"...*do what you must.* ... *You understood our cherry tree.*" It could only mean one thing: Father had no hope of leaving his prison alive. He was giving me free reign, trusting I would do the right thing, whatever that would be.

It felt as though I were watching three hourglasses: one for my father — much too small, the sand falling too fast. One for my time with Moriarty — so vast I couldn't even see its outlines, and one of unknown size — for me to find the gap in Moriarty's web and contact Holmes.

I buried my face in my pillow, thinking of the great difference between time measured and time felt.

Could live in a world without my father in it?

∽

SOMETHING HAD INTERRUPTED THE SILENCE. Or had a sudden silence woken me? Whatever it was, it screamed into my ears. Without making a sound.

I did not dare move. Twice I blinked at shadows that cut through the sheet of light beneath my door. Moriarty was standing there, waiting. Again. Or listening? Had I talked in my sleep? I squeezed my eyes shut, trying to remember my dreams, but there was only emptiness.

As suddenly as he had appeared, he walked away. His footfall was light and energetic, as it always was when he came from the woman next door. He used her like a privy. Every night he went into her room, disposed of his sperm and his urges, only to emerge an hour later, noticeably relaxed.

Not once had I seen signs of a struggle on his face or hands. No scratches or bruises. She either did not want to fight, or couldn't. The thought of her being tied to a bed, being raped every single night, was sickening.

Day 19

The day had been long. My legs felt heavy, my mind was tired. While the former rested, the latter seemed to run in useless circles: Who was in the room next to mine? Had there been others before her? Could I trust the librarian, and how was I to approach him? Even if I managed to contact Holmes, how could he possibly find my father? Without information on father's whereabouts, the only thing for Holmes to track was the occasional letter. My father was in England, I was certain. My letter had left the house, and four days later I had received an answer.

So each letter travelled no more than two days, more likely one. The translator would need time to read it and communicate its contents to Moriarty. The probability was high that my father's first response had not been what was expected or allowed, so that he'd had to write another. Might he even be in London? So close?

The envelope looked new, without kinks or smudges. Whoever had transported it was not the regular runner boy. But who was the messenger? During my nineteen days of captivity, I had yet to see or even hear the bell announce a guest or even a footman. Every evening seemed identical: I would return from the medical school where I'd spent most of my day researching the history of bacteriological warfare, as well as treatments and epidemics of glanders and anthrax. Then I would eat, and would often have a meeting with Moriarty, who would grow more and more impatient with our lack of progress in the laboratory. And then, straight to my room.

My bedchamber and clothes would have been taken care of while I was at work, and a good fire awaited my return. Before nine in the evening, a maid would have hauled coals up the stairs and stoked the fire one last time. She did this for every inhabited room. That left her with five hours of sleep at the most, before starting another day of hard work. She was in her own prison, and every day I was grateful to not be living the life of a servant.

Gooding shared the room above mine with cook and another servant. Their conversations circled mostly around the coachman. My maid seemed to be in love with him. The other women pitied her. Apparently, Garrow had a prominent scar on his left cheek that everyone else deemed unattractive, yet Gooding worried only of the pain he must have felt when he'd received the injury. All I had ever seen of Garrow was a strip of nose and eyes, for he always wore his muffler as protection from icy wind and rain. But I'd never seen him cut a brief glance in Gooding's direction. Perhaps, he was utterly ignorant of her feelings, or afraid of losing his occupation if seen flirting with her.

A noise brought my thoughts to a full stop. I pressed the cup harder against the wall. Someone was entering the house. The entrance door slammed. A gust must have torn it from Hingston's hand. There was a clacking of heels, which was soon cut off. Whoever it was must have entered one of the rooms just off the main hall. Anxious to identify the guest and the reason for the visit, I listened until my ears felt hollow from the strain. Complete silence filled the house. Durham wasn't even shuffling his feet. Was he tense?

After more than three hours, I heard movement on the ground floor. I opened my door and told Durham that I needed the lavatory. He gave a nod and walked ahead.

Moriarty's voice echoed in the hall. The other voice I recognised with a shiver — Moran. I could not hear what was being said. Only an occasional word made it up to the second floor. Among them was *Ragpickers*. So they were discussing anthrax. We were still lacking a diseased animal with clear symptoms of an anthrax infection. One could easily isolate the wrong germ if a weakened animal had contracted more than one disease. The two men were silent now. They must have had heard our approach.

I went into the water closet, bolted the door, sat on the bowl, and tried to rub the chill off my arms. I pulled the chain, opened the door, and stepped out into the corridor. It was empty. And utterly silent. My heart dropped to my toes.

As I walked back to my room, I noticed a faint odour of tobacco. Not what Moriarty smoked. Someone else's. Gooseflesh scuttled over my skin at the thought of Moran's hard face and icy blue eyes. His obsession with guns.

I pushed at the half-open door to my room. Odd. Hadn't I shut it before leaving? I couldn't even finish the thought. A hand came down on my mouth and nose, cutting off all air. Only a grunt escaped through the nonexistent gap between my lips and Moran's coarse palm. He slung his other arm around my waist and hoisted me up. I kicked air. And landed face down on my bed. I tried to scream, but nothing slipped past Moran's hand. I aimed a kick at his shin, but that didn't bother him at all. If anything, it increased his excitement. Panting, he pressed his knee onto my lower back, and shoved my face deep into the mattress. With my breath trapped between the sheets and my mouth, lights began to flicker on the insides of my eyelids.

All of a sudden, Moran stopped dead. I heard the click of a revolver being cocked and Moriarty's snarl, 'Control yourself!'

I was dropped like dirt.

Moran mumbled, 'You should be grateful that any man shows interest.' Then he stalked out of the room.

My tongue probed the inside of my mouth. I had bitten my cheek. The metallic taste of blood flicked my brain back on. A hand was placed on my head. Softly. Then taken away.

My senses were wide open. This scene felt wrong, the undertone of lies screeching like claws across glass.

'My apologies,' Moriarty said. 'I should have known better than to let him out of my sight.'

I pushed myself up. He did not move. What was he waiting for?

I got to my feet and gazed up at him. His right hand was compacted to a fist. The other clutched the revolver. The left side of his face, lit by the lamp in the hallway, showed tension.

'Well,' I choked, 'you can't see him now. Maybe he is trying his luck in the next room.'

'He wouldn't. She is mine.'

'I see. No one claimed me, so he could. You *disgust* me.'

Angry, he lifted his hand to point the weapon at my chest. I took a step forward — a stupid, pleading reflex. He misunderstood and jerked the gun farther up. Its mouth rested between my eyes. All I could think of was how awkward it was to gaze along both sides of a gun barrel, how relaxed his hand seemed, how quiet the room was.

Without a word, he turned and left. The door was slammed shut, the bolt snapped into place. A key turned.

My knees were too soft to keep me upright any longer. I

sat down on the bed, and slowly unbuttoned my dress. With my eyes shut, I recounted facts — one button at a time.

Moriarty and Moran had still been in the entrance hall when Durham and I walked to the water closet. Only two minutes later, Moran had sneaked into my room. Durham, the man who followed me like a shadow, had disappeared. I had heard no protest from the manservant. He must have been ordered to leave. Moran had caught me in my room and thrown me onto my bed, apparently to violate me. What had I heard during these short moments? Nothing. No running through the corridor, no footfall, no commotion at all. Moriarty must have been there in my room, enjoying the show for a minute before stepping in and pretending to save me. Moran would never step over limits set by Moriarty. The Colonel would only obey his master.

Moran's final sentence kept ringing in my ears. *You should be grateful for a man who shows interest.*

If Moriarty wanted to play yet another game with me, I'd certainly play along.

Day 40

❦

The petri dish in my hand contained golden brown beef broth gelatin adorned with wrinkly white splotches: colonies of the glanders germ. I held a metal lancet into the blue of a Bunsen burner's flame, waited for it to glow bright red, then drove it into the gelatin. It hissed as it cooled down. Goff was breathing down my neck. I imagined ramming the hot metal into his eyeball.

'The lancet is now cool enough that we can pick a portion of a colony.' I demonstrated the process to him. 'Which we then transfer to a fresh petri dish. To test this colony, we pick another portion from the exact same spot and put it in sterile water.'

The white clump fell from the lance's tip and sank to the bottom. I stoppered the tube and flicked it until the germs were homogeneously mixed with the liquid, then rose to my feet. Goff stepped aside, and I made for the six cages, sealed inside a glass cabinet. The mice within served as test subjects to make certain that my pure cultures were indeed glanders germs and not contaminants. I drew the deadly liquid into a glass pipette, opened the hatch, and measured exactly two millilitres into each of the troughs. Once finished, I placed the contaminated equipment into a container filled with grain alcohol.

'Should we expect the usual incubation time?' asked Goff.

'This is a fairly high dose. The mice might display the first symptoms sooner. But only time will tell.'

The germs had been obtained from the liver of a horse with glanders in its final stage. After testing various pure cultures on mice, I had found two that caused the typical symptoms. Now, it was only a matter of being certain — identifying the glanders germs by the colour and shape of their colonies — and keeping them contaminant-free and alive. Meanwhile, we kept our ears open for any sheep or cattle infected with anthrax. If any were found, we would isolate bacteria from their spleens.

One of the workbenches was lined with twenty pear-shaped glass vessels stoppered with cotton wads, waiting to be used as storage containers for large amounts of fatal bacteria. With the gaslight reflecting off them, they resembled Christmas tree decorations. Pretty bacterial bombs. My stomach roiled at the thought that my laboratory would soon be the most dangerous in the British Empire. That what we were about to produce could end thousands of lives.

Around the room were other, much larger flasks, all tightly sealed to prevent the alcohol within from evaporating. I had explained to Goff that large amounts of grain alcohol were needed as a safety measure. If we contaminated ourselves accidentally, we could disinfect our hands with it, and even soak or burn our clothes, if necessary. Although this was the truth, I kept the most interesting aspect of this explosive arrangement to myself.

∾

THE MAID SERVED a light supper of beef soup and sandwiches. Moriarty and I took it in his study, next to the fireplace. His posture was stiff, his shoulders drawn up, and he kept rubbing his eyes and neck. He was at his most volatile.

'Mr Goff reported on your success with the isolation of glanders germs. Congratulations, Dr Kronberg.' His voice was monotonous and strained.

The isolation of glanders had been simple enough, not too great a leap for a bacteriologist. I wondered whether he still regretted losing his battle for the Plague, but then wiped the thought away. Surely that defeat had not brought about this foul mood. So then, what had?

'Thank you,' I answered in the same neutral tone.

'The next thing I want you to do is test for the storage tolerance of the germs. How long we can keep them, and how the duration of storage influences infection rates.'

I had already planned on testing storage conditions. His background knowledge and how he placed the puzzle pieces of bacteriology and warfare together impressed me. And terrified me.

'I will let Goff procure more mice and cages. It will be difficult, though, to study the spread of disease in such a small room.' I thought about space, air circulation, and isolation of infected individuals. None of it made sense. The risk of transmission was too high. 'It will not be possible,' I said, cutting a sideways glance at him.

'Why?'

'The laboratory is too small. If we want to study transmission, animals in control groups must be isolated from one another. We want to test the spread of disease by wind, food, and water. But if the test subjects are all in one small room, sooner or later they will all be infected and we won't know the effectiveness and controllability of each vector. Besides, if hospital staff suddenly contracts anthrax, our project will be over before it begins.' Odd, how easy it was to sound as though I would be bothered by a premature end to our germ warfare research.

He pressed his fingertips together and shut his eyes. His hunch worsened. 'Would a warehouse be suitable?'

'If it's dry and its walls and ceiling are intact, yes. Can we guard it?'

'Of course.'

'Some renovations may be necessary. We will probably need to put up walls to form separate rooms and seal the doors between them,' I added.

'That won't be a problem.' He rose with a huff. 'To the smoking room,' he bit out, and left the study. I followed, wondering why he seemed so unworried about financial issues.

And then suspicion crept in and twisted my guts. Who else would pay for research into novel warfare technologies, if not the government and the military?

I almost laughed out loud. One essential puzzle piece seemed to have been found, but the whole picture had just grown so vast that I could barely see its outlines.

WE ENTERED THE SMOKING ROOM, and Moriarty sat on an ottoman. His hand trembled as he opened a tin the size of his palm, to reveal a brownish cake. He took a knife and pried off a small piece, then struck a match and lit a lump of charcoal sitting on a platter. He blew on it until it glowed, then held the brown substance stuck to the tip of the knife close to the heat. I could hear it sizzling.

Uncertain whether he wished me to stay or to leave, I remained near the door.

Pungent smoke began to fill the room, and its odour felt

strangely familiar. Much like that of the fireflies I caught as a child.

He picked up a slender pipe to blow air onto the brown lump, which I guessed to be opium. Then he sucked on the mouthpiece, blew at the drug again, inhaled again. And so it went, inhaling and blowing, until a minute or two later, he shut his eyes and leant back, holding his breath.

After a long moment, a thin sliver of fume exited his nostrils, curling upwards to disappear. The thought of a slumbering dragon brushed my mind.

'Sit, please,' he said softly, gesturing toward the ottoman's end. I approached, my silk dress rustling a cautious whisper. He smiled and the change that came upon him shocked me. His expression was soft and open. His hand stroked his waistcoat as though this simple gesture gave him great satisfaction. Yet his mind seemed sharp and observant. He had noticed my slight hesitation. 'You assume I am addicted? Well, perhaps I am. Rheumatism creates the need for chemical relief.'

'I doubt that.'

'Excuse me?' There it was again — the coldness in his voice that could cut through any conversation.

'I doubt your physician has made the correct diagnosis.'

'It takes you but ten seconds to know that? And what is your diagnosis, Dr Kronberg?' The lack of derisiveness in his voice confused me.

I scrutinised him, a little afraid of this new side of him, a little surprised and even relieved to see a part of him that I did not despise and fear at once. 'It is not rheumatism that causes your pain, I believe. It is not aggravated by cold weather, for example. From what I have been able to observe, it is brought on solely by disappointment. The instant you want something very much but cannot have it, your strong will bends your body. Your neck and shoulders clench, you hunch, and you develop a severe headache that causes you to be oversensitive to light and sound.'

'Interesting,' he replied, and I could hear a warning in his voice. 'Observant. How did this escape my notice?' He ran his fingertips up to his collar, his eyes half shut. 'If you are correct, it would mean there is no cure. Only alleviation.'

I found myself smiling at him to conceal my confusion. Did he mean he should have noticed I was observant, or that he should have realised that his symptoms had not been diagnosed correctly?

'How could that possibly amuse you?' His voice regained the familiar coldness, but he resumed caressing his waistcoat. How curious! Opium seemed to make him revel in his own touch. Or was it touch in general?

'The fact that you are in pain should amuse me, should it not?'

'One would think so. But I don't believe you ever leave your compassion behind. Even if it is for a man who abducts, imprisons, and threatens you. And that empathy, I fancy, is your greatest weakness.'

'You are wrong. It is my greatest strength. No one else is trying to detect a human being behind your monster facade.'

He cackled. 'What a waste of your time, my dear.'

I felt my blood rise. 'I am not your dear.'

Silence fell. His hand shot forward and grabbed my wrist. Before he could open his mouth, I replied, 'I believe you have a problem with your spine that can be solved with physiotherapy.'

The calculating part of me leant back and enjoyed the circus. One step further into the lion's den meant getting closer to the exit on the other side. The other part of me wondered why I was offering him any help at all. Why would I try to lessen his pain when I wanted him to die on the spot? Was it only because of the terror he caused me every time he transformed into rage itself? Or was he correct? Could I not let go of my compassion?

He watched me with narrowed eyes, waiting for a response.

'Did you begin hating everyone when they were beating the left-handedness out of you?' I snarled. The coldness in my voice had the desired effect — that of a slap on the cheek. A blood vessel on his temple bulged, his eyes turned black, his hand tighten around my wrist with bruising intensity. But all I saw was a little boy, once defenceless, and now possessing all the weapons of mankind.

I turned my head away, disgusted by my own naiveté.

'I know that bone-setting is not a widely accepted treatment,' I said quietly, and felt his grip loosen. 'Mostly because bone-setters are more reminiscent of butchers than surgeons. However, I still think that a gentle manipulation of the vertebrae in your neck would improve your symptoms greatly.'

He exhaled slowly and let go of me, pushed himself farther up, and with a voice straining for control he asked, 'What drives a bacteriologist to study physiotherapy?'

It felt like slowly stepping back from the edge of a cliff.

'During my time in Boston, I met Dr Still. He is a physician and a surgeon with great insight into human anatomy. He invented a treatment he later coined *osteopathy*, which is essentially a gentle manipulation of tissues and bones to stimulate the body's self-healing capabilities.'

'But you could not have been his pupil,' he noted. His eyes glazed over and his mind went to some other place. A second later he returned and said, 'Because you would have had to work in pairs for practice and study. But the good doctor's students had no need to masquerade as men. Only you.'

'Indeed,' I whispered.

'Fascinating. How hot that hatred must burn inside you.'

'For men? You think I hate men?'

'Don't you?'

'No. Yes. Sometimes, perhaps,' I said, wondering why I had volunteered this information.

'What a most peculiar situation. Here you sit, next to a man who threatens your life and that of your father. A man you despise. A man you want to kill as soon as the time is right. But you don't feel threatened now. You even offer your help. And this makes you feel guilty. Why?'

'Isn't that obvious?'

'Because you believe you allow yourself a weakness, and because you don't understand that reflex of yours.'

I offered him a compressed smile.

'But does it not require strength, and even add to it, to explore all the depths of one's character? The dark alleys, the filthy corners, the diseased limb we want to saw off?' he mused, his gaze burning with curiosity and something else I couldn't identify.

I tried to glimpse behind the speckled grey of his irises, but realised that...I didn't want to go there. Not yet. So I said, 'And you have lost yourself in that maze of your dark alleys. You hate ferociously. You desire passionately. You take heedlessly. There is no giving, no loving, no smiling in you. Because you don't want anyone using that against you.'

More time passed, a time of observation and contemplation, until he finally said, 'Am I correct in assuming that you did find a way to learn osteopathy?'

'I cannot say I learned it well. I had to practice mostly on myself. But yes, I am able to at least set bones.'

'Try it then.' His voice lacked its usual commanding sharpness. If anything, he sounded bored.

How could he not know he presented me his most vulnerable part? That fragile connection to his brain. The neck, so easily broken with the correct movement and acceleration, even by a woman. Perhaps this was the reason — was I but a woman, and therefore no threat to his life? Unable to take it by force, or so he must think.

How short-sighted.

'Take off your cravat and loosen your collar,' I said, rising to my feet. 'Then turn around and lie on your back.' My gut was quivering. If I killed him now, my father would be murdered in return. The risk was too high, but the desire so overwhelming I could barely breathe.

He did as I said, and looked up at me, relaxed and a little expectant. What an absurd situation. He was at my mercy and didn't even know it.

I knelt, and took his head in my hands. The carotid artery was tapping against the pale skin of his throat. I pictured a quick slash with a sharp blade, the gush of hot blood, the gurgles, the jerking and twisting of a man's body fighting death, long after his mind had given up. I closed my eyes and pushed my imagination aside.

'It does surprise me, though,' he said quietly.

It surprised me, too. Although he'd seemingly got what he wanted — my trust — he'd had to give me a little of his, too. Why would he willingly take the risk? He couldn't be so ignorant, could he?

My hands worked around his cervical spine, pressing at numerous small knots. Now and again, he suppressed a wince. His head lay in my palms, as I rotated it from left to right and right to left, my fingers probing the sides of his neck. His atlas — the first vertebra supporting the skull — appeared to be severely misaligned. I willed myself not to regard the identity of the man I held in my hands, to focus solely on the task at hand.

His shoulders and neck were so stiff that it took me a good deal of time to work some flexibility into them. I felt him relax. His breathing grew regular, deeper. It was time. With a quick clockwise rotation I jerked his skull toward me.

Two loud cracks announced the return of the atlas to its natural position. He sucked in air, producing a hiss, obviously realising that this dangerous moment had escaped his control. He stared at me with a mix of terror and surprise.

He was about to push himself into a sitting position when I placed my hand on his brow and said, 'Remain there for a little longer. Your body is accustomed to the misalignment of your vertebrae. The musculature will need time to rest and adjust.'

He made no reply, but did as I said. I excused myself and left the room, desperately hoping we might repeat this scene once my father was safe.

Day 49

❧

'I hear you have increased the safety measures in your lab.'
Moriarty stretched his legs toward the blazing fireplace.
A bottle of brandy flanked by two glasses stood on the coffee
table. His was empty. Mine waited in vain to be touched. He
had begun to adopt a familiarity with me that gave me a peculiar mix of relief and disgust.

'I had to. The danger of transmission was too great. I
could not allow Goff or myself to go in and out of that room
without precautions. Has he complained about the inconvenience of the daily disinfection of his apron, or does he feel
ridiculous at having to wear a cap and a mask?' My voice
carried just enough spite to let him know I wouldn't
back down.

He poured another brandy. 'I am not criticising you. On
the contrary. I know enough about anthrax to appreciate your
careful actions. And I do see that the small laboratory is now
very limiting. We will relocate as soon as you can confirm the
identity of the second batch of pure cultures.'

'You have found a warehouse we can use?'

He nodded, and emptied his glass.

I picked up my own glass and turned it in my hand. The glow of the fire bounced off its curves. 'When did you find out that I was, in fact, a woman?'

For a long moment, he said nothing. And then, 'I must confess that you fooled me. I had seen you twice from a distance and was quite taken in by your masquerade.' Upon my enquiring look, he added, 'About a year ago. I wanted to see the new recruit before Bowden sent Stark to call on you. I was also at the medical school when you began working for us.'

Back then, I hadn't even had a clue he existed.

'I should have guessed your identity then, considering the lack of facial hair and the high cravat to hide the nonexistence of an Adam's apple. Your gait was a good imitation, though. Ha! And the bulge in your trousers!' He clapped his knees, laughing, before he caught my gaze. 'My apologies. That was inappropriate.'

'Why, then, did you send Colonel Moran to the Downs? If you believed I was a man, how would an article about a woman performing a Cesarean section make you suspicious?'

'That took a while, and was the result of a series of coincidences. First, an acquaintance merely mentioned the article in passing. Then, weeks later, I remembered that Anton Kronberg had appeared somewhat...feminine. Not enough to be talked about, but just enough to suddenly come to mind, when one wonders how a woman could possibly perform a Cesarean section so well.' He smirked. 'Discovering that you were a woman was quite delightful, I must confess. I suppose you would have been burned at the stake a few hundred years ago. Perhaps not. Your masquerade was nearly foolproof.' The corners of his mouth twitched. And then his eyes grew black. 'The problem, my dear, is that I now know your qualities as an actress.'

Heat scuttled up my spine. 'Why not ask me directly?'

He raised an eyebrow.

'And I will ask a question of my own. Who is the woman in the room next to mine?' I could not specify my question without revealing how much I knew about the movements in his house. 'I heard her cry one night.'

'As usual, you combine a grain of truth with a great deal of omission. The art of lying.' A hint of appreciation lingered in his voice. 'Well, then. I will allow this little game. Can you guess why?'

'Because you enjoy it.'

He poured himself another glass and said, 'She comes from the slums and is well cared for. Let me be more specific — she is treated much better than she used to be.'

'Is she locked into that room?'

He nodded, not taking his gaze off me, constantly observing, analysing, scrutinising.

'What will happen once you are tired of her?'

He barked a laugh, tutted, and shook his head in amusement.

'You will dispose of her,' I whispered. 'No, you will have someone else do it. You wouldn't dirty your hands.' Moran's hard face and cold blue eyes came to my mind.

'Now it is my turn. How do you plan to murder me?'

I huffed a laugh. How could he expect me to answer that one truthfully?

'I thought the game was such that you answer my question to the fullest, and only then you may ask one in return?' I retorted.

He laughed again, knowing he had nothing to lose. Revealing his secret to a prisoner he would never set free, who wouldn't even survive long enough to share it, could do no harm.

'Durham will take care of her. Very soon, I fancy,' he said.

'What will he do to her?'

He put his hands behind his head and stretched his long legs. 'When he entered my employment, my dear manservant was not accustomed to uneventful domestic services, such as these. He is calmer now. You might think him balanced, but he is not. You believe I am dangerous, my dear, but compared to Mr Durham, I am a lamb. Ah, you are growing impatient! Listen carefully now. One of Mr Durham's victims caused quite an uproar last September. People thought the Ripper had come back. Cutting her up and placing her torso under a railway arch! Tut tut! How could he do such a *horrid* thing?'

There was nothing I could say in reply. My windpipe had collapsed.

'Now answer me,' he demanded.

I cleared my throat. 'I have not decided on a course. Not yet. But I have several...ideas. It depends on the circumstances, but I would prefer to run a jagged knife through your throat. Have you ever cut a throat, Professor?' Slowly, I rose to my feet.

He remained in his seat, intrigued it seemed, and arrogant enough to assume I could pose no threat to his life. I stepped closer, pushed between his knees, and observed the glitter in his black eyes as I placed my hand around his warm throat. I moved my thumb over his Adam's apple, stretching the pale skin. 'The problem is that anything duller than a razor requires substantial effort to break the skin.'

He smirked. Arrogant prick!

I lowered my voice. 'The skin moves with the blade. Either I will have to move it very fast, or I will have to immobilise you and use the knife like a saw—' He grabbed both my wrists and pulled me down.

'What you fear, you believe to be true.' With that, he released me.

My foot caught on the rug. 'Perhaps. But I am not stupid enough to believe Durham kills women for you. Moran is your man for such business. He would never dare violate me in your home, had you not given him permission to do so beforehand. *He* is the one who gets to have your mistresses once you are through with them, and I can only guess what he does to those women once he grows tired of them.'

I could have hit myself for revealing my thoughts on this matter. Satisfaction shone in his eyes, telling me that this was precisely what he had intended: to provoke an honest reaction from me.

'You are wrong on all accounts,' he said. 'Your view is clouded by fear and prejudice. None of these women have ever been violated or hurt. You are such a petty little creature. You believe your morals make you a better person, even as you never bother to ask what my morals might be.' His voice and presence were filling the room. Power seeped off his unhandsome frame. For once, he appeared to rest within himself, untroubled by rage and madness.

'You are correct. I'm a petty little creature,' I said, settling back into my chair. 'But you are wrong when it comes to my morals. I'm not even sure where I stand. On the good side? Or the bad? I don't even believe there is such a thing as *sides*. I don't believe in God or the devil. There is the church and its power, and the law with its enforcers. Religion and law are used as tools to maintain the social order. Our society, although soaked through and through with artifice to create and protect the illusion of normalcy, is highly diverse. There are cheaters, criminals, saints. People who belong to the masses are considered normal, and those who don't, are not.'

He considered that for a moment, then answered, 'You've changed your tactic. I wonder why.'

Wasn't that what he'd wanted? That I would trust him and expose my soft side? My eyes were glued to his, scrutinising every twitch. I wondered how someone could possess a mind that was at times wide open and nailed shut other times. I scrutinised myself, too. Were we truly so unalike? How far would I allow the truth to reach, and how far would I extend the lie? How far would I have to open up for him? How far to make him open up for me so I could plunge in the dagger?

He nodded then. 'We will see,' he said softly, as though he'd read my mind.

He lit a cigarette and offered me one, following my gaze all the while. I leant over, took it, and he lit it for me. The match flared up and threw a blaze of light across his face, features marked by intrigue, a sharp intellect, and something else. Could it be hunger? Was that why he let me get so close to him and let me wrap my hand around his throat? Could it truly be so easy?

I leant back and sucked in the smoke, held it in my lungs. Light-headedness followed. Slowly, I exhaled through my nostrils and watched white clouds curl toward the ceiling.

I knew he was observing me. And as I watched myself getting comfortable in the lion's den, I thought of burying my fingers in the mane of the beast, making him purr. Did he know he had invited a cobra into his house? Was he enjoying this game?

'What do you know about my morals, Professor?' I asked lightly, and not without a trace of mockery in my voice. To me, it felt like a dance. Step forward, entice, then step back and watch.

'You are not a maiden,' he began, and I snorted. The smoke burned the space between my palate and nostrils.

'I meant that in every sense,' he added calmly. 'You cheat, you lie, you've killed. But you do all of that for good reason. For a *good* cause. And you think that makes you a better person.'

I frowned at that.

'Well, then you maybe don't,' he continued. 'But it does

not make too big a difference. The essence is that you believe my cause is evil. Hence, I am evil.'

His voice was like a low hum, soothing and far reaching. He could make it crawl under my skin. I rubbed my tingling arms.

'You are a woman. One day you might be a mother. Would you not kill to defend your home, your husband, your children?'

My stare had grown cold. I would never be a mother. But I could imagine killing.

He narrowed his eyes. 'And what caused that? Something happened to your mother? No, you do not stir now. But you did before, when I said that one day you might be a mother...' He observed me, predator-like and about to pounce. 'You will never have children. Why?'

My hand moved to my stomach, protectively resting there before I could command it to retreat. His eyes followed.

'Violence,' he stated quietly. It hadn't been a question. 'I am sorry. That must be devastating,' he added without empathy.

I looked at my hands trembling in my lap, and wished I could wrap them tightly around his neck. And increase the pressure until his pulse quickened, and then wait to feel it slow to a stop.

'Yes, I can imagine killing,' I said quietly, and the intensity behind my words made him blush. 'This excites you?' I asked.

'What a magnificent opponent. I can imagine you greatly enjoyed your intellectual combat with Mr Holmes.' His eyes turned dark. 'As did he.'

I merely smiled, and tipped the brandy into my mouth. The dance had begun.

Day 52

❦

'Excuse me, Miss?' a soft voice called out as Goff and I entered the library. 'I've come to notice your fancy for historical literature.' I nearly screeched to a halt. After weeks of subtly indicating that my life and honour were threatened by my companion, this quiet librarian had finally decided to come to my rescue. Or so I hoped.

The man stood behind the counter and his eyes — enlarged through his spectacles — offered me a friendly twinkle. He must have noticed my hesitation and I was relieved he did not approach and directly hand me the book he was holding. Goff wasn't quite as dull as that.

'Oh,' I said timidly.

'Well, we've just received a copy of *The Select Works of Antony van Leeuwenhoek*. It was delivered yesterday and I was about to put it on the shelf just now. If you wish, you could be the first to read it.' He patted the large volume on his desk.

'That is very thoughtful and kind of you, Mister... Oh, I am so sorry, I do not even know your name.' I smiled, stepped up to his desk, and held out my hand, 'Anna Kronberg.'

'George Pleasant, at your service,' he answered with a

small bow.

'Later, perhaps,' I said softly, letting my eyes dart to Goff and back at the man facing me, hoping he would understand.

'As you wish. I'll put this beauty in the illustrated science literature section, and you can read it should you e interested and find the time,' he said, and pushed past us.

I turned to Goff and raised my eyebrows, as though I had not quite understood what the man wanted. Goff shrugged and we made our way to our preferred desks.

I SPENT the following hours reading every recent report on vaccine development that was to be found. Pasteur's anthrax vaccines were made for cattle, goats, and sheep. None had been developed for humans. Nor did I find anything that would protect against glanders. All the while, I was trying to decide whether or not it was wise to trust Mr Pleasant. He was a stranger. My overwhelming desire was to peek into the man's heart and mind, to make sure he hadn't been sent by Moriarty. Putting my own life at risk was acceptable, but leaving my father with his life at stake was an entirely different matter. Torn between the danger of being betrayed and the danger of never being able to contact Holmes, the zeal for action got the better of me.

Goff had grown tired by now, and his attention was not as sharp as it had been earlier in the morning. Gradually, the library emptied. I walked along the aisles as though searching for something in particular, then passed the illustrated science section, stuck my hand into a shelf and pulled out Leeuwenhoek's book. It had one dog-ear. I sucked in a breath, slipped my hand between the pages, and found a small note. My heart was ready to burst. I stuffed the slip of paper into my sleeve. The place where it touched my skin prickled with excitement.

I walked along the shelves, one eye on Goff who appeared to be oblivious to the sudden heat in the room and my attempts to calm myself. Grateful that he was not as observant as Moriarty, I picked up a journal and sat back down at the desk. When Goff began to pick at his nails, I jotted down a few words on my already crowded notepad. From his position, he could not see that notepad's surface, and it was there I unfolded Mr Pleasant's message. He had written only three words: *I can help*.

Hastily, I wrote my answer on its back: *Please advertise in* The Times: *Small golden wedding band found in the lavatory of London Medical School. To be picked up at Tottenham Court Road 11b, Miss Caitrin Mae.*

I slipped the note back into my sleeve, scribbled a bit more, read a bit more, and then made another round through the aisles. Only a minute later, the note was safely tucked back into the dog-eared book.

As Goff and I left, I gave the librarian a single nod and another timid smile, hoping to convey the immense gratitude I felt.

∾

TO STAY sane that night seemed impossible. I was tormented by fears of being discovered, of having misunderstood the librarian's message, or that he could be Moriarty's man. And the silliest fear of all — that Holmes would not understand my message. So I sat at the door, listening to the movements of servants and master. Long after midnight, once Moriarty was done with the woman next door and Durham had bolted me in before leaving for his well-deserved rest, I rose, lit a candle, and began writing two letters, careful not to leave ink on my fingers or the nightstand.

Day 53

It was difficult to focus. My hands tried to work with precision while my heart did its best to jump out of my mouth. Concerns about the librarian's loyalty and Holmes's swiftness made my head spin. If Mr Pleasant had delivered the slip to *The Times* yesterday afternoon, it should have been printed early this morning. How long would Holmes need to prepare a disguise, given he had read the papers at breakfast? Was he in London at all?

I had to stifle a groan. All I could do was wait and hope. There was no possibility of making sure all the players were positioned where I needed them. What would I do if disaster were already waiting for me? An image of Moriarty holding my note in his hand and thanking the librarian for his services, was impossible to push from my mind. On top of it all, my plan had a gaping hole. I had nothing to bargain with, nothing that could save my father if all went wrong.

I'd nearly jammed the hot metal lancet into my index finger. I sucked in a breath and glanced over at Goff, who was busy preparing media. I turned off the Bunsen burner, said, 'If you'll excuse me,' and stood. That was my way of telling him I needed the lavatory. He looked up and nodded once. We disinfected our hands, took off our protective gear, and marched toward the Ladies'.

As usual, Goff positioned himself at less than a respectful distance — three steps from the entrance. I pushed the door open and was greeted by the massive behind of a charwoman. She was scrubbing the floor and, upon my greeting, rose and turned toward me.

The door fell into its frame. I slid the bolt into place, staggered one step forward, and froze. I would always recognise his eyes. The light grey with the intense sparkle, forever mischievous.

My hand yearned to rest on his cheek. But what would I say? *How have you been? Are you happy? Do you have someone you love? Someone who loves you in return?* But I asked none of these things. Wiping emotions from my face I whispered, 'Thank you for coming. I don't have much time. My gaoler is waiting just outside the door. Here,' I pulled an envelope from my pocket and held it out to him. 'This is my will. No! Don't speak now. Read it and then deposit it at your lawyer's. Do you know a man by the name of James Moriarty?'

I had barely finished speaking when Holmes stepped toward me, eyes scrutinising my clothes, face, hands, and shoes. 'Moriarty is one of the most dangerous criminals in the Empire.'

'Moriarty was the head of the Club—'

'I am aware of that,' he interrupted. 'I have been hot on his heels for months now. As a matter of fact, the man is at the very heart of a far-reaching criminal organisation. Did he abduct you? Of course, he did.'

I nodded and held up my hand to hush him. 'We have but a few minutes! Holmes, Moriarty is holding my father captive. I beg you to free him. I believe he might even be here in London. He and I are allowed to write each other and it takes only four to six days to receive an answer.'

'Who put the advertisement in *The Times*?' He gazed down at the fine leather boots half hidden by the hems of my skirts, trailed his eyes over my clothes, which were atypically exclusive for my taste. 'Two or three months...' he muttered, and looked up sharply. '*That* long? Why did you not contact me earlier?'

I swallowed.

'Where is he keeping you?' His voice was metallic. I saw the effort it took him to remain calculating, to take facts and fit them next to one another to form a picture.

'In his house,' I replied, emotions cutting my voice thin. 'It was...difficult to contact you at all. I cannot make mistakes and risk my father's life.' I blinked the burning from my eyes.

Behind Holmes's pupils, countless questions seemed to be sizzling. He wiped them away, cleared his mind, and nodded once. 'The timing will be critical. Obviously, I can hardly split myself in two.' His hands balled up and all breath hissed through his nostrils.

I placed my hand on his arm. He looked at me, a little surprised, as though I had just appeared. 'All I need is for my father to be safe. This letter is for him. Give it to him when... *should* you find him. And please do not worry about me. I am treated well.' I held out the second envelope, gulping down the possibility that my father might never hold this message in his hands, or that this could be the only thing he would ever see of his daughter again. 'I wish I could cover your expenses.'

He was taken aback. 'Why would you say such an absurd thing? You can't possibly believe I want to be paid.'

'No, I don't think that. But I don't want you to do it because you feel sorry for me.' The instant I heard myself say it, I noticed how stupid it sounded. Yet, it was precisely what I felt.

Perplexed, he answered, 'Would a favour from a friend be more acceptable?'

Could he not see that any sympathy from him would only make my endeavour harder — near to impossible, even? No matter how much I wanted to take that last step forward and lay my cheek against his chest, it would not help me the least. All that would happen would be a weakening of my resolution. 'We have no friendship,' I said quietly. 'We are lovers who never loved. In essence, we have nothing.'

His stern face never moved as he slipped both envelopes into his voluminous bosom, and said, 'I have my own vested interest in seeing Moriarty and his entire criminal network brought to justice. That he has involved you and your father in this business complicates matters. Very unfortunate and impractical, I must confess. However, I will certainly get you both to safety soon enough. This business requires excellent planning. We will meet here again in two days' time. You had better leave now.'

I almost thanked him for that verbal slap. I found my soft self rather annoying. 'One more thing. Colonel Moran — can you tell me anything about him?'

His eyes darkened. 'He is Moriarty's right hand and the second most dangerous man you could come across.'

I nodded.

'You met him,' he noted wearily. 'Of course. Moriarty wouldn't send anyone less to capture his bacteriologist.'

'The man has an obsession with guns.'

'He is hailed the best heavy-game shot in the British Empire. I don't need to tell you to be very careful around him. He is volatile and far from being a gentleman. I am convinced he has murdered two women, but I have never been able to prove it. There are rumours that he used a child as tiger bait while he was stationed in India.'

Yes, I could easily imagine Moran doing that. He was free from scruples of any kind. My stomach revolted at the thought of going back to Moriarty's house. I wondered whether I could convince my feet to walk away from Holmes.

'Thank you,' I whispered, and watched as his eyebrows pulled apart and his shoulders sagged ever so slightly. Did he know I could read him like a book?

As I stepped out into the hallway, and the door snapped shut behind me, a feeling of overwhelming loneliness forced water into my eyes. Hastily, I blinked it away before Goff could see it.

Day 54

꧁꧂

The night was perfect — moonless, overcast, and foggy as pea soup. I could barely see the ground beneath my window. The previous day, the ice had begun to melt, leaving the ivy less brittle. The wind had settled. My scent wouldn't be carried far.

Dressed in my darkest walking clothes, I opened the window, placed a foot on the sill, and pushed myself up. With my shoes left behind in the room, my toes began to freeze as soon as I held them out into the cold and humid night air. Soon enough, the chill would crawl farther in, numbing my hands and feet and threatening to make them useless for climbing. I had to move quickly now.

The first thick vine was far to the right. I held onto the window-frame and leant far out. The fingertips of my right hand barely reached it. The heat of my own blood licked at my skin, prickling all over as I hauled myself out to catch the vine. Both my feet lost their support. I reeled down and to the side until I found another ivy branch to catch. I hugged it hard, not daring to breathe. The vines were starting to come off the wall just above my head. The thrum of my heart and the hiss of blood rushing through my head were deafening.

I pressed my brow against the cold evergreen leaves, calmed myself, and listened intently. The noise I had made while colliding with the wall must have appeared much louder to me that it had really been. The night grew dead quiet again. Nothing stirred below me or in the house.

Puffs of frosted breath clouded my view as I climbed further. Only two more yards to go. The vines beneath the other window were thicker, and I reached the sill soon enough. The ivy that had grown into the reveal was painted yellow by flickering firelight. My hand prickled as I slipped it into the brightness and slowly pushed up to peek through the window.

I don't know what I had been expecting, but it was certainly not what revealed itself to me: a large room with heavy carpets, expensive furniture, and a lit fireplace that threw light onto my hand and part of my face. There was a bed, which looked much like my own, and that fact made my stomach clench painfully. A woman with a stunning red mane sat in front of a vanity and brushed her hair with a silver brush. My head jerked back. She could possibly see me through the reflection in the looking glass.

Something was wrong, but what precisely? I closed my eyes and scrutinised the picture in my head, but could not find what it was that had disturbed me. Ever so carefully, I peeked through the window again. She was still brushing her hair. Still the same movement, over and over again. Her face in the glass was strangely unmoving, her eyes without depth. It appeared as though she saw neither herself nor her surroundings. She kept brushing the same strand of copper hair, lightly and without interest.

I began to wonder why I had risked two lives with this

excursion. Learning what Moriarty was doing to this woman had seemed important to me. Finding that there was nothing to see, that she was neither bound nor showing signs of torture, made me doubt my decision. One last look through the room and I turned away. Or rather, I meant to. I heard a shriek and saw her face turned toward me. Terror shone in her eyes.

Trying not to throw myself off the wall in haste, I scuttled back toward my window. The thick vine that had seemed close enough only moments ago, now seemed too far off. And it was loose. If it came off the wall, my excursion would be discovered. I had no other choice but to climb all the way to the ground. I tried to tread only on the few solid ice patches to avoid leaving footprints.

Barks echoed through the night. Panic struck me hard. I ran the few yards to the next vine that would lead me back up to my room. I scaled it, repeatedly stepping on the hem of my stupid skirt. The dogs were very close now and their baying would soon wake the entire household. Desperately, I flung myself through my window, tore one stocking off, rolled it into a ball and threw it as far as I could. The dogs saw the thing flying and ran after it, tearing it to pieces as soon as it hit the ground.

So that's how well trained they were.

Quickly, I yanked off my clothes, threw them into a far corner, and pulled my nightgown over my head.

The bang on my door did not come as a surprise. Neither did the low growl as he entered the room without permission. Moriarty froze in the door frame. I saw the tension in his shoulders. He stepped out of the light and snapped the door shut. Both of us in the darkness, he snatched my right hand. His was warm. Mine was ice cold.

'I'd have never expected such foolishness from you.' He

said it softly, as though speaking to a person taking her last breath. 'Let us hope your father will not contract tetanus after his hand has been hacked off.'

'Why would you want to break our agreement?'

'You cannot fool me.'

'You expect what you fear,' I quoted back to him, and the smirk was wiped off in an instant. 'The dogs were chasing after something and I watched them.' I forced my voice into monotony. 'In the thick fog they seemed to be having problems finding whatever it was they were chasing. I thought it might be a person. And I feared for him. Or her. My window was open for at least half an hour as I watched. I broke off pieces of ivy to throw at the dogs. I hoped to distract them. It did not work. Then, I saw them cornering a hare not far from the window. I rolled up one of my stockings and cast it out into the bushes. The dogs went after it and tore it apart. You can go look, the shreds should still be there. You can also look for the footprints of the hare.'

We stared at each other. Muscles feathered in his jaw. 'As you wish.' With a smirk, he pushed past me toward the window.

My heart was hammering. Each thud wanted to crack my ribcage. He leant out, inspecting the vines below the sill, then picked at the leaves and whistled. The dogs approached, yapping excitedly. 'Fetch,' he commanded. I did not dare move as the dogs' yapping, and the tapping of their paws, drifted away, and then returned.

'It appears to be a wool stocking,' I heard Durham call from outside. My breathing stopped.

Moriarty huffed. He turned away from the window and walked back to the door. Cold wind pressed against my back as he opened it.

'Have a good night,' he said.

'If you do my father any harm, I will kill you. Though I know it will be the last thing I do.'

'Not tonight,' he answered, and shut my door.

Rooted to the spot, I desperately hoped the woman next door would not mention the odd appearance of a female head in her mirror past midnight.

Day 55

❦

She had a face like a dried-up potato. Her hair was disorderly, wisps of white and grey arranged in a loose bun. Her back was bent and crooked, her hands were...slender? She winked at me and I smiled back. At him.

I bolted the lavatory door, painfully aware of Goff only inches away on the other side of the wall.

'I did not recognise you at first,' I said, a little ashamed. A corner of his mouth twitched. Something seemed to make him hesitate.

'You said you have been on Moriarty's heels for months now,' I began. He was about to open his mouth, but I held up my hand to stop him. 'We'll never again get so close to him. It's our best option.'

'You are not made for such a feat.' A simple statement.

And it split me in two. One part longed to kick his shin for underestimating me, but the other part wished to agree, sink to my knees, and beg him to free my father. But life is never that easy. I pinched my eyes shut, balled my fists, and said, 'Let that be my concern. Do you know where he keeps my father?'

He shook his head. Of course, he wouldn't know. It was too early yet.

I said, 'I believe I can gain Moriarty's trust, and gather enough evidence against him and his men.' I thought of the redhead, and kept reminding myself that she wasn't tied to a bed, that she looked unharmed. That I could do this.

Holmes's voice sounded flat as he said, 'We'll decide how to proceed once I find your father.'

I nodded, and hoped desperately Holmes might find a way to extract my father from Moriarty's clutches without Moriarty even knowing his prisoner was gone. But that seemed impossible. 'I'm aware that I represent an obstacle for you and your plan to arrest Moriarty and his gang. I am also aware that, despite the small chance that I might become an asset to your endeavour, I could just as well cause its downfall. But I am here now and we should make use of it.'

Holmes gave me a measuring stare. 'Do you have any idea what you would be getting yourself into?'

I tried a snort. It didn't sound as blasé as I'd wished. Did I see a mixture of relief and concern in Holmes's face? Or was it his hope I would soon abandon this ludicrous idea?

'I am aware of the danger,' I replied. 'Find my father. Then we will make a decision. I trust that you are able to weigh the risk to my father against that of allowing Moriarty and his henchmen to remain at large. And don't worry about me. I know how to make my escape.'

'As I already said, I will make a decision once I find him.' Holmes' hand curled around the sink's edge, his knuckles whitened. 'We need to communicate on a regular basis. I have searched this room for nooks in which to hide messages, and found certain corners to be unusually...clean.'

'This room has been searched?'

He nodded. 'Regularly.'

'Actually, I was thinking of something else. It is rather

disgusting and only a one-way communication route, but it will be safe. Moriarty has water closets installed in his house—'

'Brilliant!' he interrupted. 'Place your note in a small glass phial, then seal it with red wax. It will float and strike the eye. We need to agree on a specific time. What would be most suitable for you?'

I couldn't help but smile at the thought of Sherlock Holmes happily crawling through sewers, trying to find a message in a bottle.

'Between six and eight o'clock at night, I would think. If I should drop a glove, a handkerchief, or the like, in the morning when I alight from Moriarty's brougham, a message will be sent to you that same evening.'

Excitement shone in his eyes. How odd. The disquietude our sudden interdependency seemed to have caused him was brushed away in an instant.

Then, his face hardened. 'I have read your will. I do understand your intentions, but why would you leave your cottage to me?'

'My father wouldn't want it.'

He gazed at the door as though Goff could march in any moment. With a nod he readied himself to depart. His face collapsed into a wrinkled landscape, his shoulders hunched, his knees bent slightly. Within seconds, Holmes had transformed himself back to the tired, old woman I had encountered upon entering the lavatory.

'One more thing,' I said before taking my leave. 'The torso case last year. I remember you investigated it. Had you any suspicions?'

'Why would you ask?'

'Just answer me, please. Tell me what you know.'

He replied quietly in a machine-like *rat-tat-tat*, 'It was a woman's torso, a red-head judging from her pubic hair, and the hair in her armpits. Her skin was without blemishes and smelled faintly of patchouli. She had recently had intercourse. There was still sperm in her vagina. I found a bite mark on her hip. It was a dog's.'

Blood was ticking in my fingertips. I was glad that my back was toward Holmes.

Once I had swallowed my nausea, left the lavatory, and was walking through the corridors with Goff in my wake, I wondered whether I had just sold my father's life. And what for? For the mere possibility of saving others, and a great chance of saving no one at all?

Day 57

The brougham flew along the streets. The rattling of wheels was accompanied by the clacking and screeching of spiked horseshoes on ice-covered cobblestones. One week before Christmas, and the winter had begun in earnest and sent snow and ice all over Britain. The woollen blanket covering my legs was of little help. The only warm part of me, too warm in fact, was my head inside a velvet bag.

Moriarty had announced the inspection of a warehouse he wanted rebuilt for my tests on the spreading of glanders and anthrax. With a short apology and no further explanation, he had pulled the bag over my head. Certainly not to increase the pleasure of surprise for me.

I wondered why he suddenly felt the urge for more control. Would I have to travel blindfolded every time I went to that place, or only during initial inspections of several different buildings until one fitting our needs was found? I failed to come to a logical explanation for his behaviour and slowly, the suspicion grew that he was merely experimenting with me.

I listened to the clatter of wheels and noise from the

streets, trying to gauge the distance we had travelled. No repeating patterns were detectable, no going in circles, no detours to confuse my observations.

'You are playing a game,' I noted.

'What makes you think that?' Moriarty said.

'Hum... Maybe you're not playing, merely assessing how well I observe, something you always do. I shouldn't have asked,' I said, hoping the boredom of my tone would seep through the fabric.

'My dear, I cannot believe you would have asked without a purpose. There is nothing you do without purpose.'

How I hated to be called *my dear*. I willed my posture to relax. He could not see my face. And that was his disadvantage. 'My purpose was to let you know how annoying I find your safety measures. Besides being useless, they are dangerous. You never consider the possibility of me *wanting* to work on germ warfare. And this mistake of yours threatens my father's life and the swift success of our undertaking. It is a waste of time and resources. Or do you really believe I would invest my entire knowledge and energy under other circumstances? By the way, we are almost in East End.'

He did not answer. My brow began to sweat. The bag clung to my skin. I wished I could transfer some of that heat to my frozen feet. Finally, the brougham came to a halt. My elbow was grabbed. I was pulled up and led out of the carriage, across a street, and through a door. Only as metal fell against metal with a creak of tortured hinges, did he pull off the blindfold.

'Would this suit your purpose?' he asked.

I walked around, avoiding the mud encrusted with thin ice. Daylight dropped through grimy windows, dirtying itself on the way to the ground.

'The framework of the roof appears rotten and tiles are missing, but that can be fixed. A few windows need a new sash and almost all the panes have gone missing,' I said. 'But the dirt floor is a problem. Sewage seems to be flowing around and under the warehouse, then seeping up through the floor,' I said, pointing at stinking brown puddles. 'Do you see the salt in the walls?' I beckoned him to me and brushed some of the white flakes from the withered bricks. 'Saltpetre.'

'So?'

'This place is useless.'

His shoulders began to clench.

'The geography of the surroundings is the problem,' I hastened to explain. 'If I am not mistaken, the warehouse is built in a slight depression and above it must be slums. All their sewage flows this way. We cannot use it, because this place is probably already contaminated with half of all the diseases found in the British Empire.'

Without a word, he yanked the cloth bag back over my head.

Once back at Moriarty's house, he bade me follow him. He seemed a little more relaxed now, the wrath lurking only in a far corner of his mind.

'Hingston, the tea!' He barked before entering the study. He pulled an assortment of maps from the drawers of his bureau and spread them out on a coffee table. Impatiently, he clawed his neck and stretched his shoulders.

'Shall I?' I offered, and received a growl in response.

Hingston entered, slightly nervous. She, too, knew her master well enough to be quick and accurate now. With a soft clatter, she placed the china on the desk, owing to the lack of space on the coffee table. Quieter than one would have expected of her, she left and closed the door.

I straightened up. He seemed torn, not wanting to forgo even a fraction of his power and control. I did not move. In this one battle I was making the rules, and I was curious to see how far I could go.

'I would feel more comfortable,' I said, lowering my gaze and offering him the opportunity to save face.

He paused, then gathered up the maps. 'We will retreat to the smoking room. Durham, bring the tea,' he ordered as we walked past the manservant who was silently guarding the door.

After Durham had left, I bade Moriarty to lie down on the ottoman. He did so hesitantly.

'Would you like to ask Mister Durham to cut me into pieces, should I emerge from this room without you?' I offered.

He smiled unwillingly, but then appeared to relax a little. I would not break his neck, would not even consider it. On this day, I would take my time, and I would not think of him as the criminal dangerously close to insanity. Instead, I would think of him as someone who occasionally made an effort to be friendly. I would trick myself first, to trick him later.

My hands were warm and my eyes shut. All there was to see was through my palms. The slight bulge of blood vessels on his temples, the tapping of a pulse within. His forehead was creased, but smoothed gradually with my hands resting there. The bridge of the nose, a sharp inward bend. My finger pressed down there to tingles through his eyeballs. I heard him release a breath. His cheeks, clean shaven and smooth, skin stretched too tightly over his bones. I dug my fingers into the muscles there, found the knots and pressed them hard until they twitched and begged for mercy.

The heels of my hands slid back to his skull, over hair that thinned toward the crown. Pushing gently I noticed the stiffness of his cranial bones. Flexibly connected during infancy to allow the head's passage through the birth canal, these bones grew less pliable in the adult cranium. His skull, however, was unnaturally rigid. I undid the cravat and opened the upper buttons of his shirt. He tried to protest, but I wasn't open to discussion, and kept working on his collar-bones and shoulders. My hands slipped beneath his scapulae, searching for tension, probing ribs and vertebrae, pushing, shifting, kneading. By now, he was mine. Without looking at him, I could tell his eyes were shut, his guard down. He obeyed my hands and seemed to have no need for control. I pushed my arm beneath his neck and let his head rest in the bend of my elbow, my hand on his lower jaw. All I would have to do was twist with all my might. I felt a twinge of triumph. It distracted me, so I pushed it away. Gently, I continued to manipulate bones and flesh until it felt as though all that was twisted inside him had returned to how it was meant to be.

'Rest now,' I whispered, and walked over to the mantel-piece, retrieved a cigarette from his silver case, and sat down in the armchair. I hoped he would not open his mouth for a few more minutes. For the first time in weeks, I had no fear. For the first time in weeks, I could see myself approaching him with open arms, smiling softly, embracing him.

And slipping a blade through his armour.

Day 58

❧

The maid stood at my window, her hands resting on the sill, her lips slightly parted. The pale morning sun refracted through the frost, casting small rainbows over her skin. She looked out over the bleak premises. Her profile was vivid with longing, sadness, and, perhaps, hope.

'You are in love with Mr Garrow.'

She jumped, clapping a hand to her bosom.

'I won't tell anyone,' I said softly.

Poodle-eyed, she nodded.

'How long have you known each other, Miss Gooding?'

She heaved a sigh, walked over to me, and knelt down at the side of the bed. 'I was offered the post two years ago. And he...he's been working here longer. More than five years.' She swallowed a sob, pressed her face into my mattress, and began to cry. 'I will be sent away without reference if the master finds out.'

I patted her bony shoulder. 'As long as you are discreet, no one will know.'

'Will you promise you won't tell?' She dashed the moisture off her cheeks.

I smiled. 'There is nothing I could possibly tell anyone. All you did was gaze out my window.'

A giggle burst from her mouth. She squeezed my hand with both of hers. 'Thank you, Miss. Please, call me Cecile. If that is acceptable.'

'Cecile then. Does he know?'

'Jonathan?' A longing whisper. 'Oh, he is... Oh, I don't know. I don't think he notices me. Even if he did, he and I would have to leave. The servants aren't allowed to...to know each other. In that way.'

'Don't you think Mister Durham and Miss Hingston are having an affair?'

She blushed scarlet. The good girl was such a wonderful source of information without her even knowing it.

'Are you quite sure Mr Garrow doesn't notice you at all?'

She smiled timidly. 'Perhaps he does. At times.'

'What do you see when he looks at you?'

'Kindness.'

I wondered whether or not I should take the risk. It didn't take long for me to decide that I must — not only for her, but also for myself — to invite a little happiness into this dreadful place. 'Cecile, I think you require a secret messenger.'

She cocked her head, brow in furrows. 'What do you mean, Miss?' That squeaky voice, stuffed with hope and doubt, made her appear more fragile yet.

'You will write a letter to Mr Garrow. Jonathan, I mean. And I will deliver it. If he reciprocates your feelings, you two can write each other in secret. Later we will figure out how you can meet without anyone noticing.'

Her nostrils and eyes flared. Hastily, she dropped her gaze, produced a weak cough, and snatched my hands to press them to her forehead. 'Thank you, Miss.'

After her sniffling had subsided, she pulled herself up, her shoulders a little broader, her spine straighter.

'Cecile, may I ask whether you know the woman in the room next to mine?'

'Know her? Well, barely. She arrived the day you did. I am her lady's maid, too, but she doesn't speak much. She...sleeps a lot.'

'Is she his mistress?'

Cecile turned to the window. Her fingertips traced the edge of the curtain. 'I believe she is less than that.'

'Does she suffer?'

Her hand dropped. 'I'm sure she's...fine. She needs opium and he gives it to her. In return, she is...they are...'

'Were there others before her?'

She nodded. 'They only ever stay here for two or three months.'

'And where do they go after that?' I pressed.

'Where they came from, I should think.'

'The slums?'

She shrugged.

'Do you see them leave on their own, or are they being taken away?'

Chewing on her lower lip, she frowned. 'I've not seen them go. Perhaps Jonathan knows more?' She jumped up at footfall approaching in the corridor.

'What is taking you so long, Gooding?' Durham barked through the door.

I threw the blanket aside, walked up to the door and yanked it open. 'I was feeling poorly and Miss Gooding has been so kind as to attend to me. Thank you very much for your concern, Mr Durham.' I slammed the door in his face, and muttered loud enough for him to hear, 'That man has unacceptable manners.'

As I turned back to Cecile, she was grinning into her

hands. Then her face fell. 'Oh, I forgot!' she said, and extracted a small package from her apron pocket. 'The master wishes you to have this.'

After she left, I tore the blue crepe off the package. The small box inside revealed a crystal bottle with a note attached: *Essence of Ylang-Ylang.*

I stared at the flask, thinking of the patchouli soap Cecile had given me on my first day in this house. And I thought of the queer circumstance that when Moran had come to visit, he hadn't been greeted by barking. And there must be regular deliveries of meat, milk, butter and cheese. Of newly tailored clothing and whatever else the household might need from the outside world. Yet, no one was ever barked at or bitten. Not that I was aware of.

So, the dogs hadn't have been trained to indiscriminately kill. How, then, had they known to hunt me?

Slowly, I turned the crystal bottle in the milky daylight. The dogs knew my scent, that much I knew from that night's experiment with my stocking. They had learned to hate and fear my scent before my arrival at this house. How was that possible?

I unstoppered the bottle and inhaled. Heady. Sweet.

If it hadn't been my own scent the dogs hated, the scent must have been given to me. Was it possible a man had beaten the animals while wearing that scent? The patchouli soap was the main suspect, but it was also possible that Cecile or Hingston had been instructed to scent my clothing with something that I not smell.

But doing that would have involved too many people, and invited errors. It wasn't Moriarty's style.

Gazing at the crystal phial, I wondered what kind of murder weapon was hidden inside. Not wearing the perfume would be seen as an offence, or worse, it could reveal my suspicion a perfume was the catalyst for the dogs' killing instinct.

I washed and pulled the stopper to apply a few drops between my breasts. Patchouli and Ylang-Ylang harmonised well.

~

I WAS SURPRISED to see Moriarty at table, breakfast already set. His shoulders were relaxed, and he appeared particularly well-groomed. I tried to unclench my stomach with the good smell of scrambled eggs, warm toast, and tea.

'Ylang is derived from Tagalog, the official made-up language spoken in the Philippines, where blossoms of Ylang-Ylang are harvested. Do you know what it means?' His deep voice softly curled around my throat, leaving gooseflesh in its wake.

'No.' I sat and picked up the butter knife, turning it in the light, wondering how deep it would penetrate a skull if jammed through the eye socket.

'Ylang means wilderness.'

'Trapped in a bottle.'

His pupils snapped open, bleeding black into his irises. I would not make it easy for him, but I couldn't make it impossible either.

'The question relates to whether it is merely trapped in a bottle as you've said, or whether its essence — the purified form — is held there to prevent it from disappearing.'

'It does not matter. Wildness fades away in captivity. There is no exception to that rule.'

He tilted one eyebrow. We ate in silence, interrupted only by the crunch of teeth sinking into toast and the clink of cup against saucer.

When I alighted at the medical school, I dropped a glove

into a frozen puddle, stepped on it, stumbled, swore quietly, and picked it up without glancing around.

∾

IT WAS APPROACHING seven o'clock and supper would be served soon. I had little time left. With a pencil, I scratched a message for Holmes on a small piece of parchment.

TOMORROW, I will deposit a crystal perfume bottle in the library, behind Antony van Leeuwenhoek. I require an exact copy of the flask, filled with an aqueous solution of arsenide and belladonna, final concentration of 1% and 10%, respectively. Investigate the following warehouse locations, owners probably involved with M — (A) Limehouse Dock, at the end of Fore Street. (B) Cuckolds Point. (C) Tunnel Pier, by the river. (D) Langley Place Basin near the reservoir. (E) At the docks at Shad Thames, by the river. All should be two-storey buildings and in better condition than neighbouring ware-houses, should there be any. Yours, A.

I ROLLED IT UP, placed it into a glass phial I had taken from the laboratory, and sealed it with candle wax. After it had cooled in my hand, I slipped it into my stocking and opened the door.

Durham walked me to the water closet. I bolted the door and sat down to urinate — too suspicious if flushing were the only noise I produced.

I held on to the pull chain, pushed my fist with the phial far down into the ceramic tubing, and flushed. The water level in the bowl rose instantly. Just as it threatened to spill over, I yanked my arm back and let the flood carry my message into the sewers.

Later, when I gazed into the lightless night, I assessed the situation of the woman next door and how my fate and hers might be connected. Moriarty was playing with my fears. And he fed me more of them, only to deny any potential danger to my life a moment later. I wondered about the blackness of his heart. Had he ever dirtied his own hands? Yes. He would enjoy it, even. Would he command Moran to kill for him, or would he manipulate him into doing it? Probably both.

Moriarty seemed a master of the human psyche, knowing where to push and where to pull to mould men and women to his liking. I'd felt his force, too. His weakness was obvious, though. He believed I would not be able to harm him physically, and that his superior mind was impossible to deceive. I was, after all, but a woman.

The solution seemed so simple. I would be, after all, but a woman.

Day 59

❦

'Don't you look beautiful!' I hummed, just after the lavatory door had fallen into its frame and the bolt was slid into place. He was rather thick at the waist, with a roll of abundant bosom, hair dishevelled, and dark rimmed eyes overshadowed by sorrow and a hat.

His cheeks reddened in spite of the powder covering them. 'Thank you. I suppose both of us are at the height of our femininity.'

'Progressing age has not dampened your wit.' I quipped, punctuating with a curtsy. Although he looked like a fifty-year-old housekeeper, he couldn't have been more than ten years my senior. 'By the by, you smell of mothballs, Holmes.'

Briefly, he smiled. 'Anna.' The grit in his voice wiped away all lightness. 'I have been trying very hard to track down your father. I've been on Moriarty's heels for months, and suspect that he's aware of surveillance now. If he should see through my disguises, you would come to harm.'

And then, Holmes did something that nearly made my knees buckle: He ran a hand over his face, and inhaled a rattling breath. 'Moriarty has taken precautions. With every message he sends, four to five messengers are dispatched, all of them set off in different directions, and most of them able to evade my street urchins. I cannot show my face at Kensington Palace Gardens too often without risking your well-being, nor can I split into five of myself to track down each and every one of his runner boys.'

Leaning against the wall behind me, I tried to conceal my despair. 'Are you giving up?'

'Of course not! I will revise my tactic.'

The sharpness of his reply relieved me somewhat. I felt the perfume bottle pressing against my thigh. Turning away from Holmes, I pulled up my skirt and reached into my stocking.

'Much better to give this to you in person than to hide it in a public place,' I said, holding the bottle out to him. 'I need an identical flask filled with the ingredients described in my message.'

Hesitant, he picked it from my hand. 'Ah, expensive. Madame Rachel's.' He examined the flask before handing it back to me. 'You want to poison him, but he will expect it. Besides, there should be no need for you to turn into a murderess.'

'I am already. I killed a woman a year ago, as you well know.'

'She was killed by many hands. How much guilt you lay upon yourself is for you to decide.' After a moment of silence, he added softly, 'Should you ever spot me in public, disguised or not, and I look directly at you, you *must* run. Under no circumstances are you to hesitate. Do you understand?'

I nodded.

'Should I come to knock down Moriarty's front door, you will run the opposite way. We will meet at my lodgings or — should London become too dangerous — your cottage. If that is too dangerous, too...then the first to arrive will smash a window as a sign for the other to hide elsewhere. I know the area only from maps, but I would think the forest behind your neighbour's farm would be suitable.'

'Yes. There is a large fox and badger den. You can easily find it at the south end of the woods. Simply follow your nose. We could meet there.'

He dipped his chin.

'Holmes, I have to give Moriarty something that shows him he can trust me, or he will never share information with me. I think I should demonstrate the one weakness in his planning. Show him how easily I can escape.'

He shook his head. 'Why don't you give him what he desires most?'

I blinked at him. And swallowed. He couldn't be serious, could he? The mischievous tilt of his mouth told me that he was.

I GAVE Holmes enough time to leave the premises without haste and flying skirts. Half an hour later, our hastily exchanged words still ringing in my ears, I addressed my assistant: 'Mr Goff, I am certain that in an emergency you have the means to contact the professor immediately?'

Goff's throat blushed in anger all the way to his ears.

'Now is such an instance. I need to talk to him.' Goff did not move. 'I can accompany you, should you be worried about your...post, Mr Goff.'

The redness spread to his cheeks. 'That won't be necessary, Dr Kronberg. I am certain that whatever it is you have to tell the professor can wait until he finds the time to see you on his own account.' With that, his anger was released. He took up his usual position with hands clasped behind his back, face observant, his mind at ease.

'Well, it is your health you gamble with,' I said dryly, and turned back to the diseased rodents in front of me to puncture their brains with a metal hook. Eighty per cent of the mice that had been fed glanders germs had contracted the disease within ten days. The infection rate of anthrax was even higher.

~

I TOOK supper in my room, wondering whether Moriarty would let me wait to show that I was not in a position to demand a meeting with him. Durham had wrinkled his nose and sniffed when I'd asked to see his master. He'd led me upstairs, bolted the door, and left.

Standing at the window, I watched the breeze ruffle the fog. Footfall, a rap at the door, and a bolt snapping back announced Moriarty's arrival.

'You wished to see me,' he said, framed in the doorway, his contour sharpened by the light from the corridor.

'We may want to take this down to your study,' I replied.

He stepped aside without hesitation. As we walked downstairs, his gait appeared relaxed and I could sense no trace of his mad self. The door to his study snapped shut, and I turned to face him. 'I had the most extraordinary visitor today.'

A mask of indifference slid over his face.

'Sherlock Holmes,' I continued and his body snapped to attention, his hands curled. It seemed he wanted to take a step forward, wrap his hands around my throat, and shake the information out of me. But he recalled soon enough that I was offering this information freely.

'Go on,' he said.

'I went to the ladies' lavatory this morning, and found a thickset woman staring at me. It was Mr Holmes in disguise... How interesting, Professor. You seem greatly surprised. I had thought you installed such a blind man to be my assistant to obscure my view of other, more observant men you'd positioned elsewhere. Has no one noticed Holmes entering the hospital grounds twice in the past week?'

Moriarty's nostrils flared. His shoulders stiffened.

Holmes had told me about two men who'd been keeping me under surveillance. One of them had even entered the lady's disguised as a charwoman. I hadn't noticed either of them. And that made my stomach roil.

'Don't worry,' I continued. 'Of those you might be employing to keep an eye on me, the only one I've noticed is Goff. But Mr Goff's dullness leads me to suspect you have others.'

'You have met Mr Holmes three times now?' He kept his voice under tight control.

Despite my initial reflex to swiftly calm him, I waited and watched as various shades of rage flitted across his facade.

'I only met him today. He told me he had been watching me and had visited the medical school twice before. He meant to install a hiding place for messages somewhere under the tiles in the Ladies'.'

Slowly, his face regained its normal colouring. 'Interesting development,' he rasped.

I rubbed the goosebumps off my arms.

He caught the gesture. 'I have seen this reaction on several occasions. Why do you do this?'

'Sometimes your voice gets under my skin,' I answered, avoiding his eyes, intending to appear a bit more vulnerable and then to shake it off with anger a moment later. 'What does it matter?'

He narrowed his eyes and slowly turned away. I caught the fast pulse tapping away in his throat. What a twisted endeavour — to remain sharp and provocative while revealing more and more of my softer side, as though presenting him with an exclusive gift. Walking the knife's edge left a feeling of exhilaration in every fibre. And cold dread.

I had to be careful not to sever my self.

He strode to the cupboard where the brandy was kept, poured two glasses and carried them to the coffee table. The liquid did not quiver in the glasses. He was calm. I could not decide whether this was good or dangerous.

'Sit,' he said, lifting two cigarettes from the silver case. His gaze was scrutinising, but also seemed...new. As though we were nearing eye level. This I could not place either. Did he believe me to be as cunning as himself, or did he actually believe my charade?

'I do not find this easy, so please bear with me while I try to explain myself,' I said before filtering air through the cigarette, and letting it rest in my lungs to take an edge off. 'You abducted my father and you threaten his life. I would have willingly worked for you without all this violence. Naturally, I hate you quite ferociously, and would make an attempt on your life if that would free my father. But it would not, and so...you are quite safe. For now.'

He smiled and inclined his head.

'And then, there is Holmes. He rejected the love I offered. He ridiculed it. I will never forgive him. But I'll not sell his life for hurting my pride. I don't think I could ever hate a man so much as to wish to end it. With one exception, of course: *yours*.'

A corner of his mouth curled. 'Go on.'

'However, the situation being what it is, I am willing to sell Holmes's life in exchange for my father's freedom.'

He snorted. 'You have nothing to offer, my dear. I can have Holmes's life whenever I decide to take it.'

I answered his laugh with my own. 'So your first four attempts were merely exercise, and the fifth will be a true effort?'

Unfortunately, Holmes hadn't had the patience or time to give me details of the attempted assassinations. I flicked my cigarette into the ashtray, observing Moriarty from the corner of my vision.

A sudden cold crept into the room. My hackles rose. For a heartbeat, Moriarty looked as though he wanted to leap from his armchair. Then he settled back again, feigning indifference. It all happened so quickly and so subtly, that I would have missed it had I not known his face and his moods.

'Simply explain how you plan to wrap me around your finger, my dear.' There was a flash of his incisors.

I forced calmness into my lungs. 'The foreign secretary Mr Richard Seymour-Townsend, his wife, and their two children would do well to take a long vacation. Rather soon, I should think. Preferably in America where her parents live. I assume his mistresses won't need to go into hiding when Holmes reveals the exchange of considerable amounts of money and sensitive information between Mr Seymour-Townsend and…you.'

Moriarty's eyes drifted into the empty space between us as he reached for his brandy.

I continued, 'It appears that Mr Holmes enjoys solving crimes with me. He cannot imagine that a woman's pride might be hurt by first rejecting her advances, only to ask for her help a year later. My offer to you is as follows: I will share with you every bit of information Holmes shares with me. That allows you to save your men. Or at least the ones you choose to save. But before I begin to play this game, you will let my father go. In addition, you must agree to abstain from controlling my every move. Christmas is in four days and I wish to spend it with my father before he travels back to Germany.'

He turned the crystal glass in his hand, observing the movement of the brandy within. The refraction of the firelight. How the liquid ran like oil down the sides of the glass. 'I cannot trust you.'

I shot up from my chair and took three quick strides toward him. 'I am serving you Holmes on a silver platter and I have stayed in your house of *my own will* for almost two months now!'

He threw his head back and barked a laugh. Drops of spilled brandy soaked onto his trousers. 'Preposterous!'

'You believe I cannot escape?'

'I don't *believe*. I *know*.'

'All I need is half an hour,' I replied. 'I will pass your dogs unscathed, and you will let my father return home.'

Another cold smile. 'Accepted.'

I dashed from the study and up the stairs to my room, pulled the bell rope and began unbuttoning my dress. The maid arrived moments later.

'Cecile, I need to wash. Make haste and don't bother heating the water. The essential part is that I need your soap. Yours, not anyone else's. Please, make haste.'

She curtsied and left. I kicked off my boots, pulled off stockings, and dress, and was stark naked when she returned. She froze as I approached, and jumped as I snatched the water jug and soap from her hands.

Quickly, I scrubbed my body, washed my hair, and dressed in the male clothing Moriarty had arranged for me, but which I had never worn. Then I ran back down to his study.

'Well?' he said, slightly amused.

'Eight minutes left,' I noted with a glance at the clock on the mantelpiece. 'Will you accompany me to the door or do you prefer to watch from the window?'

He stood, and walked me through the entrance hall.

'Do you want me to climb over the gate, or is it enough to reach it?'

'Try to reach it.'

'Very well.' I took two steps forward. 'I won't apologise for this,' I said, and raked my hands through his hair before he could take a step back. I didn't wait for his surprise to subside and his rage to regain control.

I strode out the front door.

My heart did its best to crack my ribs. I ran. Ice-cold wind bit my neck. Twenty yards onto the premises, I stopped and turned. Moriarty stood in the doorway, a revolver in his hand. I wondered where he had got it so swiftly. Would he use it to shoot the dogs and save his bacteriologist, or shoot me and save face? I pushed the thought aside as I heard the huffing of the mastiffs.

I must be mad!

I stayed put, calmed my breath, and uncurled my fists. The wind gushed around the house, and pushed at my back. The dogs slowed, scented the air. They must have been able to sense a trace of what they were trained to kill. But intermingled was the scent of their master. I angled my palms into the wind. Growling, the dogs came to a halt about a yard away from me. Only the largest of them dared to get closer, hackles up, canines on display. But its tail was half way down, its ears folded. The animal didn't know what to make of me.

I took a step forward, held out my palms, and growled.

Moriarty made no noise. Was shocked by the flaw in his security? Was he waiting for the dog to lunge at my throat? Sensing my distraction, the dog jumped. I shouted and aimed a kick at its jaw. With a yelp, the dog retreated, tail tucked against its belly.

With all my instincts revolting, I stood tall and turned my gaze and body away from the pack. And I waited. The dogs yipped and huffed nervously.

On top of the marble stairs, the electric light silhouetted Moriarty. It was impossible for me to see his face, but the tension in his shoulders was obvious. And all of a sudden, a wet muzzle pressed against my knuckles, and a little later, another one. I ran my hand along the sides of their heads and talked softly, turned away to stroll to the gate and back again, all the while trying not to agitate the animals with hasty movements.

When I walked up to the house, Moriarty released the hammer of his gun.

Day 62

The morning came on tiptoe. Clouds, fog, drizzle, and wet ground melted together, drifting from the dark grey of the night into a lighter grey of the day. My heart ached. Soon, my father would be free. Or so I hoped. But so much could go wrong.

Just before lunch-time, the brougham stopped at the house. My father stepped out, slightly hunched, eyes squinting, hands trembling on the doorframe of the carriage. His legs seemed barely to support him. His hair was greyer now and his once broad shoulders appeared bony. The old carpenter had aged, and was but a shadow of himself.

As I rushed toward him, I was terrified he might be ill beyond cure, or that he would hate me for what I was doing. Or that my plan for getting him safely back to Germany would fail.

He smiled at me. It took effort and didn't reach his eyes. He saw right through me. He always had.

Moriarty received us in the hall, hands in his pockets, upper lip stiff. This was probably a tad too much drama for him.

'I want to talk to my daughter,' rolled out of my father's mouth and right into Moriarty's face. I was about to translate when he replied in fluent German, 'Natürlich. Sie beide können sich nach dem Mittagessen zurückziehen.'

Certainly. You may retire after we have taken lunch.

I nearly knocked over one of the tall vases in the hall. Moriarty was giving away a secret he could have used against me, and he did it so...lightly. Why? How many others did he have up his sleeve?

Countless, I should expect.

Lunch was served and my father ate as though he hadn't eaten for days. I felt the urge to shield him from our *host*, who was observing the two of us as a cat would eye a couple of stray sparrows. None of us spoke. But what could possibly be said between an abductor and his victims? No apologies or explanations could change what my father and I were feeling.

As soon as we had eaten, I took my father up to my room so that he might rest a little. He lowered himself onto my bed, huffed, and shut his eyes.

I placed my hand on his sallow cheeks. 'Thank God.'

He snorted in reply. He had not heard those words from me before.

'Where did they keep you?' I asked.

He shook his head, and coughed. 'One night, a man came to my house, and ordered me to drink from a small bottle, saying you and I would both be shot if I did not do it.'

'What did he look like?'

'Blond, cold blue eyes, hard face. Like a soldier. No, like a murderer. No emotion, no...warmth, regret, or...anything human in his eyes. Only calculation, and something else, flickering there. As though he floated above mankind. His accent... I think he came from Berlin.'

'And then?'

'I drank, lost consciousness, and woke up in a cellar.'

'I am so sorry, I never...' My throat closed. I pressed my face into the crook of his neck. The scent of fresh wood shavings was missing.

He tugged on a lock of my hair. 'It isn't your fault.'

We talked quietly, and soon he drifted into a slumber. His expression grew unguarded and for the first time, I saw his true age show. The creases around his eyes, so typical for his way of laughing unrestrained, now had siblings around eyebrows and mouth. The skin around his eyes had grown pale. Sorrow marked him. I tried to smooth out the wrinkles with my fingertips, being careful not to wake him, thinking of my childhood and how precious he had made it.

I swallowed a sob, and wondered what kind of woman I would have grown into if he had forced me to follow social conventions? But he'd never cared much for those. His honesty and unreservedness had set me on my own feet, taught me to go my own way. Even as a small child, I'd had a strong sense of justice, and the urge to discuss everything with him. In his endless patience, he'd informed this tiny person why God had made her short, why He had given her that squeaky voice, why she had to go to bed when she was tired, why she was growing so slowly, and why people spoke to her in ways that showed they did not take her seriously.

On my fourth birthday I'd announced that from that day forward I would be calling him Anton instead of father whenever we should debate important business, such as our ever-limited (or non-existent) family budget, or my future as the first lady carpenter the village would ever see. He would simply reach out his large, rough hand and shake mine. He could have laughed at me, about such pretentiousness, but he never did. Never when it counted.

My father stirred. His eyes fluttered open. 'Did I fall asleep? Oh. Well...what are *you* doing here, anyway? In this house? With that...man?' His bushy eyebrows bunched together as he tried to look behind my calm facade.

I placed my finger over my lips and shook my head, then spoke loud enough for any eavesdropper to hear, 'I'm staying here because the work I'm doing for Professor Moriarty is very important. But please, father, you must not ask any more about this.'

He opened his mouth, and shut it. Then he whispered, 'I do hope you know what you are doing.'

My eyes began to itch. I put my mouth close to his ear, and said, 'Tell me everything that happened. What you heard, who you met. Describe the men who gave you food and water.'

He coughed, a horrifyingly deep and rattling sound. 'It was all very queer. No one came to see me, no one ever talked to me. Food and water were pushed through a hatch in the door, as was the chamber pot. And later, your letters.'

'They kept you in a hole for two months?'

He rubbed his face. 'Today...I guess it was early morning... a servant unlocked the door and motioned for me to step out. I was provided with a hot bath, a barbing, and new clothes. I assume it was English he spoke. I have no idea what he said. Then he pulled a bag over my head and brought me to a carriage that drove about, for what must have been an hour. There was no one but me inside so I pulled off the bag. I could not tell where I was. I'd never before seen this...is it London? Ah, yes. It must be. Then we drove up to this house, and *you* were standing at the door. But what will happen now? Did the man...Professor Moriarty...say anything?'

'Has no one told you that you can go home today?'

He sat bolt upright. 'We are free to leave?'

'You will take a ship to Germany tonight.'

His expression darkened. 'You keep talking about my leaving. Are you telling me that you are staying?'

I nodded once.

He groaned. 'What *is* this? I can see you are unhappy,' he whispered and squeezed my hand. 'Ah, what am I saying? You are not only unhappy, you are suffering, child. I won't leave without you.'

I patted his hand. 'I am quite safe. And you will be made to leave. Moriarty will make sure you go to Germany, while I remain here. There is no discussing it with anyone.' I unclenched my jaw, and added, 'Knowing you are safe will make this easier for me.'

He huffed, which brought on a coughing attack. Panting, he leant back against the headboard.

'How long have you been ill?' I asked.

'The past three weeks.'

'Allow me,' I said, unbuttoned his waistcoat, and pressed my ear to his chest for want of a stethoscope. I pushed my fingers into the sides of his throat, feeling the swollen lymph nodes. 'Open your mouth, please.' The view wasn't pretty. His tonsils were oozing yellow pus.

'You have bronchitis and tonsillitis. I'll find medicine for you. Rest a little now. I will be back in a few minutes.'

'I've already rested,' he muttered, but I ignored his protest and rang for the maid. She arrived a moment later.

'Cecile, I need a jar half filled with honey, and a spoon. I'll be picking herbs in the garden.' With a glance back at my father, Cecile and I left. On the way downstairs I asked her if there was a herb garden for the kitchen, and she told me where to find it.

Winter is not a season for collecting medicinal herbs, because the plants produce fewer alkaloids than they would in spring and summer. I found a handful of limp but greenish ribwort leaves, and a few twigs of oregano under a crusty layer of snow. Back in the house, I found Cecile and accepted a jar of honey from her.

'I wish I could see you home safely,' I said to my father upon my return. I rubbed the dirt off the ribwort leaves and stirred them into the honey, then passed him the oregano. 'Chew this, please. Swallow only the saliva.'

'Witch!' he said with a grin.

'The oregano is to stop the inflammation of your tonsils. The ribwort would normally have to soak in the honey for a week. But we don't have that much time. Take the first spoonful of honey on the ship to Germany, and the rest once every two hours. Eat the leaves, too. You'll be astonished by the amount of mucous that will come out of your airways once the ribwort begins to work.'

Gently, he touched my cheek, his expression heavy with the many things he wanted to say but couldn't. 'Katherina will be so worried.' His hands clapped over his face. A sigh pressed through his fingers.

Katherina had been his neighbour and friend for as long as I could remember. He had begun courting her in the last year or so. 'Anton, listen very carefully now. I have reason to fear for your safety. You *cannot* stay at home. You must go into hiding as soon as possible.' I paused, watching his expression of dread transform into resolution. 'Will Katherina understand?'

'Of course she will,' he said.

'You never married her. Why?'

His face fell. 'We wanted to get married on Christmas Day. What day is today?'

'The twenty-third.'

'Oh, God,' he cried. 'She probably believes I'm dead!'

'You can send her a wire before the ship leaves. I don't dare send it from here. He...' I jerked my head toward the door, '...mustn't know about her.'

My father dropped his head. Fatigue made his breathing heavy.

I took his hand in mine, and whispered, 'I must finish this. I might have to do things that you wouldn't approve of. Criminal things. I might...have to kill a man. The one you met at lunch today.' I didn't dare tell him how I intended to accomplish this.

Muscles rippled in his jaw as he stared at my hands, unspeaking.

'Am I still your daughter?'

His chest grumbled a warning when he pulled my face closer to his and whispered, 'I love you more than life. But what are you thinking, child? You are but one small woman, and you want to fight these bastards?'

I put my mouth close to his ear. 'That is what I have been doing for more than a year now. But I am not alone, and it's almost over.' Those last words were more hope than truth, and he must have realised it.

'I can't lose you. I just can't!' he whispered urgently.

'And I don't want to lose *you*. So please, leave without making trouble. Go home, pack your bags, and visit your old friend Matthias. And never tell a soul where you are headed.'

He and his friend could take to the roads, as they'd done in their youth. Remote villages and small towns in the Swiss Alps would render them invisible to Moriarty's men.

My father cleared his throat and pulled me into a tight embrace.

It felt as though it might be our last.

≈

ONLY TWO HOURS LATER, the two of us boarded the brougham. I was surprised Moriarty allowed me to travel so far. On the way to Tilbury, we whispered incessantly, planning his journey to Switzerland, and how best to stay hidden. We reached our destination much too quickly and all we could agree on was that we would not write each other, as doing so would betray his whereabouts, and that he must be careful, take to the roads together with his friend, and stay away from home for at least two months. I should have expected his response. 'You want to stay *that* long with this man?'

I dropped my gaze to my boots. He sighed and pulled me into an embrace. 'Forgive me,' he said softly. I could barely hear his words over the slowing rattle of wheels.

Standing at the docks, I fought back tears. But my vision blurred, my throat constricted, and my heart did its usual, painful thing whenever it was about to lose someone beloved. The ship's horn blared, the ropes were pulled in. The figures on deck grew smaller. I would have to give him at least one week to get into hiding. Then I would act.

Garrow waited patiently. I turned to him. He gave me a nod. For a brief moment, I thought there was sympathy in his eyes. But I might have been mistaken. It was dark and the glint of the street lanterns in the coachman's eyes could be interpreted any which way.

We had been travelling for a while when a thought hit me. I knocked on the roof and called for Garrow to stop. I opened the door and jumped onto the dirt road.

'Do you mind?' I pointed up at the space next to him. He moved aside a little, and I noticed that he had just pulled his hand out of his coat pocket. The bulge remaining there must have been a revolver. So that was how Moriarty had made sure I would not run away. Would Garrow have shot me or only threatened me? I pushed the thought aside. I had a promise to keep.

'My apologies. It was rather boring down there,' I explained as I climbed into the driver's seat, and wrapped a blanket around my cold legs.

'Ma'am, you will catch a cold up here.'

'What did I study medicine for?' I snapped back. 'Oh, Mr

Garrow, I've always wondered what your scar looks like. If it is really this... er, large, as my maid keeps telling me. Would you mind showing it to me? My curiosity is purely professional, of course.'

The man froze. In one stiff move, he turned toward me and pulled his muffler down, showing me his whole face for the first time. His scar was mostly covered by a stubble, giving him a slightly dangerous touch.

'Tut-tut! Miss Gooding really does not know what she is talking about. She has never truly looked at you, I assume.'

Garrow pulled his muffler back up, but it couldn't conceal his anger. He needed another shove.

'I wonder why she keeps telling me that your scar in unappealing. I find it makes you rather—'

'She certainly said no such thing!' he grumbled without looking at me.

'Mr Garrow! Are you saying that I am a liar?'

It took him a moment or two, but when he turned back to me, his eyes held only coldness. 'That is precisely what I am saying, Ma'am.' He yanked the horses to a halt. 'This is the driver's seat,' he noted with a nod down toward the carriage's door.

I smiled at him apologetically. 'Mr Garrow, please forgive me. I needed to be certain you would be more loyal to Cecile than to me. She likes you very much, but doesn't dare show it, for she's afraid of losing her assignment.'

The reins slackened. Without a word, he turned back to the horses and gave them a gentle smack.

'I offered to act as a messenger, should you agree to take the risk. I see both of you every day, and no one else needs to know that you write each other.' He nodded, apparently deep in thought, and did not speak until we reached London.

'I am unable to read and write,' he said.

'I will read her letters to you and write down your words

for her, if you wish. One day she can teach you how to read and write.'

He laughed at that, a bitter mix of happiness and sadness.

When we arrived, the view of the large house hauled all the facts back in place: Moriarty had kept my father in a cellar for two months, with only cold stones, mould, and spiders for company. Without announcing myself, I entered the study, rushed up to him, and hit him with all my might. He groaned, pressed one hand to his bleeding nose, and slapped my face with the other. I wanted to claw out his eyes, throttle and kick him. But I forced control upon myself. Sucking in two deep breaths, I lowered my fists to my side.

He produced a single nod. I answered with one in return, and left. Durham asked me whether I needed something. I declined and walked up to my room. No one accompanied me. No one bolted my door. But I was not relieved. Bolt and gaoler merely served the purpose of decoration. Without them, the prison still existed.

Day 63

✿❀✿

On Christmas morning, the quiet and empty house filled up to suffocation with Moriarty's family. Until that day, I had not wasted a single thought on potential siblings, nieces and nephews. I never took into consideration that a man like him could have hatched from a womb.

The children with their bubbly mouths, glowing faces, and stomping feet, the happiness and chaos they carried with them, seemed entirely out of place. Did they not sense that this house was a prison?

Their mothers —well-behaved ladies with flawless pedigrees — went here and there, touched Christmas ornaments, *ooh-ed* and *aah-ed*, and occasionally slapped an overly wild youngster over the head. Men were gathered in the smoking room, where aromatic tobacco fumes crawled out a half-open door, to be stirred up by children running past every so often. Why I had been asked to take part in this celebration, I could not fathom. I could only guess that it might have been too bothersome to hide me from all those curious eyes and noses.

Trying to shut out the chattering about the royal family, I

leant my head against a frosted window pane, and thought of my own childhood Christmases. The tallow candles we had made. The neighbour's goose in the oven (if we could afford it), and the talks over hot goat's milk and barley coffee. The presents we gave each other had been small and useful: a pocket knife he made for me, or socks I knitted for him. The quality of my handicraft was an insult to all knitters. My father wore the socks anyway, although not for long, because they all died an early and leprotic death of disintegration.

I coughed to release the tension in my throat, hoping my father were safe already. Then I turned back to the merry congregation of spoiled, upper-class individuals.

The women were immersed in talk of the weather, of the news blaring from the front pages of the newspapers, the latest fashions in London or Paris, or — God forbid — America.

Suddenly, all eyes turned to me.

'Miss Kronberg, James has told us that you lived in Boston for two years. Please, sit with us and tell us everything!' A hand patted the chaise longue, several large gems wiggling on her fingers.

I smiled meekly. Two ladies moved aside so that I might squeeze in between them.

'You must know all about women's fashion in America. Surely, you think it outrageous?'

I really had no idea what she was referring to. 'I could not say.'

That caused some consternation, which was wiped away with tight-lipped sips from fragile porcelain cups, and one or two throat clearings.

'I did not purchase a single dress in Boston,' I explained.

Gasps were stifled.

The woman who had invited me to sit was Moriarty's older sister, Charlotte. I guessed her age to be close to fifty.

Her facial features revealed their shared blood, but the rest of her was probably four times as wide as her brother. And like her brother, she manipulated the behaviour of her company with ease, making them agree or disagree as she please, bending them like grass in the wind.

Charlotte laughed artificially, and everyone chimed in. 'What an *extraordinary* dislike for American fashion you must entertain, my dear.' Her voice was a little too high-pitched, but her *my dear* sounded exactly like her brother's. Perhaps it was routinely used in the family to express depreciation. Everyone joined the polite exhilaration, fingertips half-covering their mouths. Then silence fell, and their big-eyed attention was directed back at me.

'Not quite. I had no particular like or dislike for American women's fashion. My lifestyle was such that I could only wear...men's clothing.' My chest almost burst with *Schaden-freude* as I forced my face to show only naivety and innocence.

Shocked silence followed. One could have heard a flea hop, had there been any.

Some faces turned a shade of pink, others pale.

I continued, 'At the age of sixteen I cut off my hair, put on trousers, and enrolled at the Leipzig University. I studied medicine and bacteriology, was awarded a fellowship by the Harvard Medical School, and later worked at Guy's hospital here in London. I masqueraded as a man for twelve years, and I must say that it was quite refreshing. It is almost regrettable that now, women can study and practice medicine without criminalising themselves.'

I was certain that none of the ladies had ever met a female doctor. As a matter of fact, the only one I had ever seen was my own reflection.

All that was audible were the shallow breaths of my audience, and the sounds of children playing in the hallway, on the stairs, and in the drawing room. Even the men had ceased their conversation. Only the tobacco smoke dared move.

'What an adventure,' Charlotte quipped, dismissing the topic with a flick of her hand. Then she turned to the other ladies and chattered about some lord I had never heard of and his mistress I didn't know either. The men recommenced their discussion on politics and the Kaiser, while the children started making plans on which of them should venture into the kitchen to steal the candied fruits.

Hands in my lap, shoulders and waist buried in my neighbours' fashionably puffed sleeves, I tried to appear somewhat ladylike — while indifferent to all the droning about trifles. Half an hour later, lunch saved me from the brainless torture.

A delicate turtle soup was handed around, eaten, and then taken away. A turbot with lobster and sauce, oysters, patés, sweetbreads, duckling, green goose, accessories of salad and vegetables were all marched in, taken apart, ingested, and their remainders carried away.

The sheer amount of food, how it was stuffed into mouths shining with grease, mouths eating more than a stomach could take, chewing and talking and stuffing in yet more, made me nauseous. My corset's grip grew unbearable. My lungs tried to expand in vain. Even eating the little I had managed to, proved too much for so constricted a space.

The day of useless chatter and natty behaviour went on until finally — to the children's delight — the dining room was locked and secret undertakings unraveled behind its closed door. With red cheeks — still shiny with goose fat — and quivering elbows poking each other's ribs, the youngsters waited. Minutes stretched into hours. Finally, the door was opened by none other than Father Christmas himself, or rather the coachman in disguise. All the children fell silent. The man was a threat. He could withhold presents if he chose so. Seven short people were lined up, with the smallest in front and the taller ones in back. Father Christmas beckoned them in and gave each one a present, accompanied by well-meant grumbling.

The scene that followed resembled a battlefield. Children sat on the floor, trying to pry open packages, at first tentatively, and then ever more impatiently. Soon, the loot was ripped and gutted, innards spilled and greeted with happy squeals. Despite my nausea, I couldn't help but smile. And stopped the instant I spotted Moriarty on the other side of the room. He was observing me, wearing an oddly satisfied expression.

Lightheaded and aching for fresh air, I went up to my room, tore the windows open, and rang for Cecile. She helped me loosen the corset. We sat on the bed, and she pulled an envelope from her apron pocket.

I promised to covey her message to Garrow the next day, and placed the letter under my pillow. Her eyes shone with excitement.

'Now let me rest a little, for the merry company downstairs has left my brain quite wrung out.'

A giggled *thank you,* and Cecile left me alone. My throbbing head was happy to lie on the cool pillow. Just a minute, I told myself as I shut my eyes.

~

A RAP WOKE ME. The room was in darkness. I coughed, which must have been interpreted as an inviting *yes.* The door opened and the slender shadow of a man walked in. My stomach clenched and I was suddenly wide awake. My feet propelled me out of bed in an instant. He stopped, looked around in the room, stepped toward the candle on the chest of drawers, and lit it with a match. He was thoughtful enough not to switch on the electric light.

'Are you not feeling well?' His voice was kind, almost soft. I wondered whether he had smoked opium. But the scent was missing. Was he eating it, too?

'I felt poorly, and decided to rest. My apologies.' But there shouldn't have been reason for him to be offended by my disappearance. My presence hadn't been welcome during the evening hours, for dinner was a family business.

'Would you care to take a late supper with me?'

All the muscles in my body reacted in unison, snapping to attention, ready to jump. 'Your guests have left?' I asked, feeling the unavoidable...pulling me toward the dreadful path I was intending to walk.

'Yes. It is past nine in the evening. The children became quite unbearable.'

I wondered about the woman next door. He must have seen my gaze flicker to the wall and back again. 'I sent her away,' he said, before walking back to the open door, and waiting for me to follow.

THE TABLE WAS SET for two, with neither Durham nor any other servant in sight. I sat and thought about my father. He should have reached home by now.

A cough. I looked up. Moriarty pointed to my food, the fork stuck in it, nothing eaten. I dropped my gaze to my plate, just now noticing it was cold goose breast, cut into thin slices. There was fresh bread on the table next to butter that had begun to melt on its plate, and a bottle of red wine shining in the candlelight.

Romantic, almost.

'Would you care to join me in a game tonight?' he asked casually.

'What game?'

'Are you really *that* unwell to not understand me?'

'Perhaps I'm slower than you wish me to be.' I stuffed meat into my mouth to give my teeth something to do, other than clench.

'I propose a game of honesty.'

I snorted, and spread butter on the steaming bread. It quickly melted to a puddle of warm gold. 'I've already told you how I plan to kill you.'

'Very well,' he said, dissatisfied with my scant reply.

I took a bite of bread and cringed. The cooks had been too generous with garlic in the butter.

He poured wine. I drank it fast. My tongue felt heavy and almost furry. He refilled my glass without asking, then left the table and walked over to a corner of the room. A cranking noise, then music. I tipped the second glass of wine down my throat.

'Humour me,' he said, offering his hand.

I reached out and he pulled me up. My feet felt as though they weren't mine. Instead of a feared dance, he led me to the ottoman. I noticed the long pipe on the small table next to it.

'What was in the butter?' I felt...lightheaded, and disconnected from myself. The thought of having been given a drug was terrifying.

'Opium. Sit, please.'

I sat on the ottoman, paralysed like a rabbit in a wolf's maw. I knew well enough where this was heading. The knowledge tied my tongue even as my mind blared a thousand warnings.

'You'll find it more comfortable to lie down. Hold the pipe and inhale when I say so. Keep the smoke in your lungs as long as possible.'

It did not sound like an order. More like an invitation. *And wasn't this my idea? To get close enough to do what I must?*

I leant back and watched him cut a small piece off a brownish lump, the familiar smell oozing off it. My knees shook, and I pressed my legs together, fearful that he would throw himself upon me the instant the drug took effect.

He noticed my reaction, and pulled up an eyebrow. 'If I had wished to violate you, I could have done so long ago.'

'I am terrified of the drug,' I said.

'Why? You have seen its effects.'

'But I have not experienced it. Besides, you use opium as a shortcut. You manipulate. You prefer coercion to blunt force.'

The pipe sank onto his lap as he looked at me. 'Our fears are our own, and it is we who must learn to control them. Leave them behind where they belong. Only then can you see what is and what isn't.' Then, he performed the same elaborate procedure of heating the coal and melting the drug.

He held out the pipe to me. 'Opium will not make you do things you don't want to do. It will, instead, show you what your mind is capable of. Trust me this once.'

I swallowed my fear and took the pipe from his hand, blew air onto the melting lump, sucked in smoke, and was hit by surprise: Instead of the expected scorching sensation, a pleasant caress went down my airways and bronchi.

'Repeat,' he said.

Again, I blew air through the pipe onto the coal and filled my lungs to let the drug wash through my eyes and brain. I kept it in, watching him watching me. After a minute, my lungs screamed for fresh air.

As I watched him prepare another smoke, I noticed how my senses seemed to expand. Memories of my childhood came back, things forgotten or simply put aside as irrelevant. How our garden smelled just after the snow melted, how the sun painted small prickly lights onto the patches of grey slush and made them look pretty. My chest heaved a sigh and my hand wandered to my stomach, marvelling at the beauty of touch and the caress of expensive silk.

I sensed his smile before I turned my head. His face and the smoke exiting his nostrils was the last I saw before falling...

...down. I stood next to my cottage, my bare feet in the green grass. Soon, the summer sun would peek over the hilltop and dip trees, meadows, and cottages into streams of golden light.

The rich breakfast of four eggs and porridge would have to suffice for the next six hours. In the tool shed, I placed the scythe on the anvil's nose and started beating the blade's edge with a hammer, moving it slowly along the anvil to force the edge thinner and thinner without loss of tension in the metal.

After working it with a whetstone, I fastened the blade to the handle. The black scythe with its silvery edge was now so sharp I could shave my neighbour's beard off.

The sky began to pale, announcing the rising sun. I walked to my field where the rye was high and ripe.

I aimed the first sweep. Upon contact with the blade, each stem burst open, producing a popping noise. Hundreds of small blasts unified into one long rough smack with each gash I made. Smack!

The rye fell in a semicircle around me. Smack! *At the end of each swing, I tipped the scythe just enough to pour all of the stems into an even bunch.*

Two hours later, I took a short break and drank water from my pouch. The sun stood three hands above the hill. Sweat ran down along my aching spine. It was good pain. It meant I was healthy and working hard. My scythe felled the rye, smack after smack, row after row, until the sun stood high above me. As I bound the rye into sheaves and stacked them upright on the field to dry, memories took hostage of me once again. Memories of the woman I had killed, of her haggard face and her tired eyes. of how I scrutinised myself every day. Had she begged to live or to die? Was there a difference between euthanasia and murder?

I found Moriarty and I had not moved. Strangely refreshed, I sat up.

'How long have I been sleeping?'

'Two or three minutes.' His voice was calm, and the low hum of it crawled under my skin.

'It felt like...'

'Much longer,' he interrupted. 'How do you feel?'

'Like myself, but...taller.' I had to laugh. 'That wasn't the right choice of words, obviously.' My voice sounded oddly relaxed, and my mind felt very sharp. I knew with utter precision how tall the ceiling was, how far away the roof and every wall in the house, any tree on the premises.

'Don't you find your lack of apprehension curious?' he asked. 'This is the effect of opium taken in small doses. It opens your mind. Rids you of useless preconceptions. How do you feel?'

'With you next to me — intrigued, but threatened.'

'Good. I wouldn't want it to dull your mind. Only...free it, as I said already.' His eyes intense, he reached out, offering me his hand. 'Dance with me.'

I placed my hand in his again, and he pulled me up. My legs still felt foreign to me. I tested their functionality as he crossed the room to the gramophone. A scratching noise preceded a change of music.

To this day I can precisely recall the melody of what was played, although I had never heard it before and never have again. I can still feel his hand on the small of my back and the counter-pressure of his chest and stomach against mine. And the cold burning it caused, despite the softness of the touch. He led me as he led everything else — with skill and authority, while never taking his eyes off mine. My mind and my senses filled the room, enveloping us, knowing precisely what would happen, and that I would survive and he would not.

And as he leant closer, dipped his cool lips onto mine and let his breath flow over my face and neck, I fell deep into my darkest place where a dead woman looked up at me, and reminded me that I was her murderer and not the least bit better than the man who held me. I let my lips be conquered, pressed closer to him, and at last understood the entire impact of opium and why men could not withdraw from it.

The utter completeness of knowing and sensing took my breath away.

He straightened up, smiled, and took my hand into his yet again. He kissed my knuckles, then led me upstairs. At the door to my room, we stopped. I started trembling with fear. *So soon?*

He opened the door for me, kissed my hand, and wished me a good night.

Alone then, I sat on my bed, trying to piece together the contradicting information. The game had begun. Or had it? Did he guess what I was planning? Surely, he must know I wouldn't be suddenly fond of him? But what precisely was *his* plan? Why the sudden retreat? And why that knowing smile?

Groaning, I rose and pressed my forehead against the cold windowpane. All these questions itching on my tongue, and I could not ask a single one. Instead, I had taken one step closer to the man who might destroy me.

I watched the dogs play and then it hit me. He wanted to confuse. To leave no visible path. He would take detours when I wouldn't be expecting them, shortcuts where I couldn't see them. And by starting an intimate relationship, he would make sure I could not infect him with a deadly disease without risking my own life.

But could he not guess my recklessness? Did he not see that he was in grave danger?

I lay down on my bed. Sleep would not carry me away. Reality kept its firm grip on me. I would not be afraid. I would not waver.

Day 64

I didn't know where to put my hands. Behind my back, on the windowsill, or clenched at my sides. The dreaded knock sounded, and Cecile and Hingston entered my room. The older woman carried a dress, the younger a wooden box embellished with carvings and mother-of-pearl inlays.

I began to undress. All the small, stubborn buttons only reluctantly slipped through their holes. I willed myself to breathe. There was no way out. And, after all, I was being silly.

Moriarty had asked for my company at the opera that night. He couldn't know that music was like the siren call for me. It made me soft, and with him at my side, softness meant weakness. I couldn't afford that. Swallowing the clump of foreboding, I stepped out of my dress.

'Fetch water and tongs,' ordered Hingston. Cecile deftly set the box on a chest of drawers and left. Hingston picked up the dress and shook it, as if there were creases that needed chasing away. The garment was made of elaborately embroidered burgundy silk — something I could never afford. I couldn't even put it on without help.

Upon Cecile's return, the two women dabbed water onto my curls, and flattened them with hot iron tongs. They rubbed lemon juice on my face, and washed it off again. They plucked my eyebrows, and applied creams and perfumes from Madame Rachel's. A postiche of long, shiny black hair was clipped to mine and elaborately braided and pinned. I wondered to whom it had once belonged. Whether she yet had children to feed, and if she had grown her hair had long again to sell it once more.

Even though I had no fat to be pressed from the ugly places to the pretty ones, Hingston strung the corset very tight. Then, both women dropped the dress over my head, buttoned it at the back, and laced my boots. With a curtsy and a timid smile, Cecile handed me gloves, hat, and cloak.

My lungs restricted from too-tight lacing and my heart tittering, I went downstairs. When I spotted Moriarty waiting in the hall, I had to force my feet forward. The sound of my heels on the stairwell made him turn.

'Astonishing' he muttered as I reached him. I noticed the slight reddening of his throat just above the cravat, slowly spreading to his cheeks.

He offered me his arm, and this time I took it, smiled and said softly, 'You seem to neither value your neck nor your arm very much.'

His eyes flared as he suppressed a laugh. Good. He was enjoying our game of cat and mouse.

We walked down the marble stairs, to where Garrow had opened the door of the waiting brougham. He snapped down the stairs and helped me inside.

I sat by the window, gazing at the London I'd once known. The lamplighters were leaning their ladders against streetlamps, and it would not be long until warm gaslight kissed flecks of melting snow. We passed through busy streets and shot through dark alleys, disregarding people dressed in rags, the old, the sick, the poor, all jumping out of the shiny brougham's path, all staring at us, trying to catch a glimpse of wealth.

I shut my eyes, remembering the stink of the slums. The smell of home. St Giles, London's worst rookery, seemed like a long-lost paradise.

'The Lyceum Theatre,' Moriarty informed me as the carriage trundled to a halt.

With my hand curled around the bend of his elbow, I ascended the stairs to the building. A tug made me lift my gaze.

'Professor,' called a tall man clad in dark blue and black, silver hair sticking out from beneath his hat.

'Marquess, Marchioness,' Moriarty answered with a hint of a bow. The female accessory must have been at least twenty years younger than the man she clung to. Moriarty stepped forward and kissed her gloved hand. They exchanged pleasantries. It became obvious that she was well-bred and excellently trained. But what else was to be expected?

'Anna, please meet my dear friend, Marquess Seymour-Townshend and his lovely wife Marianne.' His voice carried a soft warning, as he added, 'May I introduce Miss Anna Kronberg.'

I offered my gloved hand, which was taken gingerly and almost touched by the Marquess's lips. 'I am honoured to make your acquaintance,' I answered without complimenting her on her choice of clothing, or him on his choice of bed-mate.

Moriarty brushed aside the breach of etiquette with a crisp, 'Well, my dear friend, shall we go inside?'

We were led to our seats. People were chatting all around us, an ocean of noise. The Marquess whispered into his wife's pearl-adorned ear, while Moriarty and I cultivated an awkward silence. As the heavy curtains were drawn he bent close to my face, and said, 'I hope you will enjoy this extraordinary piece. Verdi's *Otello*, performed by Francesco Tamagno.'

I felt the heat rising in my face from the contact of lips and earlobe, and knew it had neither escaped his notice nor his liking.

Only a minute later I learned that Tamagno was Europe's greatest tenor. It mattered little that I did not understand a single word of Italian. My heart was aching with intrigue, love, and despair. Tamagno's all-embracing voice reverberated from the walls, the seats, and even the audience, uprooting my very soul. Tearing at my aching heart.

In the fourth act, as Otello killed the woman he loved, I trembled and Moriarty finally noticed my torment. He watched how I tried to control myself. But the music was impossible to shut off. It seeped into every corner of my being. The emotions pouring from Tamagno's lips and washing over the audience, seemed to affect only me. Everyone else was listening solely with their ears. As the curtain fell, I heaved a quiet sigh of relief.

Moriarty took my elbow and led me outside, apologising to our company, and explaining that I was not feeling well.

Unspeaking, he led me to the brougham and helped me in.

'My apologies. I did not mean to spoil the evening with your friends. Considering they are leaving for America tomorrow, my behaviour must have upset you.' Strange, how easily I could shift into the role of the unassuming female.

He stared out the window, jaw muscles bulging. How long would it take for him to lose interest in me? How long until his fascination with an intellectual equal would no longer be exotic enough? Soon, I would be nothing but inappropriate.

'Music can break my heart,' I explained.

He narrowed his gaze at me. And slowly, his pinched expression softened. As the brougham came to a halt, he finally spoke. 'Given the circumstances, my invitation was indeed too early. Forgive me.'

My ribcage froze. I could not speak.

After supper, Durham lugged the gramophone into my room, together with a recording of *Otello*. After he'd left, I turned the crank. The buzzing and rasping of taut strings caressed by a bow, the low hum underlying Tamagno's voice, the vast diversity of sound underlying everything obvious and loud, was flattened to a dull noise. A noise people called music.

I undressed with Cecile's help, then wrapped myself in my blanket and pressed my hands against my lids until I saw lights pinpricking the dark.

A shiver ran across my skin. I opened my eyes and stared at the ceiling. Realisation hit. Even if I managed to identify every single one of Moriarty's henchmen and was able to discover the depth of the government's involvement, I doubted that I could stop the development of biological weaponry. Because ideas are a dangerous thing. Once born, they are impossible to wipe out.

And yet, my determination comforted me. Kept me on my path. It helped that I wasn't driven by self-preservation. No. I craved revenge. And I knew precisely how to get it.

Moriarty hadn't had a woman for a week now.

He would be hungry.

Day 66

The two horses impatiently pawed the ground, snorted, and shook their manes. Moriarty and I stepped away from the brougham, and walked toward the warehouse. We had chosen Langley Basin for its accessibility. With a warehouse right at the Thames' edge, the rebuilding would be swift, and we would be able us to discard mule carcasses without attracting too much attention.

A barge was tethered to the bollards and building material extracted from her belly. Steam rose from workers' mouths and intermingled with fog from the Thames — a milky soup of odours, moisture, and cold.

Moriarty took my hand and stepped through the hole that would soon be sealed by a large iron-banded door. Inside the warehouse, four men were building pens — each big enough to hold three mules. A small passageway separated four stalls on either side. Twenty-four animals would be sacrificed, and then another group, and perhaps another. To be certain our data and observations were significant, the experiment would have to be repeated at least twice.

Shivering, I briefly squeezed the hand holding mine.

'Are you cold? Do you wish to go back home?' he asked.

'The shiver was more excitement than freezing.'

He placed his palm on the small of my back and steered me through the entrance. My every fibre revolted against his touch and oppressive chivalry.

Inside the warehouse, two carpenters were pulling up the main wall that would separate the laboratory space from the animal enclosures. Another three men set the windows and fastened bars. 'Who will guard this place?' I asked.

'Do not worry yourself with men's business, dear.'

'*Men's* business? We are talking about the success or failure of *our* work. Don't talk to me as though my sole purpose were decoration!'

He stopped in his tracks and growled, 'Four of Moran's best men will guard it.'

'Well, now I *am* worried!' I cried, but quickly lowered my voice. 'Men carrying rifles and circling the premises will ensure publicity in a very short time.'

'Colonel Moran is no amateur.' He snatched my wrist and pulled me back outside.

At the water's edge, far enough from the workers' pricked ears, he yanked me to a stop. 'You dare doubt my judgement in front of those men? ' He jabbed his finger toward the warehouse.

'Let go of my arm.'

He dropped it, and frowned at the hand that had just squeezed mine so hard it bruised. 'My apologies,' he said.

'I apologise, too.' What a circus! His mind might accept the two of us being at eye level, but his culture and upbringing would always cause him to revolt over a woman with more than just breadcrumbs tumbling about in her skull. He didn't realise that he couldn't have both: a sharp woman who knew what she wanted, yet was shallow-brained enough to submit to his every whim.

I took a step back. 'You do know that I lived in St Giles for years, do you not?'

He gazed out onto the river. Murky water was lapping at the barge, pushing and pulling it gently. Anger stained his throat, the red splotches rising above the scarf he wore.

'Nothing is invisible in the slums,' I continued. 'Nothing escapes the eyes and ears of a band of ragamuffins. Have you not seen the people eyeing us? I have counted more than twenty so far.'

'I am well aware of their presence and services they can provide. Moran's men know to bribe them. And now, I'd be ever so grateful...' The last word was spoken like a knife to my throat. '...if you would stop suggesting you know better.'

'I'm much too naive to suggest any such thing, if it were even true.' With that, I walked off, climbed into the brougham, and shut the door.

I don't know what he was doing in the warehouse. I forbade myself to ask him as he finally entered the carriage and ordered his coachman to convey us home.

'I'd like to go to the medical school to re-inoculate our germs onto fresh media. If you don't have any other plans for me, Garrow could take me there after he drops you off.'

'I will accompany you.'

'As you wish.'

'You are nervous. Why?'

Had my voice revealed more than I thought it should? 'I am merely puzzled. I affronted you, yet you show no anger now. And you have seen the laboratory several times, yet you wish to accompany me.'

'I wish to see Britain's best bacteriologist at work.'

I gazed at his hard mouth. Its corners turned up slightly, his eyes betraying enjoyment. Whatever his intentions were, he would give me no clue.

We reached the medical school. He unlocked the laboratory door and held it open for me. Goff had taken a holiday while the warehouse laboratory was being refurbished. But he'd prepared Petri dishes with fresh media before leaving.

Moriarty took my hat and coat, and hung them by the door. I wiped the workbench with grain alcohol, then used it to disinfect my hands. Petri dishes were lined up before me — four with an *A* for anthrax and four with a *G* for glanders etched into their lids. 'You can step closer if you wish,' I said to him. He stood a few feet away, eyes glued to the deadly cultures that had formed small dots on the surface of the dark-golden media. 'As long as you don't touch anything, you are safe. Germs don't jump.'

With a *woof* the Bunsen burner ignited. I held a metal lancet into its flame, just above the hottest blue.

'The heat of the flame forces the air to rise, making it safe for me to leave the pure cultures out in the open for a while. Dust and contaminating germs cannot drop into the Petri dishes. Instead, they are swept up with the rising hot air.' I opened a petri dish containing glanders cultures and stuck the lancet into the gelatin, producing a hiss.

'The metal lancet is sterilised in the flame and then used to pick out part of a pure culture.' I stuck the tip of the lancet into the white, rippled surface of a glanders colony, opened a fresh petri dish, and drew sweeping lines over the entire area of the media. I repeated the procedure twice more, then disinfected my hands and switched to our anthrax cultures.

Once finished, I turned off the flame, wiped my workbench and my hands clean, and finally washed everything with water and soap, all the while observing Moriarty's fascination from the corner of my eye.

He went to fetch coat, hat, and gloves for me. 'I wish you would address me by my given name.' His gaze held mine.

The first thing that hit my brain was that I needed to talk to Holmes. Urgently.

'James, then?' I said.

'Yes, James.' He smiled. My neck prickled.

Back inside the carriage, I tested the amount of freedom he would allow me. 'I'd very much like to take a walk in a park...any park. I have been... inside for too long.' I wanted to scream, *locked up*, but that wouldn't have served my purpose. 'I'll take Cecile with me. I am certain she would enjoy an outing.'

And to my utter surprise, he acceded. 'Garrow will accompany you. Two ladies shouldn't be walking about by themselves.'

'Of course. We'll go tomorrow morning. Or do you need your coachman?'

'Tomorrow is acceptable.' He bent forward and pressed my hand.

~

'I wish I could see him,' Cecile whispered. She stoked the fire, pulled a letter from her pocket, and sat down next to me. It was her third message, and I could guess the contents. Her lines were sweet, with a pleading undertone. His were respectful and warm, yet cautioning her not to raise the suspicions of their master.

I had told Garrow about the colour of her cheeks when she received his dictated notes, which had put a boyish smile on his face. They would make a good couple. But this whole business gave me a stomach-ache. They'd lose their assignment either through flirting with each other, or else with my hand around their master's throat. What would happen to them afterwards? Without a reference, it would be nearly impossible for them to find a situation.

I pushed the thought aside, winked at Cecil, and smirked mischievously.

Confused, she squinted at me.

'I was just thinking that I will need your assistance tomorrow. I shall exercise my tired limbs on a walk. What destination would be most favourable?'

She blinked. Perhaps she thought I had lost my mind.

'Cecile, you and I will enjoy a few hours of fresh air and sunshine, while Jonathan protects us ladies from evil ruffians. Officially, at least. The two of you can take a stroll, while I will keep at a distance.'

'Oh!' She lapped her hand over her mouth, and acquired the shade of a newborn piglet. I couldn't help but laugh.

After Cecile had retired for the night, my thoughts drifted to Holmes. To meet him in the park would be suicide. Moriarty had his men everywhere. But then...I didn't need to see Holmes at all, did I?

For what I intended, he was irrelevant.

Day 67

❧❧❧

The surge of energy and joy — once the prison doors had opened — was overwhelming. I was near to bursting. It felt like spring after years of darkest winter. The air smelled so much cleaner, the few birds chirped louder, and the wind on my face was fresher and lovelier than ever.

Much to Jonathan and Cecile's surprise, I asked him to leave the driver's seat a few hundred yards into town. It took some convincing, but he relented.

Now the two lovers sat inside the carriage, safe from the ears and eyes of passersby, while I enjoyed all the freedom and speed a coach(wo)man could hope to get. I didn't care which streets I took, or what park to visit. Certain that both Holmes's and Moriarty's spies would follow us, I decided how best to justify my odd behaviour, then pushed all my concerns aside and embraced the drizzly, cold, grey day.

It was wonderful.

We rode for about an hour until we reached Hyde Park. It was so close to Moriarty's home that we could have easily walked, but that would have defied the purpose. Soaked to the bone, I knocked on the roof, and said, 'Care for lunch and a walk?'

Garrow stuck his head out the door.

'Mr Garrow, I recommend you two do not hold hands, for I am quite certain we have company. And it would be wise to return home in about half an hour.'

He blinked in surprise, nodded, and then helped Cecile out onto the pavement. They were neatly dressed, and he was freshly shaven. Each looked as if out to impress someone. It helped that they both had to huddle under one umbrella, else their proximity would have seemed inappropriate. And someone could have reason to make accusations.

I shut my eyes, hugged my freezing frame, and opened my ears wide. The scraping of the street sweeper's broom, the sharp clacking of expensive heels and the duller counterpart of those not so rich. The lazy dripping of water off trees and umbrellas. Chatter, sometimes friendly and other times agitated. At some distance, a man hawked baked potatoes, another sold oysters and eel pies. My mouth watered. I shot a glance at Garrow and Cecile who had begun to stroll back to the carriage. I did not look out for spies. Just knowing they would be close was enough.

'Would you two fancy a light meal?' I asked.

'Aren't you cold?' Garrow asked.

'I'm enjoying myself. But I'm hungry. Allow me to convey us to a food source.'

Cecile squeaked when I tipped an imaginary hat at her. Garrow shut the door, and I steered the horses toward the vendors. I handed Garrow a few coins to buy steaming pies and oysters, which we devoured with careful, though slightly burned, fingers and tongues.

I thought it unwise to enter the premises on top of the brougham for all the neighbours to see, so Garrow got his accustomed seat back just before we turned into Kensington

Palace Gardens. Knowing I'd have to face Moriarty's anger did make me nervous, but it couldn't spoil the wonderful day.

We were met by Durham, who immediately informed me that his master had left and would not return until the day after tomorrow. And that he had received intelligence of my outrageous behaviour, and I would certainly face consequences upon his master's return. I noted with relief that he had said nothing about Cecile or Garrow.

I shook the rain from my bonnet, and handed it to the manservant with a smile.

Day 69

❦

'When will you meet Holmes again?' The question was shot across the room like a dagger. Moriarty was standing by the hearth.

I snapped the study door shut and crossed my hands behind my back. 'He finds me whenever he wishes to see me.'

'But you must have a way of communicating with him should you be in danger, or something of that sort!'

'I drop a glove.'

'Where?'

'At the medical school.'

'Do so tomorrow.'

'What will I tell him?' I asked.

'That your father is in danger, and that you need Holmes to rush to Germany.'

I set the information aside, the essential part of it — he had referred to Germany, not to Switzerland, and he had not even looked at me to gauge my reaction. 'You want Holmes out of your way for how long?'

'A week will suffice.'

'How did I come to learn that my father is being threatened?'

'You overheard Moran and me talking. I told Moran to capture your father for me.'

'Why?' But more importantly: where was Moran *now*?

'None of your concern, my dear.'

'*Why* do you want to abduct my father?'

'Because I can,' he said with a smirk.

'You frighten me.'

He walked up to me and took my face in his hands. 'I know.' His touch froze my skin. 'You don't trust me and I don't trust you. That's why you get so little information. For now, at least.'

I pushed away from him. 'Holmes will expect me to have a little more insight as to your reasons for abducting my father. He will not be satisfied with a mere suspicion.'

'You will come up with something, I'm certain.'

'You don't wish to feed him with false information about our project?'

'I don't deem it necessary.'

The small hairs on my arms prickled. Whatever he was planning, he wanted to test me. 'I'll drop the glove tomorrow morning. Holmes will contact me the day after.'

He nodded, his expression turning colder. 'You were seen driving my brougham around town.'

'Obviously, I drove. I was the one sitting on top of it.'

'Have you any idea,' he snarled, 'how often I have to restrain my hand?'

'A very precise idea, I should think.' And then a rather mad thought came to me. 'If you want to know why, allow me to show you.'

He snorted. I held out my hand. After a moment's hesitation, he took it.

While Garrow braced the horses, Moriarty and I, dressed

in warm wool and furs, pulled scarves around our neck and climbed up onto the driver's seat. Garrow nodded, gave the animals a clap, and off we went.

'I will let you in on a secret, James. Something that no one but my father knows about me. But you'll have to be patient. Much like your opium, it needs to be experienced.' My decision to take a forward plunge scared me a little. But it was exhilarating too.

The *clack-clack-clack* of hooves echoed through the empty alleys, and the clatter of wheels followed.

'You have just been travelling and your senses have experienced a great many things. Mine have not had much stimulation. I have been locked up in your house and the laboratory for almost seventy days. Sixty-nine, to be precise. Yes, I do count my days in captivity, James.'

'You are not a captive anymore,' he noted.

'Indeed! Now, what would you do if you were in my situation?' I flicked the horses and they sped to a fast trot. The chestnuts' hooves clacked in synchrony, and the sharp sound bounced off the cold cobblestones, the houses lining the streets, the lanterns. I gave Moriarty no time to reply. 'Listen to the music, James. Can you hear it?' I turned toward him and saw his quizzical expression. 'Close your eyes,' I said softly, and turned back to the horses. 'The sound changes. When there are houses on both sides of the streets, it grows louder but also duller. Now, only trees are lining the street. The clacking is reflected by the cobblestones and trunks. It would sound different again if it were summer and the trees had foliage. Now the sound is very clear and...wide open, for the lack of a better description.'

I gave him a few moments of silence, before I continued, 'The loud rattling of wheels makes the slithering noises almost impossible to hear. Yet, every single one of the wet cobblestones that touches a wheel forces it to skid sideways just a little. Do you hear it?'

We drove down the Strand and onto the Mall until I slowed the horses to a stop at St James Park.

'Listen,' I said, turning to him. 'Do you hear the twigs' quiet scraping when they move in the wind? People's muffled laughter all the way from the Strand? I love this music, James. And I hear and feel it all, not just the little that meets the ear. Sounds force their way in and I *cannot* shut them out. If you were to put me in a room full of people, I could tell you what each one of them said during the course of an evening. Everyone I have met so far, including you, can focus on one conversation, while I cannot. It is extremely tiresome, but I cannot choose what my ears and mind take in, and what they don't. All is soaked up. And yet I love the noises surrounding me. I need to hear the wind in the trees, the bow on the strings, the tapping of sparrows' feet in the dirt. It touches my heart and it makes me feel alive. I spent sixty-nine days in an empty house, and I *starved*. That is why I rode your brougham through London.'

He cocked his head, listening to my words as though trying to grasp the impact of captivity and the lack of stimulation of the senses.

'I cannot tolerate Gooding and Garrow getting married and having children,' he finally said, his gaze travelling down to my mouth, his hand meeting my chin and lifting it.

I noticed his possessive expression, the parting of his lips. I tucked my observation away where it wouldn't have the power to make me flinch.

'Can you not allow them this little affair?' I whispered.

He bent closer. My throat clenched.

'As you wish.' His breath poured over my face as his mouth came down on mine.

Day 71

As the day dawned I found my limbs were heavy with fatigue. The night had been dreadful. I had barely slept, and when I did, nightmares terrorised me. I dreamt I wasn't myself anymore. I'd turned into the redhead and was drugged and tied to a bed. Or I found myself in a happily-ever-after horror with Moriarty.

His softness was precisely what I'd planned to lure out. But my web of lies and betrayal, our mind games, his threats and need to control me — all had begun to blur the edges of reality.

I'd found no rest, and had paced my room for hours, trying to push Moriarty from my mind. The flicker in his eyes when he said that Moran would capture my father for him — how much truth was in that lie? Moriarty had given up a great deal of power over me by releasing my father. Did he need more control now? Why?

I needed to find out if he was indeed trying to find my father. Asking Moriarty directly made no sense. He would not tell me the truth no matter how charming I tried to be.

I was terrified for my father. The odds were that Moriarty

had sent a man to track him from England to Germany, possibly even to Switzerland. There were too many factors escaping my control and my knowledge. I told myself that as long as I was available to Moriarty, my father would be safe. I hoped it was true. But after Holmes had made his arrests, would my father be able to return home, or would someone be awaiting him there? Someone, Holmes might not be able to catch?

Later, long after midnight, I was so exhausted that I rolled up in my blankets and shut my eyes. I pictured Holmes in his armchair across from me, smoking his pipe, and calmly telling me about the newest developments in our case. It hurt to think of him, so I pushed his image away.

Remaining only was Moriarty. *James*. I had whispered the name, and the sound alone drove icicles into my heart. I'd have to keep the coldness there for a while longer, for I knew that by betraying the monster, I would hurt the man.

Soon after my arrival at the medical school, I made for the Lady's. The smell of cheap perfume overlaying a faint tobacco aroma told me Holmes had been there already. After a minute of waiting, I left.

An hour later I got lucky, and found him with yet another middle-aged female costume clinging to his frame.

'Are you all right?' I asked. He made a gesture of pinching his lips and jerking his head toward the window. I nodded in reply.

'Anna, you wanted to see me. What is it?' he asked, his voice at half-mast. Anyone eavesdropping would just be able to hear us.

'I have reason to believe that Moriarty will soon send Moran to abduct my father again,' I cried theatrically. 'Oh, I beg you to go to Germany and save him!' I stepped closer, and he lowered his head. I whispered into his ear, 'He wants you out of England for a week. Do you have a clue why that is?' My flushed-down message had informed him of every detail of my conversation with Moriarty. The one-sidedness of this form of conversation was trying.

'Yes,' he whispered. 'Please do not worry yourself,' he said a little louder. 'I will certainly do my best.'

Much quieter, and with a mischievous glint in his eyes, he added, 'What a wonderful opportunity to be invisible for an entire week.'

I knew I could trust him to give the impression he had left for Germany, while in truth being somewhere else entirely. Yet this charade made me jumpy. I'd gnawed down my nails to the quick, and my neck was constantly itching — so much so that I checked my head for lice. But there weren't any. It was just my nerves.

I stretched up to Holmes and spoke into his ear, 'An abduction is exactly what I fear for my father.'

'Trust me.' He straightened up, and said louder, 'Why would Moriarty want your father?'

'How far did you get with Moriarty's men?' I whispered. His shoulders sagged a little, and with them, my hopes for an early escape. I tried not to show it, but probably failed.

'I don't know,' I exclaimed, 'I can only guess that he wishes to eliminate witnesses.'

Holmes bent close to my ear, and said softly, 'It appears that he has planted a seed for two secret organisations: one involves men from the military, the other from the government. I am relying heavily on my brother's information here, but each of these groups consists of only four or five men. Neither the government nor the military at large appear to have any knowledge of Moriarty's activities. And so far, neither Mycroft nor I have been able to identify anyone.'

'I might be helpful there,' I whispered. He tilted his

eyebrows. 'Trust me.' I tried a smile, which quickly dropped off my mouth. 'Moriarty knows our signal. Should I ever drop a glove when exiting the brougham, it's because he has asked me to meet you.'

'I thought so. His two men have been circling the Ladies' today. You told him?'

I nodded.

'Hum...' huffed Holmes rather too loudly and started stomping around the room. 'I will take the next ship to the continent. We must make haste!' he almost shouted, took a long stride toward me and whispered, 'How much does Moriarty trust you now?'

I frowned. 'He doesn't need to trust me.' My lips accidentally brushed his cheek. Holmes didn't seem to notice. 'I'm inferior in physical and intellectual strength, and he can dispose of me whenever he wishes to do so. He believes himself safe.'

And, in a way, he was perfectly safe. The little control I had seemed negligible.

Holmes's breath tickled my neck. 'I will have someone wait at the sewers every night,' he whispered, 'between seven and eight. If I don't receive a message for two consecutive days, I will come and get you.'

I didn't dare look up at him, certain that my cheeks were glowing like fresh apples. Instead, I gazed down at his hand, took it in mine, and squeezed it gingerly. Then I turned and left before throwing away what little strength had kept me upright.

Day 74

✦✦✦

The click of his pipe on the coffee table yanked me out of my thoughts. James's face was soft, his eyes dark. Nearly black. I remembered how the air around him had tasted different earlier that day. I remembered the shock it had brought, how my heart had wilted in my chest, how my knees seemed to lose their firmness. His intentions were clear before noon had struck, and I had used the remainder of the day to find willpower, and to make peace with myself.

And now his invitation to smoke opium, his hand on mine as he led me to the ottoman, the steady gaze, all betraying his decision to finally take what he needed.

His eyes intense, he reached out and touched my ankle. Only with the tips at first, then followed by those long and precise fingers, and finally the whole of his palm. He let it rest there, observing what my face would reveal. I let him see nothing, watched him in return, and marvelled at the dance of two intellectuals on a razor's edge.

Slowly, he pushed his hand further up and I noticed the peculiar characteristics of expensive silk stockings — a quality I had been unaware of until then: this fragile barrier amplified the tingling sensation of skin slipping over skin. I found myself focusing on his hand instead of his face.

He pushed his hand higher, together with the hem of my dress. The fabric whispered softly, caressing my skin. His fingers curled into the tender hollow of my knee and an involuntary hiss escaped my nostrils. The corners of his mouth twitched, his irises blackened.

I knew he was waiting for a genuine response as we played a dangerous game of deception, control, power, and exploration. Under lowered lids, I gazed at him. His pupils were wide open, the black bleeding into the blue grey of his irises. I shut my eyes to focus on what my skin whispered, and not what my mind was shouting. I thought not of him, but of a man I loved, with a mind just as sharp and hands equally precise.

The slender hand travelled up along the inside of my thigh, brushed a garter, and finally rested only an inch away from what had got warmer than should be considered normal. And I knew that I could — and would — do it.

I opened my eyes and was met by a scrutinising gaze.

His face hid every emotion as his hand slid away. He rose and started for the door.

'Why do you find such pleasure in torturing me?' I called after him.

He stopped. Without turning around he answered, 'I never wished to torture you. My apologies. It will not happen again.'

'And yet you walk away,' I said softly.

His hand slipped off the doorknob. I rose to my feet and approached him. We were only inches apart. My palm rested on his shoulder and his breath accelerated. He turned around. One hand went behind his back. He turned the key in the lock. The metallic click tipped me forward.

~

A STRAND of my hair was stuck to the corner of my mouth and he brushed it away. His eyes rested on my lips for a moment. Then he pushed himself up. I increased the pressure of my legs around his waist, locking my ankles behind his back, curious how he would react. There was a flicker of surprise, and then a smile as he rolled onto his side, still trapped.

'I have a question that might be a little... delicate,' he said.

I waited, and he took this as an invitation to continue.

'Were you intimate with Sherlock Holmes?'

'I don't think Holmes ever gets intimate with anyone,' I said, hoping all he would hear was annoyance and the hurt pride of a rejected woman.

'What a fool he is,' he said, stroking the scar on my stomach. He did not ask how I had received it, and I was grateful for that. His hand travelled farther down to the triangle of black curls and came to a rest there. 'Which hunger did I not satiate?'

'Curiosity,' I replied. 'You had a woman every single night from when I arrived until you began courting me. And then you were not intimate with a woman for two weeks. There was no need for you to abstain from the one to court the other. And yet, this is what you did. Why?'

Clearly surprised to hear me talking so openly about his sexual activities, he hesitated. 'I find it necessary for my mental balance to have regular intercourse. At least once a day. But the routine had become...tiresome.'

'Why would it suddenly have become tiresome?'

'It always has,' he said.

I waited, but he did not elaborate.

'How much more thrilling it is to combine necessary copulation with combat,' I noted.

He laughed. 'You have a sharp tongue.'

'I do. But you knew that already.' I pulled the blanket over us.

He slid his hand into the bend of my knee. 'I very much like both your sharp tongue and your sharp mind,' he whispered, as hunger flared in his face.

Our combat was illuminated by electrical light and guarded by his watchful eyes. There was no escaping into the depths of my own soul. He saw and analysed every one of my reactions and every lack thereof.

I had been searching for his soft spots for weeks now. Once in a while, I thought I could peek beneath the beast's hide. How astonishing it was to discover traits that deserved affection, and how despicable of me to target these most vulnerable parts.

When had he decided to put on armour and hide away the human? What would I do if he were to open the shell for me? Would I still plunge in the dagger? Yes. There was no doubt that I would.

Day 81

It was a day of great changes. Goff and a few footmen had moved our laboratory from the medical school to the warehouse at Langley Place Basin. Twenty-four mules had been delivered, together with a large load of straw, hay, and grains. The night before, I had finally convinced James that dumping diseased mules into the river would pose too great a danger of transmitting glanders and anthrax throughout London. Instead, we would ship the carcasses out to sea and sink them. By now Holmes should have *returned* from his fake trip to Germany. And my father should be safe. Must be.

And I remained, not as a captive, but as a spy and a cheat. I was the spider in the net, ready to tug at the right thread at the right moment, ready to wrap my victim in delicate silk.

Never in my life had I tried to make a man trust me, let alone fall for me, only to use him and cause him harm. Although I knew all this was necessary, I was disgusted with myself. Whether this disgust came solely from the game I played with him or from the tender feelings I had begun to develop was not always clear to me.

How ridiculous this circus was! Had I not concluded that

I *must* make myself feel for him? So that I could make him believe my actions were genuine? Why did I feel sorry for the monster now? So as not to give the impression I was cold and calculating? But wasn't that the highest art of lying? To first make myself believe the lie before I tried to convince anyone else, let alone the master of lies?

Would I soon make myself suffer deliberately, only to cleanse myself of guilt?

I assumed I would. I was foolish that way.

My short notes to Holmes contained my daily observations and conclusions. Although I never gave any clues as to my emotional state, every time I flushed the phials down the drain I was afraid he would notice that I was about to lose my mind.

THE MULES SNORTED. With a heavy sigh, I walked into each pen and inspected the animals for open wounds or sores, running my hands along their warm bodies. They answered by pressing their noses into my back, face, or side. The mules looked better than I had expected. Their eyes were shiny, ribs not visible, coats smooth. Their imminent fate pained me. And I would be the one causing their suffering and death. 'I don't see an alternative,' I told myself quietly.

'Excuse me?' asked Goff, who was waiting at the stable's entrance.

'I might have to use two or three batches of mules until we know enough about the spreading and effectiveness of our germs.'

'Isn't that what you planned anyway?'

I merely nodded.

'Everything is ready. We should feed them the bacteria today.' He stuffed his hands into his coat pockets, and stepped over a pile of manure.

'We could. But I want to make sure they are healthy. They'll be under quarantine and observation for five days,' I said and saw Goff's disappointment. 'Don't worry, Mr Goff. There will be plenty of carcasses for you to sink.'

I went outside for a smoke and to think about what could possibly be done. Soon we would have several highly infectious animals on our hands. And with every day that passed, we were getting closer and closer to the development of gruesome bacterial weapons. Our research had become too dangerous already. I desperately needed to talk to Holmes.

And I had to find a way to sabotage my own work.

∽

JAMES and I had taken up our usual places for discussing our work — the armchairs facing the fireplace in his study.

'I'd like to develop a vaccine against anthrax,' I said.

'That would slow the development of weaponry, would it not?' He took a glass of brandy from Durham's offering hand, then flicked his index finger at me — a signal for his servant to offer me one as well.

'That could well be,' I said. 'But I believe it necessary. A vaccine is like the hammer of a gun. If you had a revolver that dislodged a bullet each time you barely touched the trigger, wouldn't you want to make it safer? Wouldn't you want to protect your own troops?' Durham handed me a glass and retreated to his usual position outside the door.

'Certainly. On the other hand — war has never been safe.'

'Do you think we are the only country developing weapons for germ warfare?'

He smiled a thin line. 'I cannot tell who may be developing any given thing at the moment. But I'm certain that the Germans are considering it. The French, too, possibly.'

'Koch and Pasteur are working with deadly germs, and

you know the use of disease in war is not new. Someone else will think of it, or has already started.'

'Not many have as progressive a mind as I do.' He looked at me and smirked. 'Or you.'

I could not believe my ears. 'Thank you,' I said, and held my hand out to him. He took it. 'You have connections to politicians and the military. Don't you think it would be of advantage to know what other countries are planning?'

As I spoke, he squeezed my hand hard and yanked me to him, grabbed my hips and forced me to my knees. With one hand cradling my chin, he bent forward, about to kiss me.

Irritated, I pushed him away. 'If you do not wish to talk about it, then I beg you to simply tell me so, and spare me this circus.'

His colour drained. He ran his hand over his face as though to wipe the anger away. 'My apologies. I have other business occupying my mind. The talk about vaccines tired me. I will leave for Brussels tomorrow early in the morning and will be gone for a week. Would you care to share my bed tonight?'

'Perhaps,' I answered, wondering how I could probe this man's mind and find out what he was planning to do in Brussels. He had been evasive with me the entire evening. I would have to tread very carefully.

Abruptly, he rose and pulled me up. He was so used to women spreading their legs for him and his drugs that a little resistance now and then must feel like sabotage.

'Perhaps?' he asked, his expression unreadable. He wrapped one arm around my waist and pressed me close to his chest. His lips touched my ear as he softly said, 'May I try to convince you?'

'Perhaps,' I said again, and let myself be led upstairs.

LATER THAT NIGHT, with candles pouring soft light over us and the bed, I noticed how strong my inner prison had grown. Invisible walls held my fading personality. My will seemed to be wavering ever so lightly, my strength to be slowly disappearing. I knew this was what he wanted, what he had planned to do to me. Perhaps not consciously. Who knows where such things as habits are born?

My gaze swept over his thin body, his chest still heaving, his heat and sweat slowly dissipating.

I wondered which part of me would die when I killed him.

Day 82

✤✦✤

The message I'd sent out the previous night had been short. "We need to talk", was all there was.

Garrow dropped me off at the warehouse early the next morning. Goff was already waiting. The man observed me as I examined the mules again. They still looked healthy. I wondered whether I could infect them with something harmless, so that I would have to cure them before we could test glanders germs on them. But what then? After a two- or three-week delay, I would have to come up with yet another way of sabotaging. I couldn't afford a pattern. I needed something major and long-term. My gaze flickered toward Goff. Wouldn't it be handy if my personal parasite disappeared?

There was no sign of Holmes the entire morning. Around noon, Goff and I took a hansom to a public house and had lunch. Just after Goff had paid for us, a familiar looking woman pushed past me, heading to the lavatories. A minute later, I excused myself and followed.

'Refreshing,' I commented on the privy, filled with excrement and covered in a buzzing sheet of flies. The room was small, Holmes hardly fit in with his voluminous dress.

'You look dreadful,' he said.

'Why, thank you! Holmes, I need to sabotage my own work, and I'm not certain how to go about it without drawing suspicion. And I can't run away, either, because Moriarty would simply find another bacteriologist. I need to create a delay, without an obvious pattern of sabotage. A delay of one month or even two would be perfect, but I fear I would have to burn down the warehouse to win that much time. But I can't, because Goff sticks to me like a fly to shit. If possible, I would very much like to get rid of him. At least for a few hours.'

'The warehouse is guarded by ragamuffins and four gun-toting men,' he said.

'Yes. I know.'

Eyes narrowed, he stared at me. 'Any valuables other than the mules in your warehouse?'

'Grain alcohol, glassware, workbenches.'

His eyes twinkled. 'Wonderful.'

'But...whatever you will do, do *not* open the Petri dishes! You may move them about, but under no circumstances are you to open them.'

He inclined his head, his mind already working away on the details of his plan.

'Could I throw them on the floor?' he asked.

I frowned. 'You could, but stay at least six feet away. And after they are opened, you must leave at once. Oh, and wash—'

He waved my concerns away. 'I handle concentrated acids quite regularly and, as you can see, my hands and eyes are still intact. I will certainly disinfect myself after having touched anything in your laboratory.'

'Good,' I said, a little relieved. 'Thank you.'

He nodded and pointed his chin toward the door.

'Goff?' I whispered.

'I believe so.'

My heart stumbled. I couldn't squeeze out the door without Goff spotting Holmes in the lavatory. Holmes and I gazed at each other, simultaneously raising our index finger to silence the other.

After a long moment, we heard a rap, and a 'Dr Kronberg, are you all right?'

'No, Mr Goff. I am not all right. This privy is disgusting and my stomach has decided to rid itself of the oysters I just had. If you'd be so kind as to order a strong beer and another serving of oysters and bread for me, so I may eat it far away from this place.'

He coughed, then answered, 'Yes, er...I certainly will.' His footfall faded.

'You have an impressively strong stomach,' said Holmes.

I grinned, pinched his arm, and made to leave the lavatory.

'I might need a few days,' he said quietly.

I nodded at the door handle and left.

Day 89

I entered the smoking room, ignoring Moran and the other men as I stepped up to James and showed him with a smile. He still looked a little weary from his trip.

'Allow me to introduce our guests to you,' James said to me. 'You've met Colonel Moran.'

That was an understatement. The man's name alone was worth a nightmare or two. I tried a timid smile. Moran took the bait, and lifted my hand to his lips. I twisted it from his grasp, and said calmly, 'Should you ever try to touch me again, I will castrate you.' He huffed. The other men ceased their muttered conversations, but none of them seemed particularly surprised that a woman would utter such words to the Colonel.

James cleared his throat, and motioned toward one of his guests. 'Colonel Dr Colbert Brine from the Veterinary Military Academy.' The man took my hand without hesitation.

'Mr Ridgley from the Foreign Office.'

A nod from him. 'My pleasure.'

'Mr Erving Hooks, a talent in finding useful friends on the continent.'

Hooks stepped forward, breathed onto my knuckles, and smiled widely. The word *espionage* brushed my mind.

'And Mr Whitman,' finished James without mentioning the function of said man.

'Gentlemen, it is my pleasure to introduce our bacteriologist, Dr Kronberg, to you.'

Silence lowered itself onto us like a wet blanket. And then Witmen huffed. 'Outstanding! We had already heard you were a woman, but seeing it with my own eyes...'

None of them seemed shocked. Perhaps James had forbidden any depreciative remarks on my sex. But then, all were gentlemen and any such thing they felt needed saying would be said behind my back only. I wondered whether James would join in. Maybe not today, but one day he would.

We took our seats. It was a casual meeting. The guests stretched out their legs, and James stood leaning against the mantelpiece. Everyone seemed relaxed. Odd. I was certain that everything I said and did would be scrutinised, compared, and measured. If I didn't prove sharper than the average male (though this shouldn't be too hard to accomplish), for them I would just as well be dumb as a cabbage. If I were too sharp, though, they'd probably be shocked if not outright scared. I would bite my tongue once in a while, I decided. That would at least give the impression there was a woman inside this dress, and their world wouldn't be turned upside down just yet.

'Would you do us the honour of introducing our work to these gentlemen?' James said, offering me his silver case. I noticed his look as he bent close to light my cigarette. He seemed appreciative, maybe even proud.

I blinked my confusion away, and decided that I would observe now and analyse later. When alone in my bed. 'May I ask how much the gentlemen know about our project?'

'They know the essentials. No need to introduce the

concept of germ warfare.' James answered while I watched the faces in the room. They were either very good at lying, or genuinely interested in bacteriology.

'Very well. The purpose of our work is to spread disease among equines and soldiers. We have isolated glanders and anthrax germs, and tested them on mice. More than eighty per cent of the rodents showed symptoms of the disease. We are now about to test our germs on mules.'

A head went up. 'Why these two diseases? Why not use only one? Both types of germs can infect and kill men and mules alike.'

'You are correct, Dr Brine. I chose the two for different reasons. Disease and death are only the *results* of germ warfare, but the success of our weapons is greatly determined by how well we can store them, how easily untrained men can handle them, how fast the disease spreads, and how controllable the entire process is. I would be betting on only one horse if I had isolated but one bacterium.'

There were nods — some thoughtful, some appreciative.

'Can you give us any details on the factors you mentioned? Have you tested storage conditions, for example?' asked Brine.

'Yes, but please keep in mind that the results are preliminary. When it comes to long-term storage, glanders germs need a bit more care. One needs to keep them relatively fresh. A two-months-old culture infects only ten per cent of our test mice. That means one can keep the stock of glanders for months, but before transmission, one must make a fresh culture. This is uncomplicated and adds a mere two or three days to the entire procedure.'

'Why use glanders at all?' interrupted Moran. 'Anthrax kills in less time. I have seen it with my own eyes.'

'Yes, glanders is less dangerous for men. But I urge you to see germ warfare as a chain of events. Glanders has a great advantage at the very beginning of that chain — the isolation is simple, and diseased specimens are easy to procure. The only disadvantage, compared with anthrax, is the storage. But does one need to store them at all if one can isolate them whenever one needs to? And the advantages towards the end of the chain are even more important. Glanders is primarily an equine disease. It spreads quickly among horses and mules but rather reluctantly between men. That means that men handling the germs are less likely to get infected. If they were — how easy do you think would it be to find men to spread it for us? Do you think anyone would willingly handle a bacterium that would surely cause him large, painful boils and a dreadful, prolonged death?'

The faces darkened. 'A good soldier doesn't ask such questions. He does what he is told.'

'My apologies. I understand little of a soldier's mentality and motivations,' I said to Moran. 'All I know is that when fear is involved, men tend to make mistakes. The more dangerous the disease, the greater the fear and the greater the potential for errors.'

'Soldiers are *not* to fear death! What does a woman know about that, anyway?'

'Control yourself,' James murmured, cutting a sharp glance at Moran.

'I know precisely what you are talking about, Colonel Moran.' I said. 'But please believe me, if you gave soldiers the choice between dying of these terrible diseases or being gutted with a bayonet, every single one would choose the latter. I'm not talking about the fear of death, I'm talking about the fear of prolonged and excruciating suffering.'

Silence fell, interrupted only by the crackling of the fire and the singeing of tobacco as air was pulled through pipes and cigarettes.

'Men will bleed from their anuses and vomit blood if they

contract intestinal anthrax. The mortality rate is eighty per cent. They will bleed from their lungs when sick with pneumonial anthrax. The mortality rate is very close to one hundred per cent. We are talking about one of the cruelest ways to kill.'

They looked at me as if seeing me in a different light. Did they see themselves differently as well? None of these gentlemen appeared to have spent time considering *not* using germs in warfare.

'Can you tell us more about anthrax germs?' asked Ridgley, the man from the Foreign Office.

'Anthrax is more complicated to obtain, but very easy to store. Anthrax bacteria form resting stages called *spores*. These spores can be stored for years in a dry place. In fact, spores can contaminate soils and pasturage for decades and every time cattle graze there, they will come down with anthrax. It might seem like an advantage, because you can spread the disease and infect people and animals for years to come. But this, gentlemen, is in fact a great disadvantage. Claiming anthrax contaminated territory is...foolish.'

Frowns showed hesitation.

'That would indeed render this germ much too risky,' said Ridgley, tapping his front teeth with his pipe. 'But you are the bacteriologist. Shouldn't you know a way to kill spores or develop a cure for anthrax?'

'Reading a pile of scientific books doesn't make me a magician.'

Chuckling, followed by consideration and silence.

'Dr Kronberg was thinking of developing a vaccine against anthrax,' said James, and this time it sounded as though he considered it a good idea.

'How long would that take, and what costs are involved?' Ridgley again. Was he the man pulling the purse strings?

'I can only provide a rough estimate. Pasteur's vaccines

took months to develop and test. I suppose we would have to double our budget.'

Ridgley nodded without hesitation, and I willed my breath to come regularly. The vastness of their financial resources was shocking. I hoped my face did not betray my excitement and relief. Prolonging the project, delaying the production of biological weapons for the sake of vaccine development was precisely what I had wished for.

I noticed that Mr Hooks had remained silent, all the while listening and observing, not taking part in the discussion at all.

Later that night, in the pitch dark with only a sliver of moon to chisel faint outlines, I lay next to James who had just quenched his greatest thirst.

Mine, however, was still burning: curiosity.

'You have been staring at me for the last ten minutes. What is it?' He tucked a stray lock behind my ear. The gesture was so familiar. Garret used to do that after making love to me. Usually on the rug, because all too often we had found the bed too far away. When I gave James the soft smile I reserved for Garret alone, my heart iced over. 'You were away for eight days, and have not spoken a single word about your trip.'

'I forbade you to ask me about it.'

'And so I did not ask.'

'I am certain you are entertaining your own theories,' he said, apparently bored and tired.

How could he not see how obvious his plans were? The government, the military, a man *who knows how to find friends on the continent* and a trip to Brussels. Did he believe that his mounting me had drained my mental powers? James had formed a secret organisation that extended into all vital parts of Britain. The question was, whether to serve in her defence, or for an entirely different purpose? If Holmes should even *try* to arrest James and his men, his life and reputation would be at stake. I was sure of it.

'Indeed, I have one,' I copied James's bored tone and turned away, showing him my back and pulling the blanket over me. I heard his breath catch. 'But I herewith forbid you to ask me about it.' I added.

He slid his hand down my back. 'Tell me.'

'I'm just about to doubt my judgement,' I answered, my voice softening.

'You cannot possibly think I visited a mistress?' His breath ran down my back, as did his kisses.

I must dispatch a message to Holmes tomorrow, I thought, before pressing closer to James.

Day 90

I awoke in my own bed. Each night I would share James's, then leave after we had finished with each other. Neither of us had the need to sleep afterwards. He usually went back to his study, while I went to my room to think my own thoughts, unaffected by his presence and the need to pretend.

A sudden commotion in the corridor brought Holmes to mind. Since our last meeting, I had wondered how and when he would sabotage the laboratory. It appeared as though he had just done so. It was probably Durham rushing up the corridor to James's room. Soon after, James knocked on my door.

'What is it?' I called.

James stepped in, looking ruffled and wild. 'Something has happened at the warehouse. Get dressed. We leave in five minutes.'

The door snapped shut. I propelled myself out of bed and into my walking dress. Hingston held out a cup of tea and a sandwich for me as I strode through the entrance hall. James was already waiting in the brougham. The whip cracked and the carriage made a lurch.

'What happened?' I said, wide-eyed for fear of discovery, and trying to conceal it as anxiety for our project. How many more days before I wouldn't even notice the selling of one emotion for another?

'Moran's men were walking their beat early this morning. The warehouse appeared normal, but they heard noises coming from within. When they unlocked the door, they found mules scattered throughout the laboratory, glassware shattered, and alcohol fumes saturating the place.'

'A burglary?'

'I am not sure.'

Only a few minutes later, the carriage stopped. Four burly men were guarding the warehouse entrance.

'We didn't touch nothing,' one of them said. James ignored him, opened the door, and stepped inside.

I noticed that he had not looked at the dirt in front of the entrance, nor at the hinges or the lock. Hopeful, I followed on his heels.

Mule faeces and straw were distributed all over the floor.

I had to bite back a laugh. 'I have never before seen drunk mules.'

Four of the animals lay on their sides, their breaths coming in low grunts. The others were leaning against walls or workbenches with their eyes half closed and their heads hanging low.

The floor was mostly dry, save for the faeces and occasional puddles of urine. The entire grain alcohol must have been licked off the floorboards, or must have evaporated and been inhaled.

'How is this possible?' I exclaimed. James turned to me, his expression dark. 'Are you thinking sabotage?' I asked.

'Perhaps.' He gazed at the ground.

'What is it?'

'I am searching for evidence.'

'I will help,' I said, taking a step toward him.

He blocked my approach with his arm. 'You will remain where you are.'

'Well, thank you for your trust,' I said, folding my arms across my chest. 'Am I allowed to recommend you protect yourself against infection?'

Without another word, he began examining the floors of the laboratory, the corridor, and the stalls. Soon Goff's exasperated cry of, 'Let me through!' sounded.

Apparently, the guards were holding him where he was. What perfect timing! Holmes had chosen the one night Goff had been working at the warehouse all by himself and I had been discussing germ warfare with James and his men.

James walked back to the laboratory, and poked a stick at the remnants of our Petri dishes. 'Would you take a look at this?'

I walked over to him and bent down to gaze at a mess of broken glass and chunks of gelatin. 'This is terrible. Not only have the cultures been contaminated, but the grain alcohol has certainly killed them all.' I groaned and pressed my face into the bend of my elbow.

James kicked a petri dish across the room. It shattered on the wall. He stalked outside and examined the lock on both sides of the door, then the hinges, and finally the ground.

'Mr Goff!' he barked.

Goff walked up to us, chin set, shoulders drawn wide in full defence. He was about to speak when James cut across him, 'The lock has not been tampered with, and the windows are all intact. There are no footprints apart from yours, Dr Kronberg's, and the guards' walking up to this door. There's nothing to indicate a burglary.'

Goff looked as though his hanging had been announced. 'I would assume your footprints should—' the slap across his face stopped him. Silly boy.

'The stalls were not locked, Goff. Dr Kronberg wasn't at the warehouse yesterday. It was you alone who could have let the mules out.'

'I swear, I didn't—' Another slap made his jaw rattle.

'You will speak only when asked,' said James.

Goff dropped his gaze to the mud.

'You will move the mules to their stalls, clean up the laboratory, and repair the damage you have caused.'

Goff nodded, head still lowered.

'And you will retrieve the germs I asked you to safe-keep.'

My heart stopped. I looked at Goff, then up at James.

'Not all is lost,' James said. He grabbed my elbow and led me to the brougham. 'Home,' he called to Garrow.

'You did not tell me that Goff had kept a batch of pure cultures.' I said.

'No, I did not.'

'Why?'

'It was not necessary,' he spoke to the window.

I swallowed and tried to slow my desperate heart. Mud-covered pavement and ramshackle houses flew by. We struck pothole after pothole. At least James could not see my shoulders shaking. We steered out of the slums and the ride grew smoother. I said, 'You should have told me. It would have spared me the shock.'

He acknowledged my presence with a flick of his gaze. I leant back and shut my eyes, unwilling to play this game.

Upon our arrival at his home, we retreated to the study where Hingston served tea and toast.

'What do you recommend,' he said, his cold stare stuck to my face.

'The laboratory will be clean and fully functional by tomorrow morning, I should think. Goff should have procured new material from the glassblower by the day after tomorrow. Then I will have Goff prepare fresh media, and I'll re-inoculate the germs. I assume the mules are infected, but I would like to wait two or three days. Perhaps not all of them will show symptoms, and we could even use one or two for vaccine development.'

James covered his brow with his hand and exhaled slowly. 'That was close.'

'I am glad he did not leave the warehouse door open. Those mules would have been sold or eaten, and the diseases spread. With a glanders and anthrax epidemic in the neighbourhood—'

'—we would have had to relocate,' he finished my sentence.

'When did you ask Goff to keep pure cultures in his apartment?'

'I did not mention his apartment, dear.'

'Well, then I'm even happier, because keeping two diseases in a jar on a kitchen counter is not the most intelligent thing to do.' I mirrored his cold voice.

'I will not discuss this with you. And I have other business demanding my attention now.' With that, he strode from the study.

I stared at the door he'd left ajar, and the sliver Durham's profile as he waited in the hallway. I felt nauseous. I had run out of ideas on how to prevent myself from developing bacterial weapons.

Day 91

✿❦✿

I placed the petri dish back onto the workbench. Despite the distance, the Bunsen burner's flame pressed heat into my forehead, chest, and arms. Sweat itched on my skin, and my eyes burned. My throat clenched with nausea.

'I fear I am getting ill,' I said to Goff. His eyes shot to the bacterial cultures and back to me. A nod and a decisive huff, and he rushed off to fetch our coats. He was afraid I'd infected myself with anthrax. And to be honest, so was I.

I turned off the Bunsen burner, and wiped down my workspace, unsure if it made a difference now.

James wasn't at home when I arrived. I shut the front door in Goff's face. He probably muttered a few pleasantries, but I didn't hear any of them. I was barely able to make it to the stairwell to sit down. The hallway tipped aside, the floor approached swiftly, and I felt a dull pain on my forehead before darkness swallowed me.

I awoke in my bed with Cecile holding my hand, and a chorus of church bells clanking in my brain. 'How long have I been unconscious?'

'Half an hour, I believe.' Her chin trembled and her hands squeezed mine as though she needed to be rescued.

I tried to sit up, but that was a mistake. The room spun and bile jumped up my throat. What was wrong with me? These were surely not anthrax or glanders symptoms! Or were they? The influenza season hadn't yet begun. But perhaps it planned to begin with me this year?

A knock, then the door opened and James stepped in. A stranger followed, holding a doctor's bag in his hand.

'Anna, this is Dr Mark Blincoe.'

'Madam,' said the doctor, as he took my wrist to feel my pulse.

Irritated, I wrenched my arm away. 'I can feel my own pulse and hear myself talk. My guess is that I'm still alive,' I said to the doctor, and then to James, 'I don't need a physician.'

James looked down at me, then at Cecile and the quack. 'I will leave you two. Follow me, Gooding.' He turned on his heel, and left with Cecile in his wake.

Blincoe nodded with a frown that was supposed to make him look seriously concerned.

I waved him off. 'It's nothing.'

'It might well be nothing. But you lost consciousness. Your husband sent for me and I will examine you.'

'My husband? Ha! I suppose we got married while I slept.'

The skin over Blincoe's cheekbones stretched tightly. His nostrils flared. 'I can wait here for hours until you allow me to examine you. I'm not to leave without knowing what the problem is.'

'Are you the quack who told my *husband* that he suffers rheumatism?'

The doctor placed his hands behind his back, and stared down his nose at me.

I looked at the window, the ceiling, my gnawed-off fingernails. And still, he stood there, oozing patience and annoying me.

I groaned. 'Get on with it then.'

He felt my pulse again, listened to my breathing and heartbeat, prodded my chest and back, and pushed his fingers into my abdomen. He examined the reaction of my pupils, and checked my mouth and ears. After some huffing and frowning, he straightened up and asked, 'Do you feel soreness in your breasts?'

'Yes, as I usually do when running a fever.'

'You do not have a fever now.'

'No, but I felt feverish about an hour ago.'

'Hum. And yet, I don't believe you are sick. I think you are with child.'

I snorted. 'What utter tosh! I am barren. You keep making hilariously wrong diagnoses. You should be ashamed of yourself, Dr Blincoe. '

He tugged at his cravat, packed up his stethoscope, and snapped his bag shut. 'Why do you believe yourself barren?'

'That's none of your business.' Despite the utter impossibility of a pregnancy, my mind began calculating. My menstruation came only once or twice a year. At the most. The last one had been a week before Christmas. One month.

'Are you experiencing morning sickness?'

'No.' The slight queasiness I'd felt at the sight of kale on my plate hadn't bothered me enough to remember it an hour after it occurred. Now the fact struck me.

'Well,' he said, straightening his lapels. 'You know my diagnosis. Rest, and eat well. Take daily walks in the fresh air and abstain from tight lacing your corset. This is not the time for vanity, Madam.' With that and a raised index finger, he left.

James entered my room a few minutes later. His expression was unreadable.

'The man is a quack,' I said.

He sat down next to me. 'And what is your own diagnosis, dear?'

'Probably a cold. You know I'm not able to bear children. The man has a history of wrong diagnoses, as you well know.' I pointed to his neck.

'I know,' he said and rose. 'I will send your maid.'

As the door snapped shut behind him, I could do nothing but stare at it while my mind marvelled at the peculiar distortion of perception that fear produced.

Day 93

❧

I entered the study. Moran and James rose from their armchairs, the former offering me his seat.

'I prefer to stand.' With Moran close by, I'd rather be ready to jump. Hingston brought tea and biscuits, then left us alone.

'I believe it is time to discuss options for the transport and spreading of our bacterial cultures. As we will be using soldiers for this particular task, I invited Colonel Moran.'

Arms crossed over my chest, I leant against the mantelpiece, close enough to the fire to warm my frozen limbs. 'Both glanders and anthrax can be transported in liquid media sealed in small glass phials. These can be opened by pulling a stopper or breaking a seal. The contents are then poured into fodder. Simple enough for even an untrained man.'

'How high is the risk of infecting the messenger?' asked James. It sounded odd. He had never cared much about collateral damage.

'Well, if a man transporting the germs were clumsy or in very much of a hurry, he could break the phial, cut himself, and get infected.'

'What about the... What did you call them?' interjected Moran.

'Spores?'

'Yes, the spores. You said they can be stored as a dry powder. How do we transport it?'

I could not recall ever having mentioned to Moran that spores were a dry powder. That they were stored in a dry place, yes. The information on spore powder must have come from James. He was the only one I had told. 'The spores can be transported in a small phial, too. I am not certain how we should spread them, though. Whoever opens the phial will be at great risk of inhaling them and dying of anthrax.'

'Hum,' Moran said, and began shovelling sugar into his tea.

Silence fell. The clinking of Moran's spoon in his cup and the crackling of the fire were the only things to be heard. After a few moments, I noticed James staring at his friend. Moran poured even more sugar into his already sticky tea. As if in trance, he stirred it, then dropped his spoon onto the coffee table.

'Mules *love* sugar,' he said.

James's spine snapped to attention.

'Sugar cubes,' Moran muttered, and looked up at us. When we didn't applaud, or whatever it was he expected us to do, he slammed a fist on the table, effectively spilling his saturated sugar solution. 'Sugar cubes, for crying out loud! Hide a tiny phial inside sugar, the mules and horses will chew it to pieces, swallow it and contract whatever disease it contains!'

Stunned, I grasped the mantelpiece for support. That much brain power coming from Moran was...unexpected.

'This is an excellent idea,' James said, and turned to me. 'But can it be done?'

I swallowed. 'Easily. Each glass ampule needs but a few

drops of liquid media and germs.' No need to tell them that the use of solid media would considerably increase the storage potential of each of the deadly vessels.

'Very well. Now, all we need to come up with is a way to infect men with anthrax spores. They wouldn't bite down on sugar cubes. Well, children would—'

My icy stare stopped this narrative.

'Spreading via spores comes with a high risk of killing your own men,' I said.

'Refresh our minds about the different types of anthrax infection, please.'

'Ingesting germs or spores will result in gastrointestinal anthrax. The natural causes are, for example, eating under-cooked food. Symptoms are primarily nausea, abdominal pain, bloody diarrhoea, and ulcerative lesions. The second form is cutaneous anthrax, and it has no relevance for us, because the germs or spores have to be transmitted through a scratch or stab wound. When you get that close to your enemy, you can simply stick the bayonet all the way through.' I cast a glance at Moran, whose face hardened.

'Could one spread anthrax germs attached to bullets? To kill even those men that were only grazed by a shot?' Moran's mind seemed to be in hunter mode.

'Possibly. But again, the risk of infection when handling the bullets would be very high.'

Both men shared a brief glance. Something silent passed between them and I knew they would most likely make an attempt, with my cultures and Goff at their disposal.

'Shall I continue?' I asked and James nodded. 'Compared to the other two anthrax forms, pulmonary anthrax is the most lethal. It can only be caused by inhaling germs or spores. The patient will experience a septic shock within two to three days and will die twenty-four to thirty-six hours later.

There is no treatment for pulmonary anthrax, and the mortality rate is almost one hundred per cent.'

'Extraordinary,' breathed Moran, and stuck a pipe between his teeth.

I felt the urge to kick it all the way into his brain. 'Moran, I thought I made it perfectly clear that lethal germs are not to be confused with toys. I've come to think I should demonstrate it on *you*, so you will be more motivated to believe my statements.'

Moran curled his fingers around his armrests, and pushed up from his seat.

James stepped between us. 'Enough! Anna, it was your suggestion to use anthrax, and it is you isolating and testing it. I am certain Mr Goff would gladly take over should you decide this operation is too dangerous.'

I leant back against the wall, arms crossed, exhaling the tension. 'This operation is dangerous in nature and will become lethal if we don't show respect. Colonel Moran had an excellent idea on how to transmit disease. Forgive me, but you both tend to choose the most dangerous options germs have to offer. When I object and give you reasons as to how this weaponry can turn against us, you rarely listen and you believe it to be but a woman's foolish drivel. You take me seriously only when it suits you.'

The blood vessels in Moran temple were bulging. But James considered, and after a moment, he nodded at me. Moran threw up his hands and groaned.

James said, 'I see what you mean. Regardless, I want us to discuss all our options and only then make a decision.'

'As you wish.'

Moran rubbed his bushy eyebrows, and went back to sucking furiously on his pipe back. 'Whenever a country is about to lose a war, men grow desperate.' He puffed a large cloud. 'At the end, when the lives and the well-being of their families are threatened and their homes are about to be burned to the ground, nothing seems too cruel a measure to prevent that from happening. You will not find gentility on the battlefield, Dr Kronberg. Governments will break their own laws to prevent invasion. As to your lethal germs: We will use them when circumstances call for them, no matter the risk. It is your task to supply us with germs and instruct us on how to handle them. It is not your responsibility to tell us what, and what not, to do.'

His eyes glittered behind a wall of tobacco smoke.

'Is there anything you'd like to add?' James asked me. It sounded very much like, *We've heard your opinion. It's time to hold your tongue.*

And there was so much I wished to add. A knife between Moran's ribs, for one. Or my own ribs for that matter, because I had been naive enough to choose anthrax as the less dangerous alternative to the plague. But anthrax in the hands of these two — men who were practically in love with this germ — would be an extremely dangerous toy.

I reached out to the silver case James held in his hand and picked a cigarette while sorting through all I knew about anthrax. Taking a step closer to him, I smiled. He struck a match and held it out for me. His expression appeared gentle, his hand calm.

'Thank you, my dear,' I said. 'Gentlemen, you have obviously noticed that my preference for a bacterial weapon is glanders. I will now tell you why, and give you the essence of all the information I possess so that you can make your own judgement. Equines are the main means of transportation in a war. An army without horses and mules is painfully slow and will be overrun. Food, clean water, and medicine will run short. Glanders primarily infects equines, but can spread to humans, too. Both man and horse will die within two weeks. The disease has a mortality rate of eighty per cent. Transporting and spreading glanders is as simple as transporting and spreading anthrax.'

I looked at both men, waiting for a sign of understanding. They nodded and I continued, 'And this is the essential part: glanders slows both advancing and retreating troops. Starving, injured, and ill soldiers make an army painfully slow because no one wants to leave them behind. Not so with dead soldiers. The enemy will simply step over the corpses of their fellow soldiers on their way to the front lines. Corpses are not much of an obstacle. Anthrax can reach a mortality rate of nearly one hundred per cent in both men and equines. At first, this disease appears to be the perfect solution for us. But it is not. Its most aggressive form is pulmonary anthrax, which can only be contracted from inhaling spores. And here is where the problem lies. One cannot see these spores. One cannot smell them. They poison the air we breathe. I could infect you with anthrax this very moment, without needing to force infected food or drink into either of you. But in the course of doing so, I would most likely infect myself, and would only realise it when I was already dying. You tell me that a soldier goes out to die. I have always believed soldiers try to survive, to kill the enemy and win the war.'

Moran snorted.

'There is only one more thing I'd like to add,' I continued. 'Anyone who plans to use anthrax in warfare must keep in mind that the *wind can and will turn*. Spores are spread by wind and water. They stick to food and soil. They survive the coldest winters and hottest summers. If you spread anthrax on your enemy's land, you will reap what you have sown even one hundred years later. Your children will get ill and die, your produce will become infected, as will your cattle and sheep. The more anthrax germs you use, the more severe the after effects.'

I jammed my cigarette into the ashtray, and resumed my position next to the fireplace.

A slow smile spread on Moran's visage. 'As I already said, you are to provide the germs. We will decide where and when we will use them.'

James produced an appreciative nod.

Day 94

✤

Goff had invested all of his energies to make our laboratory look like new. He had prepared fresh media, purchased glassware, and ordered new test animals. Our mules had to be sacrificed, though. They were coming down with both diseases. Although Holmes's sabotage had been very well planned and executed, one small circumstance had ruined it all. If Goff had not kept copies of our pure cultures, the development of bacterial weaponry would have been thrown back by two months. Or even more.

I needed an alternative, but was afraid that a second major *accident* would raise suspicion.

The creaking of Goff's footsteps snagged at my nerves. He walked into the laboratory — a little out of breath — and announced, 'All mules on deck.' He brushed off his hands as if he'd been the one who'd dragged the carcasses out of the warehouse. The belching and rattling of the barge seeped through the half open door. A cloud of fog crept in.

I watched how Goff fumbled for a smoke in his coat pocket. My gaze strayed to the large flasks of grain alcohol. What if I were to target not the warehouse but...us?

The barge grew louder for a brief moment, and then its noises petered out in the distance. The mules would be sunk off the coast. And all Holmes and I had managed to gain were four days to fix the damage, plus another five to observe the new animals in quarantine.

I turned away from Goff, and focused back on my work. Or pretended to. Leaning on the workbench I tried to squeeze a solution out of my mind. The Petri dishes before me. Anthrax and glanders. One very dangerous, it being James's favourite. The other a little less so.

And an idea began to blossom.

~

Durham handed me a brandy and left the study.

I tapped my fingertips against the glass, cleared my throat, and said, 'I would like to conduct an experiment, James.'

'I cannot tolerate yet another extension of our project without outcome.'

'Obtaining the pure cultures was not an outcome? Testing them? Determining their effectiveness?'

Irritated, he ranked a hand through his hair. 'Yes, yes. Certainly. But we are far from a functional weapon.'

I wondered what had made him so impatient. Without a war at his doorstep, there should be no reason for haste.

'It might be worth it,' I said softly

He showed mild interest, and so I added, 'You want anthrax and I am reluctant to use it because of the great danger it poses to our men, as well as the spores' resilience once they have been spread in enemy territory. However...' Here I paused, gauging his mood. But his face showed no emotion. Which was usually a bad sign. 'I believe I can develop anthrax vaccines. If our men were immune to anthrax, we could use it widely without much risk to ourselves.'

He turned his glass in his hands, emptied it, and rose to fetch the cigarette case from the mantelpiece. I observed him. A slender figure, always a little stiff and under constant tension. He sucked smoke into his lungs and stared into my face for several long moments.

'We discussed vaccines before, but I never quite decided whether or not you should invest the time to produce them. You should start to brew large batches of anthrax and obtain sufficient spores for storage. But I do know this is a deadly business. Given the circumstances, it might be better if you developed vaccines as well.'

'What circumstances?' I asked. He pointed to my stomach. I snorted and tipped the brandy down my throat.

'At what time will you need human test subjects?'

'What a cold-blooded bastard you are, James! There is no need to murder people just yet. I will have to balance the germ's inactivation against immunisation efficiency and the morbidity of our test animals.'

'I repeat the question. At what time will you need human test subjects, *dear?*'

My throat closed. 'Three... Three months.'

'Excellent. Time enough to make preparations.' His glass clonked as he placed it on the mantelpiece.

He strode to the door, his movements calculated and fluid. With the handle in his hand, he turned back to me. 'Are you coming to bed?'

Day 104

James sat next to me, our cold legs sharing a blanket. The brougham had almost reached the medical school, where I was to meet Holmes to give him a list of men working for the government and the military. None of them were connected to our project and their arrest would be used as evidence for Holmes's ineptness. I found the plan rather superficial and suspected James was trying to gain time for whatever he was planning behind my back. His constant tension indicated that Holmes was beginning to pull in his net.

James put his index finger under my chin and turned my face to his. Smiling, he let his hand wander to my bosom. The message to Holmes that was tucked between my breasts crackled lightly. 'Why did you hide it there, of all places? I detest that he is allowed to touch what has touched you so intimately.'

'Would my stocking, specifically the inside of my thigh, suit you better?'

He glared at me, then reached for the blinds.

'The curtains have never been drawn before. If they are now, his suspicions will be raised,' I said.

He dropped his hand. The carriage came to a halt.

'Behave well,' he said, and slid low on his seat baring his incisors in a smirk.

Garrow folded the steps down and helped me alight. As my feet hit the pavement, my knees knocked together. And would not stop until I entered the medical school.

∾

'THIS LIST SHOWS ONLY the names of innocent men,' I whispered into Holmes's ear and handed him the scrap James had given me. 'I am not certain why he wants me to give you this. He claims he wants to taint your reputation, but his planning appears...hasty. Something is very wrong, and I don't know what his true intentions may be. Three weeks ago he and I met with several men to talk about germ warfare, as I wrote you earlier. You have their names, but...' I rubbed my itching face. 'They might be false.'

I was a wreck of nerves. Holmes looked at me with puzzlement, and whispered, 'Mycroft can prove connections between Moriarty and Colonel Dr Colbert Brine from the Veterinary Military Academy as well as Mr Jaran Ridgley from the Foreign Office. Your description of the men fits those individuals,' said Holmes.

'Are you quite sure? Why would...Moriarty reveal his men's names to me? And why did he want to get you out of England for a week?'

A small smile tugged at the corners of Holmes's mouth. 'He had several meetings that were planned and executed in great secrecy. If I'm not mistaken, and I dare say I'm usually not, they plan to move the entire operation abroad.'

'Hum... I have seen no indication of this. But he keeps

most information from me. Holmes,' I added urgently. 'If Moriarty is, as you've already suggested, forming a secret organisation with the sole purpose of defending Britain — or perhaps even to pull all expertise together for an attack against another country — how can you possibly arrest such high-level people?'

Holmes straightened up and said loud enough for any eavesdropper to hear, 'Thank you, Anna. This is valuable information. I'll need only a little more preparation, but soon enough Moriarty and his men will be arrested.'

Then, he bent down again and spoke into my ear, 'Let that be my concern. But we must tread very carefully now. Especially *you*,' he squeezed my shoulder. Urgency sharpened his features. 'Do nothing that would further risk your well-being. Abstain from too many enquiries into Moriarty's actions and try to be a compliant and well-behaved lady for a while. Should the danger become too great and you need to leave in a hurry — you will always find one of my boys close by. They follow you wherever you go and if you should drop your glove anywhere other than in front of the medical school, I'll know you need help making your escape. Do you understand?'

The word *compliant* rang in my ear. I snorted and answered for the eavesdropper to hear, 'Well, goodbye then,' turned on my heel and marched out of the lavatory.

How fortunate that Holmes had no clue how compliant I already was.

Day 131

❧❦❧

S not dribbled from the weakened mules' nostrils. They kept shaking their heads, catapulting strings of mucous onto their neighbours' necks, heads, muzzles. Goff watched from a safe distance, fascination singing in his every bone. He was looking forward to sinking corpses off-shore and I hated him for it.

In two days, we would receive the third batch of test animals. The glanders infection had caused strong symptoms in twelve of our first twenty-four animals. The other twelve had been immunised with heat-inactivated glanders germs twice during the last three weeks. However, all the mules were to be sacrificed, as not to mix diseases and obtain false-positive results.

Moran's men were already on their way. Soon, twenty-four shots would mark the end of our first test run. I would stay and watch. Perhaps it was a ridiculous notion, for the mules wouldn't care either way, but I believed I shouldn't turn away from the suffering I had caused.

The metal door creaked. Two men stepped through its frame — men I wouldn't wish to cross in bright daylight.

Moran's undertakers had the swollen hands and reddened, enlarged noses of alcoholics. The most unreliable sort when it comes to *not* spreading information.

Upon seeing the sick animals, one of them fingered his revolver.

'Go ahead if you'd like to die of a gruesome disease, gentlemen. I wouldn't want to hold you back,' I said.

They eyed me from the rim of my hat to the hems of my skirts, and started cackling.

'Mr Goff, if you would,' I said, and stepped back. He tied a grain sack on each mule's head to prevent them from slinging the infectious mucous at us. Then he injected a generous volume of chloroform through the fabric. The mules protested loudly. Until they grew sluggish. Goff injected another dose. And another. The animals collapsed and he threw blankets over over them, and then ordered the two undertakers to kill them with a bullet to the head.

Strangely detached, I watched it all.

Goff's gait was springy with excitement as he led the men to the barge. Their huffing and grunting produced clouds in front of there face, their arms bulging with the weight of the first carcass. A loud thump on the hollow deck of the barge, and then they returned for the next animal.

About an hour later, they began mucking the stalls. They washed down the remaining excrement with Thames water. And finally it was Goff's responsibility to wipe off all surfaces with grain alcohol. He would probably be intoxicated from the fumes once he was done cleaning.

Nauseous and angry, I scrubbed the workbenches and moved the glanders cultures to a far end of the laboratory. Our work on anthrax would begin the following day. James wanted us to test the more dangerous disease as soon as possible. All the while I silently implored Holmes to finish his investigations. How much longer could I pretend to be someone I wasn't without losing myself and my sanity?

After the barge had left, I paid the waiting street urchins five shillings each. An outrageously high wage for staying around doing nothing. But I didn't care. James would, I was sure.

'I have the impression you are replicating faster than I can count,' I remarked to the largest boy. He drew himself up defiantly, all four and a half feet.

'Ma'am, beg'n yer pard'n, but the more the better.'

'Any movements to report?'

''scuse me?' he said, picking something from the depths of his nostrils and flicking it into the river.

'Have you seen anything suspicious?'

'Only suspicious folk wus usselfs,' he said with a wink, and darted off.

I watched them run away, wondering how shocked they'd be if they knew I had lived in the slums for years. The smallest of them caught my eye. Her thin legs stuck out from dirty trousers that were too short for her, revealing grimy ankles. Her boots were too large and threatened to come off as she ran. She was dressed like a boy but her long hair and girlish features betrayed her easily. Yet she seemed to be accepted in the crowd of street arabs. Poverty had no space for most social restrictions the upper classes had invented. Perhaps she was the only girl among many brothers and her mother had no money to buy her a second-hand skirt or the materials to sew her one.

Or she had no mother at all. What if I...

What if...

≈

'YOU ARE NOT WITH ME,' James said softly.

'My apologies.' I took the brandy from his offering hand, and tried to recall what we had been talking about. Ah, vaccines.

I took a sip. The alcohol burned down my throat. 'Louis Pasteur developed anthrax vaccines for sheep and cows. According to his publications, he made the vaccine by exposing the bacilli to oxygen. But anthrax germs tolerate oxygen well enough, and the spores would only laugh at oxygen, and infect anything they come across. I am not entirely sure Pasteur told the world all his secrets.'

I rose and placed my hands on his clenching shoulders. His gaze softened. 'Remember that I was a student of Robert Koch,' I said. 'Pasteur's rival Toussaint used potassium dichromate as an oxidant to create an anthrax vaccine. And that is precisely what I will try next.'

'You should write down the procedure, so that Goff can take the lead should you... get ill again.'

'James, *I am barren*. How often do I have to tell you this?'

He stepped back from me, lowered himself into his armchair, and did not speak to me for the remainder of the evening.

Day 142

⚜

J ames changed over the next days. Tense, hurried, and impatient, he was gradually changing back to the monster who had abducted me. Madness twitched behind his controlled facade. Soon it would pounce.

When he was around, I spoke little. It was a matter of self-preservation. His mood would change so swiftly that I was unable to gauge when he would react with violence, and when with deadly silence.

Late one night, when his expression had softened and his hands relaxed, I allowed my guard to lower. Just a little. And I tried to find some rest before the storm that would hit us both.

I watched him stroke my abdomen and trace circles around my navel. 'Is your diagnosis still the same?' he asked softly.

My heart hiccupped. 'There hasn't been much time to think about it. But I fear your physician might have been correct after all.' Fear wasn't the right word. *Terror* would have described it better. There was nothing lovely or innocent about the thing possibly growing inside me. I felt as though I would be producing a perfect copy of James Moriarty. A copy that was invading my insides while its father tried to control the rest.

'I thought so,' he said, his fingers still stroking my stomach. 'Would you be my wife?'

I clamped down on all emotions, else I would have vomited. 'What? Why?' tumbled out of my mouth.

His expression darkened. 'You don't want my child.'

I wanted to grab his shoulders, shake him, and scream *Precisely!* 'I have never wanted to be a wife, and I've never wanted to have children.'

He nodded, head lowered, gaze attached to my stomach. It was still flat, but for how much longer?

'Your life has changed. And mine has, too. Have I not shown you often enough that I love you?'

It was a slap to my face. How could he even *think* such a thing? He had not the slightest clue what love was! And how could I not have seen this coming?

He must have seen the shock I felt. He drew back.

I touched his wrist. 'I always thought it was merely... physical.' My voice thinned as my mind worked frantically on possibilities for extracting myself from this trap. 'I don't want to be a mother. Once the anthrax test trial is over and you can do without your bacteriologist for a few days, I will see a surgeon.'

'You are planning to murder my child?'

Of course! Meekly, I blinked at him. His eyes were wild.

'What about your other progeny?' I asked.

'Other progeny? You think I would ever have allowed that to happen?'

'I don't know what to think.' Again an entire sentence spoken without a single lie. I doubted he noticed the difference.

'Nothing ever happened. They all used a sponge, they douched, none of them ever had a child.'

I nodded.

'You will *not* murder my child. And I will *not* permit you to put the mark of illegitimacy on my son or daughter. We will get married.'

'And what then? I'm to stay here in your house, the house of the man who abducted me and my father. Marry the man who kept my father in a hole for two months?' My voice was shrill with desperation.

'It was necessary then.'

'It was *never* necessary, James! Do you plan to lock me in my room again? So you can have full control? Am I to be strapped to a bed and filled up with opium?'

'Of course not!' he said, groaning and running his hand over his face.

'The last thing I want is to be a wife, to serve only my husband, and to have one child after the other. *Plop plop plop.*'

His palm made sharp contact with my face. 'It's about time you grew up.' Without another word, he dressed and left the room.

I barely felt the sting on my cheek. Every fibre was in uproar. I was cold to the bone. Mechanically, I rose and slipped into nightgown and robe. To find a skilled abortionist would be difficult. The chance of surviving such a procedure was, at best, eighty per cent. Should I be so unlucky as to have a quack extract the child, I would most likely bleed to death. Doing it myself was out of the question. At least surgically.

But what about...a poison? I had a flask with arsenide and belladonna, and could use some of it. But the remainder would not be enough to use against James.

I felt pressed into a tiny cage. I could barely breathe. I

longed to flee, to leave everything behind, and to find my old life with all the freedom it provided.

I began pacing the room. Would a great amount of alcohol induce early labour and bleeding? I wasn't certain. And James would know what I was attempting. No...I needed something that would make me ill, as though I suffered from a disease, not a poisoning. I stared out into the garden. There was a yew tree. Very toxic and it might kill me before it would affect James's brood. I was shocked by my own cold-ness, my detachment.

I tried but failed to imagine the alternative. I could *not* be mother to James's child.

A juniper bush. Its old German name was fitting: *Kindsmord* — child murder. I had no clue what the correct dose might be. But then, I didn't really care much about the consequence of overdosing myself.

∾

WHEN I WALKED through the entrance hall I heard James call for me. I met him in the study. He sat in his chair, head in his hands.

'Close the door, please,' he said, and I did so. 'Sit.' His motioned toward the armchair.

'I have been married before,' he began. 'My wife and our son both died within days of his birth.'

'I am very sorry,' I said softly. I even meant it. Whenever he showed his vulnerable side, he hurt me more than any of his cruelties ever did.

'I beg you not to kill our child, Anna.'

Words were stuck in my throat, impossible to swallow, impossible to retch up. I was torturing the monster before I attempted to kill it.

'Look at me,' he said, and I did. 'I know you cannot

imagine being a wife and a mother. But who insists that you stay at home all day, that you have one child after another, that you not work as a bacteriologist? You will have a nurse-maid and another maid for yourself. You can get back to your research whenever you wish.'

How interesting that his well-meant words sometimes felt like a knife to my guts.

'Why are you weeping?' He rose and walked up to me, knelt at my side, and wiped my tears away. 'Marry me, Anna,' he pressed. So much pain and want in that voice. I would have felt better if he'd punched my face instead.

'My father would never allow it,' I squeezed out, hoping that this one straw I had left to cling to, the only socially acceptable objection I could have, would count at all.

'He cannot want you to have an illegitimate child.'

'I beg you, James, do not even think of asking my father.'

His heart would break, or rather he would try to save his daughter by running a crowbar through James's heart.

'Very well, I will not ask him if that is your wish.' He looked expectant and a little smug.

'You want me to lie to him.'

'It is none of my concern whether you lie to your father or tell him the truth.'

If not for Holmes, my father, and all those men knowing too many details about our germ warfare project, I would have closed my hands around James's throat and not let go until one of us was dead.

'Give me time, please.' I said, taking his hand and pressing it against my forehead.

'Of course,' he answered.

Day 151

❦

My days were marked by anxiety. I slept little and had excruciating nightmares about James and his child. Becoming a mother had never occurred to me before.

Since the rape, my menstruation had come so infrequently that I was certain I would never conceive. I was nineteen and had just defended my thesis when three of my fellow students wanted to check the size of my cock. How shocked they'd been, and how swiftly that shock had changed to pleasant surprise. They knew I wouldn't tell on them — that would have destroyed my newly-won career as a male medical doctor and bacteriologist. They had hurt me. Badly.

How much bad luck must one have, to then be impregnated by James Moriarty of all the monsters in this world?

For a week now I had been contemplating what toxin I would use and which dose might be best. I'd finally settled on my first choice — juniper, a toxic plant that caused symptoms a sloppy physician might confuse with severe influenza. It seemed so easy. I sent Holmes a message that I had caught the flu and wouldn't be able to write for a week or two. Then I told James I wasn't feeling well, retreated to my room, and asked Cecile to bring tea. After she had left, I placed the juniper tops on the saucer and crushed them with a spoon. I scraped them into the cup and poured tea over the remains to wash them into the liquid. I kept stirring until the tea had cooled, then drank it all and picked the few remaining twigs out and ate them, taking care not to leave any traces of what I had done.

Half an hour later, I began feeling sick. Just a little at first, and then nausea hit ferociously. My stomach contents hit the chamber pot. I wiped the sweat off my face, then picked bits of juniper twigs out of my vomit, and threw them out of the window. I wiped my hands on the pillow which I'd soiled earlier. My muscles were hurting. A twitching and trembling spread through my body.

I pulled the bell rope.

Cecile entered. Seeing me hang over the side of my bed, retching, she squeaked, 'Are you poorly, Miss?'

'God bless your powers of deduction,' I grunted, and spat into the chamber pot.

Cecile put her hand to my forehead. How wonderfully cold her skin was. She said she would get the master, and rushed from the room.

I must have lost consciousness, or perhaps time was flying, because the very next moment, James's hand brushed my face.

I scrambled to recall what I'd planned to say. Something about our project. Ah, yes, there it was. 'Better not touch me. I don't know what this is and...and I can't really think straight. Might be influenza. Or maybe not. But...' I coughed. 'Make sure you and Cecile wash hands. Thoroughly. Just to be certain. You know what...what I mean.'

'Impossible.' He spoke so low that I had to look up at him to check he had spoken. Was there mistrust or only concern in his expression? Before I could analyse it, he turned on his heel and left.

I DON'T KNOW how often Cecile changed my chamber pot. My body expelled the juniper poison as I anxiously waited for blood. My uterus cramped, together with most other muscles. Trying not to moan too loudly, I shut my eyes and rolled up into a ball.

Footfalls woke me. The first thing I saw of Dr Blincoe was his black bag. Then his hands, wandering all over my body, prodding my abdomen, opening my mouth, and feeling my pulse.

'Disinfect yourself,' I managed to say just before he stuffed two or three carbon tablets into my mouth and showed them down my gullet with spoonfuls of cold tea.

I drifted in and out of consciousness. And whenever I woke up, I spotted Blincoe sitting in an armchair across from me. He watched, felt my pulse on occasion, and urged me to drink more tea. My mind was sluggish. My body ached. Until I drifted off again.

Day 152

I opened my eyes. The morning sky was milky grey.

'How are you feeling?' James asked.

'Weak.' Despair crawled into my heart. No blood wet my thighs. My uterus seemed to contract only ineffectually. 'How is my temperature?'

He placed a palm to my forehead. 'Not as high as yesterday.'

'Would you help me to the vanity?' I pushed myself up, fighting the urge to vomit. He helped me out of the bed and to a chair. I gazed at the looking glass and opened my mouth to examine it. From the corner of my vision, I saw him frown.

'I don't see any lesions.' I huffed a sigh of fake relief. 'Yesterday, I feared I might have contracted intestinal anthrax.' I grabbed James's hand, pulled myself up, and let him walk me back to my bed.

I tugged the blanket around myself and asked, 'What did Dr Blincoe say?'

'He said you might have been poisoned.'

'Nonsense.'

'Or that you poisoned yourself to abort the child.'

'And of course, you believe him. Or is it that you believe what you fear to be true? As you said to me the other day?'

A muscle feathered in his jaw. His pupils bled into his irises, staining them black. 'I swear to you, if you kill my child...' He let the words hang in the air like vultures.

'And here we are again. You threatening my life if I don't do as you say.'

A derisive snort. 'You will obey me.' Then he stalked from the room.

Some time later, Cecile brought tea. She helped me wash, and change into a fresh nightgown. The procedure drained me. Exhausted and aching, I lay back down on my bed. 'I need your help, Cecile,' I said quietly.

She sat down on the bed. 'And how may I help you, Miss?'

'Do you think you are brave enough to do something behind the back of your master?'

Her eyes widened, but then she must have remembered the secret messages between her and the coachman. She blushed and nodded.

I was not sure if I could trust her with this, but I saw no alternative. 'I need to be ill for a few days and for that I need tops of the juniper bush down in the yard. Pick a handful and stuff it in your bosom. Take utmost care that no one sees you. Don't walk down directly now and don't come straight to me after you have picked them. Do you understand?'

'Is it because you are with child and you don't want it?'

I was thunderstruck. 'Did you overhear Dr Blincoe and your master?'

She smiled apologetically.

'What else did they talk about?'

'Nothing much. The doctor said that it could be the flu or a poisoning. The master said he suspects the latter and Blincoe answered that under these circumstances you should be forbidden to leave your room. So as not to give you the opportunity to poison yourself again.'

'I can't stand the thought of carrying his child,' I whispered. My voice nearly broke. 'Would you help me, please?'

'And you will...you will not kill yourself, Miss?'

'That was never my intention.'

She swallowed and said, 'I will help you then.'

An enormous weight fell off my chest. I pressed Cecile's hands. 'I will hide the carbon tablets under my mattress. Ignore them when you put fresh sheets on my bed.'

She lowered her head, her posture tense with anxiety.

'Cecile, I am a medical doctor. I will not harm myself beyond repair.' That was the plan, at least.

~

AROUND NOON, after I had refused a light lunch much to James's dismay, Cecile came to stoke the fire. Before she tended to the fireplace, she slipped her hand into her dress and extracted a small bundle of slender green twigs.

'I'll be forever in your debt,' I croaked. Anxiety flashed across her features. I added, 'If he discovers our ploy, I will tell him that I forced you and that you bear no guilt.'

'I fear for you, Miss,' she pressed out. Her fingers crumpled her apron.

I wondered how I could possibly make up to her, her imminent unemployment. She and her lover would have to leave this house, as would all of James's servants as soon as their master was dead or in prison. New employment was hard to come by without a reference.

After Cecile left, I began my procedure of crushing twigs, stirring them into my tea, drinking it all, and removing the telltale signs.

Everything contracted at once. My stomach expelled its

contents, and my guts did, too. My lower abdomen cramped so badly that I couldn't help but cry out. Soon my room was crowded with people. Durham and Blincoe held me down while the latter pushed a tube down my throat. The resulting pain melted into yet another contraction. But none of the pain mattered. When Blincoe said, 'She is bleeding,' I could have sobbed with relief.

～

'Miss?' Cecile's voice. I liked that lilt, although her fear made it a little squeaky.

'Is she unconscious?' James, a little bored, a little exasperated, and cold. How curious, no one seemed to have taught him compassion.

A hand on my forehead. My abdomen cramped. I was already rolled up in a ball, but tried to compact myself just a little more. The contraction slowly subsided.

'Drink this,' Blincoe said, and lifted my head. He pressed a cup to my lips.

I allowed the bitter concoction to fill my mouth before I spat it all over my nightgown.

Day 160

❧❧❧

I spent my days in bed, guarded by the doctor's watchful eyes. Occasionally, James would come in to ask how I was doing. 'Recovering,' was Blincoe's answer.

Cecile had brought me sanitary towels earlier. I didn't know who had put them there, but I felt them between my legs. I slipped my hand under my blanket, palpated my lower abdomen and probed for blood on the towels.

'The bleeding stopped this morning,' Blincoe said.

I looked across the room.

His expression was soft. 'Do not worry yourself. You did not have a miscarriage. Your child is alive, I believe.'

The room began to swim, I clapped my hand over my face and wept. Close to hysteria, I managed to squeeze out, 'Thank God!'

Blincoe grew uncomfortable and rose to his feet 'I will find your husband.'

'No! Please, don't. Allow me to collect myself. I don't wish to upset him further.'

He sank back in his chair. 'You did not use an abortifacient?'

'No, I did not. I confess, I considered it. But then I thought that this might be my only chance to be a mother.' I rubbed my wet face with a corner of the blanket, shocked how much control I was able to haul out of the depths of my exhaustion. 'You may call him in now.'

Blincoe left and a long moment later, James stepped in.

'You convinced Blincoe, but you cannot convince me. I know what you did.'

'I planned to. But I couldn't...'

He placed his hands on the bed, his face close to mine. 'You called me a cold-blooded bastard. And here you are, unable to distinguish your truths from your lies. I have found vegetable matter in your vomit. You collected toxic plants from my yard, yew perhaps, and you took it to kill my child.'

'I collected oregano, James. The same plant I picked for my father who had contracted tonsillitis and bronchitis in that hole you locked him up in. I felt my tonsils beginning to swell and grow sore. I used oregano for its mild antibacterial qualities.'

'I don't believe you.'

'Get out of my room then.' I glared up at him. A blink of his eyes and he turned away and left. The sound of the bolt sliding in place shouldn't have surprised me.

I lay perfectly still, with only my mind moving about. Escape was the only solution. I would have to get my strength back, eat better, walk about, use my weakened muscles. Then I would destroy everything James and I had created. The first anthrax trial should be completed, and—

The sensation of butterfly wings softly brushing the inside of my lower abdomen brought my thoughts to a full stop. What a force this little touch had! I placed my hand there, eyes widened in terror, shoulders trembling.

Moriarty's child was moving.

~

A TIMID KNOCK and Cecile entered. She rushed up to my bed. 'How are you doing, Miss?'

'I am fine, thank you, Cecile. How is your master?'

Her head drooped. 'He is...furious. Everyone is walking on tiptoe, the slightest noise upsets him. But I think he will be calmer soon.'

'Is he smoking opium?'

She nodded.

'Would you bring me tea and a sandwich, please? And I'd like to wash.'

'Yes, Miss,' she said quietly, and left as though the slightest noise would send me into raving madness, too.

She helped me wash and dress, and patted my back as I caught my feeble breath. Surprisingly, the sandwich made me feel a little stronger, although I had to force it in. The tea helped to wash it down my dry throat.

I felt ready. A little.

'I will go down to see him now,' I said and rose to my feet. My knees were weak and I had to hold on to the bed frame.

'I will help you, Miss.'

Slowly, we made our way to the study. I knocked and stepped in. James lay on the ottoman, eyes directed at the ceiling.

'May I come in?'

'I am tired of your lies,' he answered.

'Me, too.'

Slowly, his head turned toward me, his face unable to conceal the surprise.

'Thank you, Cecile,' I said and shut the door.

The few steps toward him seemed very far. It took a moment for him to realise that I wouldn't be able to walk all the way by myself. He rose, caught my arms, and walked me to the ottoman.

'Just let me lie down next to you for a while. I'm quite out of breath.' There wasn't even a need to feign my weakness.

I felt him watching me, waiting.

And so I began, 'Our relationship is based on control and manipulation. Neither of us has relinquished even a fraction of power. Can we agree on that fact?'

He nodded once.

'Learning that I am with child tipped that balance. Suddenly, I saw myself being forced to give up every ounce of control. I felt I had no power at all, not even over my own life. Can you understand this?'

His eyes scrutinised my face. Gradually, he lost his cold expression.

'I took juniper to abort our child.'

'I should have killed you the first time we met.'

'Yes, that would have spared us a lot of pain,' I whispered.

He did not react. Exhausted, I placed my head on his shoulder. 'Your child is moving.' He stiffened. 'The fact that I will be a mother soon changed...everything. I will not take part in your germ warfare project anymore. I will only develop vaccines. I want to save lives, not take them.'

His ribcage heaved. And all of a sudden, his arm shot out and wrapped around my back. He pressed me to his chest and his face into my hair. I began to shake and promised myself that he needed a fair chance to become human again.

'Marry me,' he whispered.

'I can only marry you when you abstain from murder.'

'Is that all you ask of me?'

'Yes,' I answered, shocked by how far I had gone already.

'A simple request,' he mused. 'I will certainly grant you this wish.'

Day 171

James had grown more and more obsessed with Holmes. My tension grew with his, but for a very different reason. I hadn't spoken to Holmes for weeks and had no clue how far he had come in closing the case. Since the day James had proposed to me and I had consented, he freely shared sensitive information. And I sent my water closet messages to Holmes every day, stuffed either with a few names and the nature of the connection between these men and James, or with observations of James's everyday routine. I also learned that he had indeed attempted to influence a new draft of the Brussels Convention. Apparently, men were listening to him, but no new draft had been made thus far.

While I was working on vaccines, I kept a close eye on Goff. The man had turned into a maniacal germ-producing machine, brewing batch after batch of anthrax germs, and developing variations of a spore dryer that would prevent spores from escaping into the surrounding air to infect us.

I rearranged the laboratory set-up every day, explaining that I was worried about his spores and wished to increase our safety. The changes were small. But gradually, I was turning the warehouse into an oversized bomb.

～

THE BROUGHAM WAITED next to the river. What was James doing, coming to the warehouse at this time of day?

I frowned at him as he opened the carriage door for me.

He gifted me a brief smile and motioned me to climb in. 'I'm making sure my fiancé and my child get enough to eat. You are working too much, my dear. Come, I've reserved a table for us.'

I climbed in. Just before he closed the door I spotted one of Holmes's street urchins. Wiggins was his name, I believed, but I might have been mistaken. The boy looked hurried.

Garrow drove us up to Richmond, folded down the stairs, and opened the door. James exited the carriage, then he froze. I followed his gaze.

Holmes! Without disguise he stood just across the street, looking me full in the face. I forced my head not to shake. He was too early!

'What does this man want now?' snarled James.

With pain in my chest, I took James's hand, and gave Holmes a cold stare, hoping he would understand. James tucked my hand in the bend of his elbow and marched us off to the *Castle*, a nearby dining hall.

Judging from James's constant tension and Holmes advising me to run, Holmes must be very close to arresting James and his men.

Three days before, James had begun to hunch again. Headaches were bothering him constantly. Although my treatments gave him some relief, every evening he was to be found on his ottoman, smoking opium. The ageing cat was trapped, and furiously pacing his cage.

James pulled up a chair for me, and I sat. He didn't speak until the waiter had taken our orders.

'We will move to Paris,' he announced.

'Is it Holmes?' I asked softly.

'We will live in an apartment for a while until we find a house that suits us.'

'What about the laboratory and our project?'

'Goff will begin packing up tomorrow morning.'

'Our first trial is almost finished, James. In eight days I could infect our immunised mules and the control group. Then we would know whether our anthrax vaccine works. Please, I need another two weeks!'

It would be a catastrophe if our laboratory were moved before I could destroy it.

James stared at the tablecloth, his jaw muscles working. 'Very well, a fortnight. Not one day longer.'

'Thank you.' I placed my hand on his.

Day 183

❦

I felt translucent. Prolonged hardship can make personalities stronger, but it can warp them as well. I had believed myself strong enough to escape this fate. How curious was the capability to live through mental torture and physical pain minute by minute, day by day, while the mind allowed no glimpse of the future self for even a second. Had I known James Moriarty would keep me for half a year, only to be invaded by his child and handcuffed in marriage, I would have let his dogs eat me that first day. Yet it had been I, only I, who had taken every single one of these steps, one by one, half-blind to the consequences. There was no one to blame but myself.

As we drove up to a small cathedral outside London, I gazed at James's face and wondered what hardships had removed his humanity.

The ceremony was short and only Jonathan and Cecile were present to witness the unification of bride and groom. Cecile, in her naiveté, smiled happily, while Jonathan's eyes betrayed suspicion.

A simple *"I do"* and I belonged to James. Now he owned all

that I had, and I owned nothing. My clothes had been his before. I felt sorry for my cottage, though. He could sell it or burn it down. Whatever he chose to do, no law would hinder him. He could lock me up in my room and violate me, and it would be legitimate. By signing the marriage papers, I was robbed of freedom. Should I ever regain it, I would shed my female identity forever. Being Anna Kronberg only meant a constant struggle with society and its laws that I would always fail to recognise and obey.

I was too tired to do this any longer.

I put a timid smile on my face as James took my hand in his to lead me back to the brougham. We had been quiet for a long moment, with him gazing at me as I observed the streets and houses flying by.

'You are not with me, Anna.'

'I am sorry, James. I haven't been myself lately.'

'To be honest, nor have I,' he replied, slamming a fist against the window frame. 'This Holmes is getting on my nerves. He is like a bloodhound that won't be led off track. He's all over my men lately.'

The brougham came to a halt, James alighted, and offered me his hand. 'Mrs Moriarty?' he said with pride. I tried a smile and his face fell.

'I shouldn't have rushed you,' he said.

'Perhaps.' I gazed at my shoes, fighting for words. 'We had no time to get to know each other as man and woman, James. We've worked and slept with each other, but we never considered spending our lives together, let alone having children.'

'Well, what is done is done,' he said, kissing my hand. 'You could not have a child and be unmarried. Come.' He led me up the marble stairs into the house. Lunch was awaiting us. The odour of fish pudding made me sick. Upon my request, Hingston removed it from the table. The vegetables looked inviting enough, though.

'It is time to change tactics with Holmes.'

I swallowed. 'What do you mean?'

'I will put an end to this. The man is a nuisance.' James tried to shovel peas onto his fork, but they wouldn't obey. He began to stab them ferociously. Silverware screeched on china.

'Are you breaking your promise?'

'No. I will have someone else murder Holmes. But let us not talk about such gruesome issues, my dear. We have a wedding to celebrate. I would very much like to see every inch of you in the afternoon light.'

Hingston blushed and left the room.

Day 184

✦✦✦

Friday, April 24th, 1891

I stepped out of the tub, and paused to watch water run down my body and steam rise from it. The Moroccan soap coloured the air heavy and sweet. What I felt would be hard to describe. *Precise,* perhaps?

The decision had been easier than I had anticipated. While taking supper with James, the certainty fell upon me as light and cold as April rain. James had been trying to murder Holmes. First attempt: in person, at Holmes's apartment, but Holmes had had his loaded revolver ready. Subsequent attempts were carried out by James's men, be it stones thrown from rooftops or horse carriages trying to run him over. I had let James know that I was shocked. There was no way to disguise what I felt. And why should I not be shocked? My husband was putting himself in danger. I was entitled to be upset.

I worked almond oil into my wet skin, then dabbed excess moisture off with a towel. A crystal phial waited on a chest of drawers, the clear liquid inside refracting the candlelight into sparks of red, blue, and orange. I watched the small rainbows, marvelling at the beauty of my murder weapon.

I pulled the stopper.

The treacherous fluid clucked through the phial's neck and fell onto my palm. I applied it to my breasts, and let the dew soak into my skin. I spread another handful on my vulva and pubic hair, and a final droplet on my lower lip. Then, I opened a tin of activated carbon tablets and swallowed them all. His kisses would transport some of the poison into my mouth and I would inevitably swallow it. The carbon had to absorb it all or I would not survive the night.

I brushed my wet hair which now reached past my chin — the same length it had been before the injury to my head a year and a half earlier. My fingers probed the scar. It still felt sensitive to the touch. I stepped closer to the looking glass and wiped its cloudy surface. I met my gaze. *You will murder a man tonight,* I whispered. *Yes, as you should.*

Condensation crept in and obscured my face.

I put the camisole on and strung myself into the corset. He fancied unpacking me. No drawers, only garters and silk stockings covered my legs. He liked that, too — immediate access to the most important parts.

I walked out of the bathroom, the Moroccan perfume trailing in my wake. The clacking of my heels sounded in the corridor, and I knew he was listening for it, awaiting my arrival at his bedroom door. I knocked and heard his approach on the other side. He opened and smiled at me. I smiled back, feeling a surge of excitement over the imminent murder by intimacy. He saw my slight trembling, curled his hand around the back of my neck and pulled me close. His kiss was demanding. I surrendered to him and our final battle.

'You are different tonight,' he whispered, his breath brushing against my neck.

'Yes.' I titled my head to offer more of my sensitive skin.

'Why is that?'

'Tonight, I wish to surrender.'

His hands stopped in their tracks, his expression darkening in mistrust.

'I've never given myself to you completely. I never could, and never thought to. I am a headstrong woman. You know that.'

'Why the change of heart?'

'I thought about it while bathing. How it would feel to not be in control of myself for a few moments.' I took a step back from him, feigning disappointment. 'My brain is always analysing, and it distracts me from being with you. Thinking of surrender aroused me. But we don't have to—' His lips came down on mine, his tongue swept into my mouth and spread the taste of opium.

We fell onto the bed. He pushed up my dress. I struggled to get it off, and he helped me, found the corset and whispered, 'Lovely.'

Slowly, he untied the arrangement of hooks and strings, silk and whale bone; whispering, crackling, rustling intermingled with staccato breath and the sound of kisses.

His hand wandered from my breasts down to my stomach, coming to a halt just above my clitoris. Impatiently, I grabbed his wrist and pushed his fingers closer and deeper. With a growl he dove down, greedily kissing my toxic vulva. I did love him then. All of him, who trusted me now and did not know that this would be his end. I loved him for what he was, and for all he had done. Because tonight I was the one murdering, and he the victim. Sending him off without anyone loving him felt wrong.

SPENT, he rolled off me. A few moments later, his face began to redden unhealthily. He opened his eyes. His pupils were dilated, his eyeballs bloodshot. He blinked. I could see the realisation sink in and the shock it brought.

'I'd always suspected... the wine,' he croaked. His feet began twitching. His eyelids fluttered.

'You took precautions?'

'Hrmm...' His jaw would not follow his orders.

'Carbon?' I asked. He did not reply, but his eyes betrayed him. If he had taken his last dose of activated carbon before or after dinner, there must only be very little left in his stomach. Too little to save him now.

His hand moved up, his index finger trying to enter his throat to help expel his stomach's toxic contents. I held on to his wrist and pulled his arm away. He feebly shoved at me. His eyes were brimming with water, as his body gradually relented to the belladonna's debilitating effect. He blinked, squeezing tears onto his cheeks. I wiped them away and said softly, 'I cannot allow you to bring suffering upon thousands of people, and I will certainly not let you kill Holmes. But we both lost this battle, James. I allowed you to break me.'

The twitching intensified. I rose and dressed, then opened the strongbox and took his revolver, munition, and all the money and papers from it. I cocked the gun, picked up my shoes, and walked back to James's side.

Froth seeped from the corners of his mouth. His abdomen appeared to be cramping. I turned him onto his side, for drowning in vomit would be an even crueller death.

I kissed his brow, whispered my farewells, and left.

I tiptoed to my room, and put a wad of bills into an envelope and marked it "Cecile." With cloak and purse on my arm, I climbed the stair to the attic and pushed the envelope under the door of her room. Then I went down into the study and collected the papers from the top drawer of James's desk.

With my back to the entrance door and observing the stairwell for any movement, I laced my boots. Then I sneaked outside. The dogs came running and greeted me with wagging tails. I made my way to the gate and tried it. It was locked, so I climbed over it. The hem of my dress tore as I jumped down on the other side.

I stuck my finger deep into my throat until black vomit splashed onto the pavement. The carbon that held the toxin captive needn't go through my digestive system. Then I walked down Kensington Palace Gardens and with every new step I took the turmoil inside of me worsened.

Running, I turned into Bayswater Road, then slowed to a casual walk, wondering where Holmes's street urchins were. Soon, I heard a cab approaching. The hairs on my neck prickled, but I willed myself not to turn around. The hansom passed me and stopped after a hundred yards. The cabbie climbed down and checked his horse's front hooves, swore, spat, and climbed back up again. I decided to go for it.

'Cabbie!' I cried and walked up to him. 'I need you to take a message to Mr Sherlock Holmes, 221B Baker Street,' I said, hastily writing a small note and extracting a gold sovereign from my purse — the smallest of the coins I had found in James's strongbox. 'Be quick and Mr Holmes will give you another.' I held the money and the message out to him. The cabbie's eyes bulged. He appeared close to heart failure, but pulled himself together soon enough and snatched the money as if in fear I would change my mind.

'Yes, ma'am,' he said, flicked his horse hard, and raced away.

I walked for about ten minutes before another cab came into view. I hailed it, gave the driver an address, and climbed in. He appeared rather taken aback by my choice of destination.

I handed the man a sovereign, thinking that the news of a

madwoman paying outrageous fares would spread like fire. I watched the hansom drive off, then turned around to unlock the warehouse.

I entered and the metal door fell into its frame with a loud crack. Heavy odours of swine blood, beef extract, and mule manure saturated the air. My trembling fingers searched for the lantern on the floor, found it, opened its hatch, and lit the wick. The small bubble of light did not reach far. I walked all around the room, lighting oil lamps and checking the positions of the large flasks filled with grain alcohol. I took a scalpel and cut my petticoat into slices, then twisted them into wicks. The end of a wick went into each flask, sucking up the liquid and releasing its vapour into the air, biting my nostrils. The other ends were laid out on the floor and unified in the centre, one large, white spider-web with globules at each tendril's end. I dumped all my notes and James's papers — the sum of our work on germ warfare — next to one alcohol bottle, then walked over to the dozing mules, bracing myself for my next task.

Two days ago, we had poured anthrax germs into their fodder. By now, half of the animals stood on shaky legs, hindquarters soiled with diarrhoea. I strapped fodder bags over their heads and soaked them with chloroform. I waited until they collapsed, then I stepped back to shoot each of them in the head.

Reload and shoot.

My hand and wrist hurt from the recoil, but everything else felt numb. I dropped the revolver into the straw, and walked back to the laboratory, struck a match and threw it into the spider-web's centre.

With a mighty *woof*, flames shot up the wicks. I darted toward the exit to escape the explosion. Before I could even touch the handle, the door flew open. Moran's face and his flying fist were the last things I saw before darkness fell.

WHAT A CURIOUS SENSATION! Flickering light. Flickering memories. Reality slipping into dream slipping into reality. My lungs were burning. I opened my eyes to stare a wall of fire. Thick smoke floated inches above my head. The only cool place was the ground on which I lay. My breath was barely a whisper. Labouring, heavy, painful. My left eye hurt, my head throbbed, my throat clenched. So much effort to push myself forward. Inch by inch.

Why wouldn't my hand let go of the bulky purse? The walls were on fire, the ceiling invisible, the metal door probably too hot to touch or too heavy for me to push open now. I thought of crying then, but why should I? Dying wasn't too horrible a thought. I wouldn't even feel the flames lick my skin. The smoke would make me unconscious in but a moment. I rested my cheek on the cold floor, forcing myself not to think of fire eating flesh and slowly drifted off.

SOMETHING RUMBLED. *Clack clack clack*. Smoke. Smoke! My eyes opened. Or rather, one eye — the other was swollen shut — and looked up at...Holmes?

He touched my forehead.

'Something is burning.' I managed a croaky whisper.

'You are safe. It is the smoke on your clothes and hair you smell.'

I shut my eye. For the first time in my life, my brain refused to think, and I was too tired to coax it into analysis mode.

He carried me up a flight of stairs and laid me down on his bed, then disappeared.

'Drink,' he said upon his return, holding a glass of water in one hand, lifting my head with the other. My mouth and throat felt like sandpaper. I tried to ask what had happened, but only a rasp came out. He bent closer, and I repeated my question.

Slowly, he placed the glass on the nightstand.

He looked worried. 'I should have foreseen that Moriarty would instruct the cabbies working the area to keep their eyes open for any woman fitting your description. And for a substantial reward, they would certainly make for a good surveillance army. It's what I would have done.'

'He did that?'

Holmes pressed his lips together and nodded.

'How did you find me?'

'Wiggins clung to the hansom, took a ride to the ware-house and back to Kensington Park. Then he came to me, asking whether I had got your message. Of course, it never arrived here, it was delivered to Moran instead! Moran must have run to Moriarty first, else he would have been at the warehouse before it went up in flames.'

I coughed and he gave me more water. 'Thank you,' I squeezed out. 'All his notes and our germs are burned. James is dead, Moran will be caught soon.'

He placed his hand on mine. 'Yes,' he whispered.

I heard a door open and close, a rustle, and footfall.

'Watson, finally!' Holmes exclaimed. His friend gazed down at me, bushy eyebrows drawn low.

'By Jove,' Watson muttered, as he examined my face, chest, arms, and hands. He pulled out his stethoscope, leant over me to press it between my chest and his ear. Humming and huffing, he probed my heart and lungs.

'Any signs of pulmonary oedema?' I rasped.

'No, nothing as yet. But it needs to be observed. I am more concerned about your eye, to be honest.' He reached for it. I held his hand back.

'I can do it,' I said, and gingerly pushed around the swollen left eye. 'I cannot feel any bones shifting.'

'Good. Are you hurting anywhere else?' he asked, while checking the reaction of my right pupil.

'No. My head hurts, but given the circumstances—'

'Indeed!' interrupted Watson, straightening up. 'Holmes, she needs fresh air, lots to drink to compensate for the loss of fluids, and Mrs Hudson should help her wash. That soot has to come off. She needs to breathe.'

Holmes patted Watson's shoulder. 'Thank you, my friend. You are, as always, most reliable. Please forgive the harsh welcome.'

'Never mind. Never mind.' Watson seemed a little miffed all of a sudden, as though he had just noticed Holmes's roughness.

'Thank you, Dr Watson,' I said. 'You always rush to my aid when I get myself beaten up.'

He squeezed my hand and told me he'd be back tomorrow morning to examine my lungs once more.

'Holmes?' I asked, after Watson had left.

'Yes?'

'Have you seen Moran?'

'Yes, I saw him leave the warehouse.'

'What is it?' I sensed that he was withholding information.

'I could swear he looked triumphant.'

'Did he see you?'

'No. I saw his face for but a moment, illuminated by the fire. I might be mistaken...' He did not sound doubtful, though.

'Tell me your suspicions. I don't feel able to think much at all right now.'

'Moran did not appear like a man whose best friend and employer had just died.'

'He was dying as I left him...' My mind raced around the last scene with James. Had he managed to retch up the poison? Could this be? Or could Moran have possibly pumped his stomach?'

'How far from James's house is Moran's?'

'Five minutes,' he answered. 'By foot.'

I closed my eye as the threat of failure and utter disaster came crashing down. 'Holmes?'

He threw an analytic glance at my hand that still held in his.

I couldn't bear it. 'Watson is right. I need to wash. But without Mrs Hudson's help.'

He pushed himself up and left the room only to return with a jug of water that he poured into the washbasin.

I pushed myself into a sitting position. My head spun and I felt sick.

Quietly, Holmes left the room.

'Please,' I called after him. 'Leave the door ajar.'

I heard him walk to the armchair, stuff his pipe and light it. The calmness he radiated felt like my float in the middle of a wild ocean.

I peeled off my dress and undergarments to wash off James, together with the remaining poison. It took three changes of water to get the soot off. But no matter how much I scrubbed my skin, the feeling of being dirty would not subside. My breasts still felt sore and tight. I gazed down at my stomach. A week ago, it had been quite flat. But now...

My chest heaved and my throat contracted, I felt unable to breathe and started sobbing, trying to hold it in and not let myself be heard.

'Anna?' asked Holmes from the other room.

'Don't come in!' I slapped tears and snot from my face, dried myself with the towel, and pulled on Holmes's fresh shirt and undergarments, wrapped his dressing gown around myself, and walked toward him to sit on the floor, close to the fireplace. I was trembling, and it wasn't from the cold. Holmes walked to the window and cautiously peered down into the street.

'Hum.'

'What is it?' I asked.

'One of Moriarty's footmen.' Holmes looked at his pocket watch, then slid it back into his waistcoat. 'He has been standing there for about ten minutes.'

'Is he waiting for the artillery to come and take revenge?'

'Possibly, but not very likely. He's observing the house. He seems quite relaxed. If Moriarty were dead, there would be more than a mere look-out. The most likely explanation is that his master is forging new plans while he spies on us.'

Holmes turned to me. I could see his brain rattling. 'Thank you,' I said quietly.

'For what?'

'Anyone else would empty a bucket of pity over my head now, trying to make me believe I hadn't failed, making me more miserable yet and even less able to function. You don't, and this is the more respectful and considerate thing to do. Thank you.'

He raised his eyebrows, blinked the puzzlement away, and said, 'I recommend we lie low tonight. Tomorrow morning I will initiate a chase through London to keep them busy. On Monday, all of Moriarty's men will be arrested by the police, including Moriarty himself.' Holmes rubbed his hands, eyes shining, limbs vibrating with anticipation.

I could not get the images of the poisoned James and Moran's flying fist out of my head. They came in constant repeat, making me blink every time the imaginary knuckles hit my eye.

Holmes pushed a glass of brandy into my hand. Just then, the bell rang. 'Into the bedroom!' he commanded. He fetched his revolver from the coffee table and went down the flight of stairs, taking several steps at once. I ignored his safety measure and eavesdropped at the open door.

'It is a little late for a visit, don't you think, Mr Durham?'

My heart sank.

'My master sends me to give this to you. Have a good night, Mr Holmes.' The door fell into its frame and Holmes climbed the stairs, again taking several steps at once.

'I think that might be for me,' I said, stretching out my hand toward the letter he held. He passed it on with reluctance. I tore it open and almost fainted, seeing James's handwriting.

MR HOLMES,

I propose a challenge. The final destination will also be the price: the carpenter's life. We will begin our game tomorrow morning. Any earlier movements at Baker Street 221B will result in a telegram being sent instead. The better man shall win.

J.M.

'HE DOESN'T SAY where to. He has an assassin waiting for his orders, but he isn't telling us where.' My hoarse voice was about to give in. Holmes took the letter gingerly, read it several times, then dropped it on the coffee table.

'Three and a half months ago I went to Meiringen,' he said. 'Your father and his friend had taken to the road.'

'So you did leave London as James wanted you to?'

He grunted in response. 'This is where Moriarty has had a clear advantage — he has as many men at his disposal as he needs, while I have only myself, Mycroft, Watson, and you. The trip to Switzerland had to be very short because I needed to be back in London only four days later. But it did indeed help with the charade. I had wished for more time, to be more thorough with my investigations into your father's well-being. Do you happen to know when your father plans to return to his home?'

'No. I told him to hide for at least two months. He could be with Matthias still, or on his way back to Germany, or even back at home already.'

'We can only hope Moriarty doesn't know your father's whereabouts, either. Hum...'

'What is it?'

Unspeaking, Holmes retrieved his tobacco and lowered himself into the armchair. When stuffing his pipe, he would occasionally pause to stare into the void. Wrapped in smoke, the only noise that would come from him was the occasional clicking of mouthpiece against teeth. I rested my head on my knees and closed my eye. The view of Holmes was replaced by images of Moran's approaching fist and of James — his shocked face, the cramping of his abdomen, the froth on his lips.

Holmes clapped his hands and jumped from his chair. 'To hell with it! What we need is an army.' With that, he snatched his coat and was out the door.

To the Continent

❧❧❧

Holmes was dressed as an Italian priest, and I as a random young man. We made our way through unlit alleys toward Piccadilly. A stranger followed us the first few blocks after we left Baker Street, but we lost him soon enough. Our luggage was waiting to be picked up by Mycroft Holmes in two hours, and Watson would join us in three. I had neither run nor walked far during the past months, and my chest ached as my lungs begged me to stop hurrying so.

My abdomen began cramping, and the thought of a miscarriage made my heart lighter. Although the timing would be anything but perfect. Loving James's offspring was impossible to imagine. I flicked the thought away and almost ran into Holmes, who had come to a halt at Oxford Street. We pressed into a dark corner. His gaze searched the street before he turned to me.

'We will cross casually,' he said just before strolling off. I followed him at a few yards distance, hands in trouser pockets, strutting with my feet and knees slightly bent outward, as though I had large testicles. Holmes caught me at yet another dark corner. 'You are overdoing it.'

'No, I'm not. I look precisely like a young man who aims at impressing a pretty woman.'

'There are no women on the street at the moment. Not even the one-legged sweeper could be confused with one.'

'Perhaps I was trying to impress myself,' I retorted and pushed on. 'Holmes, I need breakfast before we board the train.'

We found a public house. A dingy place, and despite the early hour (or the late hour, for certain clientele) it was quite filled with an assortment of odd people. Holmes manoeuvred me into a far corner, and sat down so that he could observe the entire room while I had my back to it. It felt wrong, but I trusted him.

The porridge that was served smelled stale, but the bacon and eggs looked edible. Holmes folded his hands, mumbled an Irish drinking song, and added a loud *Amen* at the end. The odours of food made my stomach roar like a bear. How odd, the child could not be half as large as my hand and yet it demanded all that was on the table.

We did not speak. Holmes observed the room and all the people in it, while I observed him. His hooded eyes were sharp. Once I thought he had seen someone or something suspicious, but upon my enquiring look, he shook his head slightly. Long after my food was eaten and the teapot about to be emptied, we still had an hour to catch the train.

I pointed to his breakfast. He didn't react so I touched his arm and said, 'It will be a long journey.'

His eyes made contact with mine. 'Oh, certainly,' he mumbled, pushed the plate toward me, and commenced scrutinising the room.

Hopeless, I thought, and ordered two cups of coffee for us.

Even as Holmes paid, his long antennae remained pointed in all directions.

'We will run another mile now. Do you think you can manage it?' he asked once outside.

'I may not have moved much in captivity, Holmes, but I still have legs to run with.'

'Very well,' he said and off he went.

As agreed, we split up at Victoria station. He made his way to the front of the train to meet Watson, while I went to the back, and waited for Mycroft Holmes. Soon enough, a large man appeared in coachman's clothing, a muffler pulled up high onto his face, almost to meet the brim of his hat. He pushed past me onto the train. I lingered, pretending to wait for someone, repeatedly checking my watch and tapping my foot. The train hooted, the conductor blew his whistle. I threw my hands up into the air, shook my head at the non-arrival of my imaginary friend, and climbed into the carriage.

Pushing past other passengers, I made for my seat. Mycroft was already occupying the one next to it. He tipped his hat, then resumed ignoring me. We waited until people had settled down and no one was pushing past us anymore. Then he pulled his muffler down and wiped the sweat off his brow.

'I'm honoured to make your acquaintance,' I whispered, and reached out to him.

'The pleasure is all mine,' he replied, squeezing my hand lightly. 'We will relocate to first class in a minute or two.'

I nodded, loosened my cravat, and dabbed a handkerchief at my moist forehead. Once we had both cooled down a little, we made for the front of the train. A compartment with drawn curtains came into view, and Mycroft Holmes slid the door open without knocking.

'And now the company is complete,' announced Holmes. With that, everyone went back to looking grim.

'Dr Watson?' He turned to me, huffing a 'Yes?' through his moustache. 'Could I talk to you in private?'

'Certainly, my dear.' He spoke like a physician to his patient. Watson had a good sense for people's needs. I rose to my feet, but the Holmes brothers waved at me to sit back down, and they left the compartment.

'Dr Watson, I must ask for your absolute discretion on what I'm about to tell you.' My expression caused his mouth to compress to a thin line.

'Of course,' he answered.

'You cannot even talk to Holmes. I prefer to tell him my secrets myself, and you can be assured that I will. In time.'

Watson reached for my hand and pressed it. 'You can trust me. What can I do for you?'

'My first request is small. Do not mention me when you write about your friend.'

'As you wish. I can certainly use a different name—'

'No!' I interrupted. 'Do not even mention there was a woman or a bacteriologist acquainted with Mr Holmes. Not a single word about this case, I beg you, Dr Watson!'

Watson coughed at my rather intense speech, but finally nodded.

'Thank you.'

He exhaled, his moustache bristling.

'My second request is...illegal. I was abducted by James Moriarty and spent one hundred and eighty four days in his house. To reach my goal, I ended up sharing his bed.' A surprised puff and a reddening of cheeks were Watson's only response. 'I believed myself barren. An injury, long ago. However...' I lowered my head as though this would lessen the shame. 'I am with child and I need an abortion conducted by a skilled surgeon.'

'By Jove!' cried Watson and jumped from his seat.

The door opened abruptly and Mycroft's head stuck through the gap. I held up my hand. He nodded, and retreated.

'May I,' Watson said while pointing at my lower abdomen. I rose and took a step forward. Gently, he pressed his fingers into my flesh, his gaze measuring. 'It might be about four months now.'

'Yes, I believe that is correct.'

'We will have to be quick,' he said hoarsely. 'Are you certain?'

'I tried an abortifacient twice. It was unsuccessful. I am absolutely certain. Dr Watson, I cannot raise James Moriarty's child!'

He took my hand and patted it. We sat back down. I stared out the window, and Watson said, 'As soon as we are done with this excursion, I will remove the child from your womb. If we wait any longer, it will be too big to be extracted.'

'Thank you,' I said, leant my head against the cold window pane, and shut my eyes.

Watson called the Holmes brothers back in.

'Moriarty missed us at the station,' noted Holmes with concern. 'I wonder what he thought our plans were to reach the continent? This is puzzling...'

'He must be in pain and extremely furious — his weakest and least predictable state, but also his most dangerous.' Upon the men's enquiring looks I added, 'He has a problem with his spinal column which causes severe pain in his shoulders, neck, and head. Did you see him hunch and blink his eyes yesterday morning?' Holmes nodded. 'He grows highly sensitive to light, noise and odours, and to disappointment in general. *Rabid* is the word that comes to mind...'

I turned away, trying to force dark memories of the nights with James out of my head. The compartment suddenly seemed too crowded. I excused myself and went to the lavatory, and opened the window to let the wind ruffle my hair.

Upon my return, Holmes announced, 'Moriarty will

engage a special — or rather, that is what I would do. So we will exit the train at Canterbury, travel cross country to New Haven, and from there set off over to Dieppe. Then, Watson and I will make our way toward Switzerland while you, Mycroft, will accompany Dr Kronberg to Leipzig. Do you have your revolver?'

Mycroft snorted, holding up two fingers. Good, then I would have one, too.

'I do hope a wire is waiting for us at Canterbury,' he said, with a look to his elder brother.

'There will be, trust me,' said Mycroft.

～

CANTERBURY CAME SOON ENOUGH and we got off the train, Holmes all the while scanning our surroundings. Suddenly he cried, 'There he comes! Here, hide,' and pushed us toward a pile of luggage.

Far away in the woods of Kent rose a sliver of smoke, that quickly approached and dashed past us. Oddly uncomplicated, I thought, and my mistrust grew to nausea. What was James up to?

Mycroft Holmes went to the stationmaster to enquire about a message, returning only a minute later, a half-smile on his face.

'My friends have done excellent work. Your father is rather hard to find, Dr Kronberg, which is of importance given the circumstances. He and his friend Matthias Berger left Geneva two days ago. Unclear is whether both are returning to Meiringen or have parted on the way. I suppose you two,' he nodded at his brother and Dr Watson, 'will have a splendid time in the Rhone valley.' He gazed down at me. 'How is the eye?'

I shrugged. 'Black, I guess.'

He barked a laugh, then said softly, 'You and I will begin our search at your father's home. If he's not there, we will work our way toward Switzerland.'

~

WE BOARDED the ship to Dieppe in the afternoon. When Holmes went out for a smoke on deck, I joined him.

Before I could utter a word, he began, 'Moriarty has set up an astonishing criminal network all over London and Europe. It was impossible to find them all, but the main players will be arrested on Monday.' Holmes peered over my head, assessing the proximity of other passengers, then beckoned me over to the railing. 'Moriarty had a wife and a son. Both died of tetanus only days after the child was born. Four months later he initiated the Club to test this same disease on paupers. I learned about this only three days before you were able to free yourself. The cold-bloodedness of this man is unmatched and I deeply regret having let you stay there for so long.'

'It was my decision.'

'I sincerely wish you had a greater sense of self-preservation.' His gaze was penetrating, as though he wanted to climb behind my facade and extract all there was to know.

I set my chin. 'I do not wish to talk about James and myself. Someday, perhaps, but not now.'

Without delay, he changed the topic. 'Mycroft and I have been taking Moriarty's network apart. Carefully putting pressure on the weaker links. We are preparing to arrest the more stubborn men very soon. Come Monday, and that man's organisation will be non-operational.'

I gazed out across the sea. The sun was preparing to set. Gulls sailed quietly over the waves. All spoke of beauty and peace, while inside me raged a chaos of foreboding, shame, guilt, and pain.

'Were you able to find out who supported Moriarty's idea for a new draft of the Brussels Declaration?'

A hollow breath was followed by a crestfallen answer. 'As it happens, I wasn't. The entire business is rather complicated and I'm not entirely certain why Moriarty wanted to change the Convention at all. It forbids the spreading, by any means whatsoever, of disease on enemy territory, while at the same time it lacks any enforcement provisions. Whatever laws there are for warfare, no one is ever arrested for not abiding by them. Although he must have known this, he invested a great deal of energy in convincing them to remove that section on disease. I am not quite certain why, but it is highly alarming.'

'It has already been changed?'

'Yes, unfortunately.'

'More work for us, then,' I said.

He nodded absentmindedly.

'Holmes?'

'Hmm?'

'You look pale and worn. But what worries me most is that you appear...far away. What troubles you so much?'

He showed me a smile that didn't reach his eyes.

I never got an answer.

Anton

We parted in Dieppe. Without looking me in the eye, Holmes tipped his hat and walked away. Watson squeezed my hand longer than necessary.

Mycroft Holmes and I boarded the night train to Hamburg, and then another to Berlin and Leipzig. We talked little. Tension and fear tied my tongue.

Late the following morning, we hailed a carriage to take us to my childhood home. The closer we got, the worse the anxiety that dug into my stomach. As the cab would have drawn too much attention, I let the driver drop us off before entering the village.

The way up the hill was steep, and Mycroft was sweating and huffing after the first yards. I had no patience to wait for him and ran the last half mile to the house after given him instructions on how to find it.

Without the chickens, the garden looked abandoned. I ran through the small gate, searched for the key in the cherry tree's knothole, and opened the door to the house. The curtains were drawn, but the stuffiness and dust I'd expected were missing. If my father had been absent for months, who had cleaned the house recently?

'Good morning, Dr Kronberg,' a voice crept from the darkness. The man spoke perfect German. His black silhouette — relaxed with hands in his pockets — moved in the far corner. He stepped into the dim light. A hat overshadowed his eyes, the glint of a smile flashed across the room.

'Where is my father?'

'Ah, well. Who can know for sure? Heaven, maybe? Or hell?'

'Did you...are you...' Like a fish on the sand, I could only gape.

'You stupid girl. Did you really believe you could with play us? Your father is currently in the church, but he will not be buried on sacred ground because he took his own life. Ha! Who would have guessed?'

'You are lying!' I cried. Saltwater crept down my cheeks.

'Of course I am. Or maybe not? After all, he *did* take the poison I gave him. Does that make him a victim, or does that make him a man who commits suicide to avoid the bullet? A philosophical question, clearly, but what the neighbours believe must be the truth, mustn't it?'

I couldn't breathe. My mind was blaring so loudly, my heart aching so badly that I was about to lose control.

'What now?' I asked, voice quivering.

'What kind of question is *that*? Shouldn't you first marvel at the plan that got you here, all alone, then show some fear and maybe scream for help?'

Finally my survival instinct flicked the switch and my mind came back to life. 'I have never screamed for help in my entire life. And the plan is obvious, don't you think?'

By now, Mycroft should have reached the house. I dearly hoped he would eavesdrop before rumbling through the door.

But what good would eavesdropping do, if he did not understand German?

'I could make you scream, but I was told not to. What a pity. Now, how is the plan obvious?'

'The night before yesterday, James Moriarty sent a wire to you and ordered you to kill my father. I guess you have been following him for a while now, because he just arrived here, cleaned up, and was about to feel at home again when you came to end his life. James's plan was to separate Holmes and me. It was likely that I would come here while Holmes searched the other end of my father's trail. So you waited here for me. But I'm surprised James would dirty his hands by killing Holmes himself.'

'Close enough. The Professor has a personal issue with Mr Holmes, and I think that should be all cleared up by now.'

'He has no chance against Holmes.' Desperate hope spoken aloud.

The man facing me shook his head. 'Silly girl. Holmes has no chance against the Professor and Colonel Moran. You see, the two of you willingly ran into the trap he set.'

'Brilliant,' I spoke through my teeth, my mind racing around possibilities, or rather, the lack thereof. 'And how am I to die?'

'Slowly, of course, but not quite yet. The professor forbade us to harm you. He will allow you to give birth to his child, and raise him to the age of three. Then the two of you will be found.' With that, he tipped his hat and slunk toward the back door. My legs wouldn't move at first, and I almost fell forward in an attempt to catch him as I heard Mycroft snarl 'Stop!' Next came a bang of a door against its frame, three shots, grappling, and yet another shot. Something heavy dropped.

I slithered to a halt. The heap was moving, inching toward the revolver on the floor. I kicked it away. Mycroft held his gun in his large hand, perfectly steady, his face a mask of fury.

I bent down and saw blood seeping through the man's waistcoat. The shot must have gone straight through his lungs. His chest tried to heave, without success.

I had no pity for him. 'Mr Holmes, are you all right?'

'Yes, thank you. He was about to shoot me as he spotted me behind the door. But how are you? What did he say to you?'

'Your brother and Watson are in great danger. Moriarty's plan was to separate us. Now he and Moran are hunting your brother and Watson. You must leave immediately.'

Mycroft Holmes stared down at the man, slowly pocketed his revolver. I picked up the other gun.

'We thought it likely that this would be Moriarty's plan. That is why I accompanied you. We were also aware of the possibility that your father would be dead. Where is he? Did he say?' He stuck the tip of his shoe in the dead man's side. The blood was already beginning to coagulate, turning the black puddle into a flat lump.

'He killed him,' I whispered and turned away. 'Mr Holmes, the neighbour next door will bring you to Grimma, the next city with a post office. Keep your brother and his friend alive, please.' With that I left to notify the neighbour, and to see my father.

IT WAS COLD INSIDE, colder than outside, but it had always been that way. The church was never quite inviting, with its tall walls and distant ceiling. With the hollow echoes of heels on a stone floor. And the bleeding Jesus — always suffering, always in the distance far up behind the altar, so intimidatingly large.

They had laid my father down in front of the altar. A

sheet was covering him. I could almost hear their heated discussions — how he had always been a good man, that he should be buried at his wife's side in sacred soil, and the other voices that said it would be a sin to allow a man who had taken his own life to rest on church grounds.

I didn't quite know whether I wanted to run to him, or to never approach his body, this fragile husk that no longer contained my father. My feet decided on a slow walk. My knees folded, and I sank down next to him. Mechanically, my hands removed the sheet that covered him. Only a little at first, then I flung it aside.

The rustle of linen against the cold stone floor sounded like a scream. Or maybe that was me.

His face was white as cheese, his lips blue. I touched his chest. No heartbeat, no breath was lifting his ribs. What had I expected?

I bent down to smell his lips and the faint odour of cadaver exiting his nostrils punched my stomach. I licked his lips, cold and stiff, and I tried not to retch. Nothing — no metallic taste, no stinging or burning. What poison had been used? My mind spun in circles and my eyes flew over his body, trying to analyse what had happened during those last minutes of his life.

What was I doing? Was it important to know which poison had killed him? No antidote could bring him back to life! Wasn't this just my brain wanting to work on something, solve a problem, a puzzle, so as not to let the heart feel the pain?

I swallowed and told my mind to shut up. I placed my hand on my father's cheek and curled up next to him. Perhaps sharing a little of my warmth would let him feel that I was close.

～

I HAD LOST track of time, or time lost track of me. I didn't really know. The police had come, had taken the murderer away. They questioned me, frowned and didn't understand. But how could they? The story was long and all they'd got to see was but one end of a severed thread. A thread that was part of a far-reaching web of murder, betrayal, abduction, and torture.

My father was buried next to his wife — my mother — while Katherina, his lover and almost-wife, stood by crying quietly. I felt nothing but curiosity about my own emptiness.

∾

I SAT in my father's living room with tobacco and a bottle of brandy as companions. The knocks at the door couldn't motivate my legs to move. I stayed put and refilled my glass.

Perhaps mothers should not drink too much, rang in the back of my head. But I didn't care. I would shed motherhood like an oversized cloak. But wasn't it too late, the child too big? I shook my head ferociously at this thought. It would be too late when the child's kicking could not be confused with bowel activities any longer, when my stomach was so large I could no longer hide it.

Would I really kill—

My thoughts were interrupted by Mycroft Holmes rumbling through the door. Without a word, he sat down opposite me, took my glass, and poured it down his throat. It was then that I knew I didn't want to hear what he had to say. My head wanted to tip forward, rest on the worn tabletop, and invest not a single thought more on loss or pain.

'My information is based on only a few telegrams,' I heard him say. He sounded oddly far off. 'One from Watson, the others from two reliable friends.' He bent forward and refilled the glass, pushed it over to me. Automatically, I tipped it into my mouth, greeting the dullness it would bring.

'I am afraid he is dead,' he exhaled, face falling into his palms. The large man shrank, but I could not move to place a consoling hand on his shoulder.

'I am sorry for your loss, Mr Holmes.' My mouth spoke without involving my brain. 'Please, feel welcome to stay overnight. The next train to Berlin should depart tomorrow before ten o'clock. Would you like supper?'

He coughed, sat erect, and nodded. 'Yes, thank you.'

Was that how floating felt? Detached from everything? I did what needed doing to finish that day and start another. The decision came so easily.

I'd loved. I'd lost. And I couldn't go on.

The Fallen

❦

How I reached my cottage, I cannot recall. But at some point, I found myself at the front door. There were wisps of memories: the decision to come here and not defile my father's house with a suicide. Sitting on various trains, a ship, and wandering through the countryside. It had rained the entire day, I thought. My trousers and waistcoat were sopping wet. I had forgotten to put my coat on. It hung limply over the bag I'd carried. Did I travel all the way with this revolver in my hand? No, that seemed unreasonable. I held the gun up. Water ran out of the drum, down the gun's butt, and into my sleeve. I shook it, wondering if it still worked.

There was no need to go inside. I could do it here and watch the sunset. I dropped my belongings, sat down on a small rock near my cottage, and closed my eyes. I soaked up the sounds of water dripping off the roof. The quiet sizzling of warm compost turning rain into steam. The blackbird's song announcing the end of the day. The end of me.

Swimming in music and the aroma of washed earth, I opened my eyes.

And three things happened simultaneously: the cloud cover tore open, a red sun slashed through to hit the wet ground at a sharp angle, and Death appeared at my side. All sound died.

I expected Death to be a haggard man clad in black robes, stretching out his skeletal hand to close it around my throat. I braced myself and turned toward him. A billowing cloak. Or was it...a dress? Softly flowing along curved hips, caressed by the wind, without beginning or end, its hems melting into thin air. I was stunned. Death was a *woman?* Or was it my Death only? Perhaps I wanted her to be female in the hopes she might be gentle.

But then, how I took my life was not for her to say.

I felt her touch on my shoulder. Her hand was neither warm nor cold. Her outlines melted away whenever I tried to see her clearly. It felt comfortable to have her at my side. I wouldn't be alone when I left this world. Her hand on my shoulder was protective, neither pulling nor pushing me in one direction or the other.

What I would do next was my decision. Mine alone.

The blackbird's voice tore at my marred heart. I turned the gun and stared into its gaping black mouth. Would I see the explosion? Would I see the projectile before it entered my head and ripped my brain apart? I pushed the hammer down. The clicking noise washed exhilaration through my chest, dulling the pain within.

Keeping my eyes wide open, I moved my thumb to the trigger.

Death dropped her hand, abandoning my shoulder and pulling my attention toward my cottage door. The handle moved. A shy creak. The door opened. In one swift move, I rose to my feet and pointed the revolver at the tall silhouette in the shadows.

'You bastard!' I cried.

He plunged back inside the instant I pulled the trigger. Nothing but a wet click happened. Chasing after him, I pulled it again and again with the same result. I ran through the door and slammed it shut. With a cry of despair, I flung the useless gun in his direction. The clatter told me I hadn't even hit my target, only an innocent wall or cupboard. I pushed into a dark corner and forced my breath to come silently so as not to betray my location. It was impossible to reach my kitchen cupboard to fetch a knife, but fury would make my hands strong enough to wring his neck. Certainty and foreboding vibrated in my limbs.

Soft footfall. A floorboard creaked, and a hand emerged from the shadows.

'Anna.' That unexpected voice sent me into a numbing suspense. How still everything was. Had it ever been so quiet? A second hand, followed by shoes, trousers, a waistcoat and Holmes's face. Bruised and limping, his right shoulder hanging so low it looked about to come off its hinge.

I blinked and lifted my hand to touch his cheek, to feel whether he was real and not a product of my imagination.

He shut his eyes and pressed his face into my palm. I stepped closer. He punched all air from my lungs with his embrace. We just stood there, quite still, him holding me and blowing fragile breath into my hair.

'What happened to you?' I didn't dare think of James.

He straightened up, took a step back, and answered, 'It was a short fight. Moriarty was mad with fury and flung himself at me to throw us both off a cliff. He is dead now. I saw him fall.'

I touched his shoulder. 'Was it dislocated?'

'It was. I set it.'

'Let me take a look.' Stoically, I grasped his other elbow and led him to a chair. The same chair I'd sat on as Moran and... I wiped the thought away.

'Does this feel numb?' I gently squeezed his deltoid muscle. He nodded. 'The axillary nerve is injured, probably from an anterior dislocation. In normal language: You fell, caught some handhold and swung rather violently, thus dislocating your shoulder joint. But you obviously know that already. I'm amazed you had enough control that you did not lose your grip. The pain must have been overwhelming.'

'I am amazed at how much you sound like me.'

I dropped my hand and walked to the kitchen, numbness accompanying me as I made a fire in the stove and fetched a kettle to get water for tea. He must have searched the house earlier — dried meat and bacon were still on the counter. That and a few beans and rye were the only things I had. 'I'll be back soon,' I said and left.

Death was still waiting. She smiled at me while slowly dissolving into the blood-red sky.

Purpose held me upright. I walked to my neighbours' and then back to my cottage, feeling as though I had no substance and the gentle evening breeze might blow me away. I carried a loaf of bread, butter, fresh ham and the hen Mary had plucked from the roost, swiftly beheaded, de-feathered, and gutted. Also, the bottle of cider John had pressed into my hand, his face stern and puzzled. Neither had asked a question, not even as I'd taken Wimp the goose home with me. Holmes had spoken of James's death, but no word about Moran. He might still be alive.

'What...' got stuck in Holmes's throat as I entered the cottage, arms loaded with food and a grey goose in my wake. 'Wimp,' I explained. 'She will sleep on the roof. She's the best guard one can think of.'

'A rather odd name,' he remarked.

'When they found her she was not two days old, and very weak. The name stuck and she was too nice to be cooked.'

The goose walked through the kitchen, a *flap flap* of

webbed feet, a *rat tat tat* of her beak investigating everything she could reach, and a *plop* as she left a dropping on the floor. Beating her wings, she announced her delight.

'Time to sleep, Wimp,' I said and picked her up. She pinched my earlobe in reply. We walked outside, and I climbed on the bench next to the cottage, to lift her up onto the roof. Honking softly, she settled down, and I wished her a good night.

'I forgot the water,' I said. His glance showed understanding. I couldn't stand still now. The collapse would come, but only after everything that needed doing was done.

The moments of bustling and eating were over too soon. Silence lowered itself heavily. An uninvited, but necessary guest. Two exceedingly tired people and only one bed. The thought made me stiff.

Holmes had found my tobacco pouch — a cow's horn with a rubber stopper from my laboratory in London. He rolled a cigarette. Avoiding his proximity, I declined his offer and made one myself. He poured the cider and I decided to get drunk. At least a little.

'Moran knows I am still alive,' he said. 'At the moment, he should be on his way to Paris, thinking I'll be there. I laid a false trail.'

'How much time do we have?'

'Two days, maybe three. We should leave tomorrow.'

One day of peace. I wished it might be a year. Or a lifetime.

'I need to tell you what I did,' I murmured. The silence broke, a crack running through the space between us. He turned toward me, his expression soft.

'Do you really believe I'd judge you for marrying Moriarty?' he said. I stared at him in disbelief, holding onto my glass so as to not fling it at him.

'I do not care whether you judge me or not,' I lied. 'I will pack my belongings tomorrow. I'm too tired tonight.' With that, I left the room to sit outside, with the crooked cottage wall at my back, the forsythia drawing lines in the pale moonlight at my feet.

I heard him step through the door. 'May I?' he asked, pointing to the space beside me. I nodded. For a long time neither of us spoke.

'I'd very much prefer if you'd let me tell you my secrets when I am ready, not when you have observed and deduced them.'

'My apologies. It was not my intention to intrude. It pains me to see you so...small. I saw it happening gradually, but everything was explainable and logical. Then at my lodgings I told myself you were hurt and very tired. But on the train to Germany, I had to admit to the facts. I was shocked at how much you had changed. I've known you as a strong and decisive woman, both feet firmly on the ground, chin always a little high, defiantly set, knowing precisely what you want and what the right thing to do is. Then, on the train, you appeared so fragile, smaller — for lack of a better word — as though you had turned away from the world. And now as well.'

I gazed up at the stars. Venus appeared — a flickering pinprick, in a moment followed by others more faint.

'I think that in an odd way, James loved me, and that breaks my heart. Although the love he gave was selfish, it was the only love he knew. Who am I to judge his love as less than mine? He always loved himself first and so never lost himself, never broke himself or let another break him. He died with his soul intact, or as intact as it ever was or could be.'

I had to control my breathing. 'He killed my father, and I must ask myself how much of the guilt I carry — all, or only half? Had I been able to love James, had I not betrayed him... would my father be alive now? But then...if I'd told James from the start that I would not work on a weapon that could kill thousands of innocent people, might he have not killed my father, and only me?'

I turned Holmes. 'What is the truth, my friend? Do innocent people exist at all? Don't we all carry guilt? The child causes pain to its mother during birth. Should it feel guilty for the rest of its life? A man loves a woman without fully giving her his heart. Is he guilty of causing her pain every single day? Or is she guilty because she cannot love him who does not love her as she expects? Because the only love she knows is the all embracing one? The one that must give up all to gain all? Where and when did I make the wrong decision? I *cannot* see it. And I cannot trust my own judgement anymore.'

'May I?' he said again, his hand offering to take mine. I shook my head. I wasn't ready yet.

'I am tired, Holmes.'

'The thought of retiring has appeared very attractive to me lately.'

'You would be bored within hours.'

'Most likely,' he said.

'What did you plan for Moran?'

'Not much for now. I find it more important to get you away from him than to try capturing the man.'

'If I ever run across Moran again,' I growled, 'I will gut him. I might even enjoy it greatly.'

'Precisely. Another reason to get you as far away from him as possible.'

'How odd. As long as I've known you, I've felt a strong wish to pull you close and at the same time I want to run away from you. A constant push and pull.'

'You will not feel better if you kill Moran,' he said softly.

'I've almost lost my mind. I saw my own Death today. She was a woman. Isn't that strange?'

'Why did you try to kill yourself, Anna?'

'I would think that obvious.'

'No, it is not. You have succeeded in bringing Moriarty down, you gave me identities of men I had no clue were involved with him. In fact, the very heart of his organisation within the government was revealed by you.'

'I cannot find that very significant at the moment,' I said.

'Wasn't that why you insisted on staying in his house?'

I laughed bitterly. 'Yes. That was what I wanted. But now I weigh these small accomplishments against the price. A price others had to pay.'

'Many more people would have had to pay that price if we hadn't stopped Moriarty.' He sounded a little exasperated.

'It will happen anyway. Technological and scientific advances happen, regardless of what you and I believe is right or wrong.'

Silence fell. The goose had moved to the roof's edge to sleep closer to us. 'It isn't your fault that he murdered your father,' he said.

'I thought I couldn't live, if he and you were both dead. What an odd phenomenon time is. Often, a single minute is insignificant. And then, the flightiest moment decides life and death.'

'Your revolver was wet.'

'I would have used a knife.'

'You will have to live with the push and pull for a while, Anna. I will not let you out of my sight. You and I will pack our bags and go for a long walk.' He said all this in his typical matter-of-fact fashion, as though any opposition would be futile.

'What were his last words?' I asked.

He cleared his throat. 'Moriarty said that he was dying and would make sure you and I were taken down with him. I saw his blackened fingertips from the arsenide you gave him. How were you able to accomplish that at all?'

'I don't want to talk about it.'

He tipped his head. 'He said his legacy will grow and impact the whole of Europe.' He paused.

'Tell me,' I urged.

'He said he enjoyed domesticating you.'

'What precisely did he say?' My voice quivered.

Holmes exhaled slowly. 'My wife was a lovely toy to play with. A wildcat that needed taming, domesticating, and finally breaking. I enjoyed it greatly.'

My head fell into my hands. My shoulders began to shake.

'I am with child,' I whispered, and it sounded as though I had screamed it, so overbearing was the reality as soon as the words were spoken. Then I broke.

I grabbed his hand as though it were the only thing that could hold me, wept his shoulder wet and then his chest. How curious that one can endure so much when there is no alternative. But once safe, and the tale told, reality rises to bring all the pain, guilt and shame. One is left to wonder: How did I survive all this? Or maybe I did not survive at all, and another self must emerge from the dark hollow I am in.

He whispered into my ear and I had to staunch my weeping to understand what he said. 'Whatever happened, you are alive and he is dead. You have memories, while he is only one of them. You feel guilty, and he never felt remorse. You go on, and he will not. This is essential, Anna. He will *not* go on because you stopped him.'

END

Keep reading for a preview of book 4

THE JOURNEY

Preview of Anna Kronberg Book 4

I

❧❧❧

Hear my soul speak.
  Of the very instant that I saw you,
  Did my heart fly at your service.
W. Shakespeare

May 1891

H unger, exhaustion, and cold stiffened my every move. We had been walking for three days. Our provisions were reduced to two handfuls of salted meat and a sliver of stale bread. A curtain of drizzle surrounded us. The dripping of water from above merged with the *squish-squish* of two pairs of feet: mine and the ones of the man walking a yard ahead of me. The broad rim of his hat hung low, feeding streams of rain down on his shoulders, one of which was still drooping. He had dislocated it while throwing my husband off a cliff.

With my gaze attached to his calves, I placed one foot in front of the other, imagining him pulling me along on an invisible string, forward and ever forward. Without his pull, I wouldn't go anywhere. My knees would simply buckle.

Holmes led the two of us with stoicism. His trousers were rolled up to his knees, bare skin splattered with mud, feet covered in it. He avoided the coast, with all its roads and people. We walked through the heath without cover from view or weather. Half way into the moorlands we took off our boots. Sickly white feet had emerged, toes wrinkled like dead raisins, heels raw from friction and wetness. Water had stood ankle high in our footwear.

When the day drifted toward a darker grey, I saw him growing tired. The slight sway of his hips became stiffer and his gait lacked its usual spring. Within the hour, he steered us to a suitable place to set up the tent and protect our few dry belongings. One frigid night followed another. A series of dark and restless hours, all lacking a warming fire, all without enough food to fill our stomachs.

There was nothing to be done about it.

'Over here,' he called, his hand motioning toward a group of trees. I was hugging myself so hard now, I felt like a compacted piece of bone and skin. He took the rope from his bag and strung it low between two crooked firs, then flung the oilskin off my backpack and over the rope, securing it with rocks on its ends. As I hunched over the rucksack to protect it from rain, I watched Holmes, knowing precisely which move would follow the last, as though my eyes had seen it a hundred times and his hands had done it as often. As soon as the oilskin was in place, I stepped underneath, pulled out another piece of oilskin and spread it out on the ground.

I extracted our blankets, and anxiously probed for moisture. But my fingers were so numb they felt little but the needling cold. As exhausted as we were, wet blankets would bring pneumonia overnight. Brighton, the closest town large enough for a chemist and a physician, was a brisk six-hour walk from where we were. No one would find us but foxes and ravens.

During our first day on the run, we had established a firm evening routine. One might call it effective. And it was indeed so. But I, for my part, didn't care too much about how quickly we got out of the rain, as long as I could shut out the world and the struggle.

The peaceful moments between closing my eyes and beginning to dream were all I looked forward to.

In less than three minutes, we'd shed our soggy clothes and let the rain wash the stink and dirt off our skin. We hung our shirts, trousers, skirts, and undergarments out in the rain. They wouldn't dry in our makeshift tent anyway.

We squeezed water out of our hair and dove under the blankets. Holmes opened my rucksack to pull out the one set of dry clothes we had for each of us. We stuck our trembling limbs into these shirts and trousers, then clung to one another, sharing our blankets and the little heat that was left in our bodies.

While necessity demanded close proximity, we avoided each other's eyes, even as we avoided talking. Attached to Holmes, I felt like a foreign object with my flesh about to wilt off my bones.

He had to spend an hour each evening attached to the woman who had bedded his arch-enemy. How uncomfortable he must feel, I could only guess.

But I tried not to.

Holmes shot his wiry arm out into the cold and retrieved the meat from his bag. He cut off a large slice and gave it to me, then cut off a smaller bit for himself. This was the only trace of chivalry I allowed. The day we had left my cottage, he had insisted on carrying my rucksack. I told him I'd have none of it, and walked away. The topic was closed.

But I sensed his alertness, his readiness to run to the aid

of the damsel in distress should the need arise. His chivalrous reflexes annoyed me greatly.

We chewed in silence. The food dampened the clatter of teeth. Gradually warmth returned. First to my chest, then to my abdomen. As soon as the shivering subsided, we each retreated to the solitude of our own blanket. And only then did we dare talk.

'How do you feel?'

I nodded, taking another bite. 'Warm. Good. Thank you. How is your eye?' I had seen him rubbing his right eye frequently.

'Not worth mentioning.' He gazed out into the rain, as though the weather might be worth conversing about. 'We need to replenish our provisions,' he said, and added softly, 'We have two destinations from which to choose, one of which has a city large enough for a skilled surgeon.'

'It's too late. Choose what place you judge best for your needs.'

'Too late?' Again, that soft voice as though words could break me.

'Five months now. The child is as large as a hand. It cannot be extracted without killing the... mother.'

He lowered his head in acknowledgement. The matter required no further discussion. 'We have to talk about Moran.'

I didn't want to talk about that man. All I wanted was Moran dead.

'Tell me what you learned about him,' he pressed.

'Nothing that you wouldn't know.'

'Anna!' He made my name sound like a synonym for pigheadedness.

'Damn it, Holmes. I tried to avoid that man whenever possible. All I can provide is what you already know: best heavy-game shot of the British Empire, free of moral baggage, in the possession of a silent air rifle, very angry, and out to avenge his best friend and employer, James Moriarty.'

I stuck my hand out into the rain where the oilskin was collecting water in a thick stream. I filled my cup, and washed the salty meat down my throat.

'You lived in Moriarty's house. I didn't. It follows that you must know more about Moran than I.'

'If he cannot find us, he'll set a trap. It was *you* who said that he once used a small child as tiger bait.' I coughed and rubbed my tired eyes.

'Precisely. Now, what trap would he arrange for us? I cannot use information of his behaviour in India ten years ago and extrapolate it to the near future. How does this man's mind work? You *must* have observed something of importance!'

I pulled up my knees and tucked in my blanket, trying to keep the heat loss at a minimum. 'Just like James Moriarty, Moran doesn't have the slightest degree of decency. He made a fake attempt at raping me so James could stage a rescue. Perhaps they hoped I would be naive enough to sympathise with James after he *saved* me from Moran. But whatever their true intentions, they enjoyed themselves, I'm certain.'

Coughing, I turned my back to Holmes and shut my eyes. Sleep would take me away in mere minutes. 'Moran's brain is exceptionally sharp when he is hunting,' I added quietly.

'Your cough is getting worse,' he said.

'So I noticed.'

Listening to his breathing, I wiped the memories of Moran and James away, knowing it wouldn't be long before they returned. As soon as the dreams woke me, I'd take the second watch.

∾

SOMEONE SCREAMED. My eyes snapped open. Oilskin above my head. The gentle tapping of rain. A hunched figure next to me. I wasn't in bed murdering James.

'You can sleep now,' I croaked and sat up. Tinted with fear, my voice was a stranger to me.

He settled down and rolled up in his blanket. 'Wake me in two hours.'

I didn't want to talk about James, nor did I seek consolation. On our first night, Holmes had accepted my wishes with a nod. I was glad I'd never detected pity or disgust in his face.

He could conceal his emotions well.

The sound of water rolling off leaves and cracking down onto our tent, along with Holmes's calm breathing, were all I could hear. Nature's quietude was a beautiful contrast to London's bustle. It almost felt as though we were silent together, nature and I.

Holmes's feet twitched a little. Only seconds later, his breathing deepened. I waited a few minutes, then struck a match. A dim golden light filled the tent, illuminating his face. It amazed me every time. He looked so different. His sharp features were softened, his expression left unguarded.

I flicked the match into the wet grass, peered outside, and thought of the day I'd kissed him. The memory was far away. Violence and betrayal had bleached it to a dreamlike consistency.

A shy flutter — as though I had swallowed a butterfly and it now brushed its wings along the inside of my uterus. I put my hand there, trying to feel more than just the touch. Where was the love I was supposed to feel for the small being inside? For the first time in my life, I didn't know what to do. I didn't know where to find the energy to keep fighting. Hadn't I found solutions to the most impossible situations? Even the fact that women were prohibited from studying medicine hadn't kept me from entering a university.

My abduction by James Moriarty — a master in manipulating the human mind and will — hadn't stopped me from manipulating him in return, and breaking free.

But giving birth to his child, and raising it, seemed a very high mountain to climb.

Too high for me.

I listened to my own heartbeat. How fast was the child's heart beating? Like a sparrow's, perhaps?

Was this non-love based on my hate for its father? Or was I so egoistical and driven that I could not endure the life of a woman?

Being of the *lesser* sex and unable to disguise it any longer, medicine and bacteriology were out of my reach. A single mother was hardly acceptable, but a widow and mother who refused to marry long after her mourning year was over wouldn't stand in much higher esteem.

No medical school would take me as a lecturer. The only alternative for me was to open a practice. But who would choose to be treated by a woman if there were plenty of male practitioners? No one, certainly.

But these were mere difficulties, easy to overcome with enough willpower and energy. Why could I not welcome this child? Was it truly so dreadful to be a mother? Until a few weeks ago, I'd had no reason to even think about it, for I had believed myself barren.

Mothers were other women. I was something else entirely.

Gradually, realisation crept in and a chill followed suit. I was terrified of never being able to love my child, of not being the mother a newborn needs. All my accomplishments were based on lies. I had pretended to be a male medical doctor, affected a wish to develop weapons for germ warfare, and faked love for James.

I would never be able to feign love for my child, the one person who would surely see through my charade.

Holmes began to stir, coughed into his blanket, and cracked one eye open. 'You did not wake me.'

'You said two hours.'

'How long did I sleep?'

I shrugged. How would I know? His watch had produced its last tick yesterday when it fell in a puddle.

'It stopped raining a while ago,' I said. 'Sleep. I'm not tired.' At that, my traitorous stomach gave a roar. Holmes reached for the bag, but I stopped him. 'At my rate of food intake, we'll have nothing left by tomorrow morning.'

When he gazed at me I wished I were far away. 'I'll hunt fowl,' I mumbled.

'We cannot make a fire.'

'Humans must have eaten raw meat before they discovered what fire is good for.' I pulled my crossbow and the bolts from the rucksack. It was an old and worm-eaten thing, made for a child to hunt rabbits and help provide for his family. I had found it hanging on the wall of my cottage, and its small size and lightness served me well.

I pushed the oilskin aside. Water dripped from the trees. The ground was muddy.

'I will stay close and watch for any movements. This,' I held up a bolt, 'makes even less noise than Moran's rifle. Go back to sleep now.'

Holmes grunted, pulled his blanket tighter around his form, and shut his eyes as I slipped out of the tent.

The Journey will be released on January 21.

Get pre-publication access to the newest Anna Kronberg books:

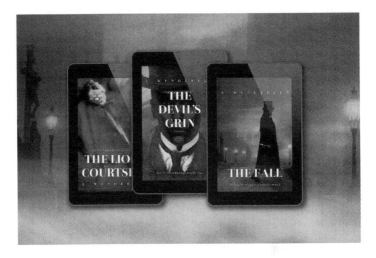

www.silent-witnesses.com

Acknowledgments

I'd like to thank my husband for all his patience with that obsessive-compulsive, pigheaded wife of his. I love you, even if I sit up all night and write.

Béla and Lina, who still remember my name although all I do is write and be grumpy—I love you dearly!

My two wonderful editors, Carrie Ann Carlson and Jennifer Nissley who rearranged my prose, pointed out the funny plot holes, and killed the boring chapters. You girls are brilliant! Thank you so much for your help. Should there be any typos, grammar nits, or historical facts gone awry - all my fault. I had the last word in that matter.

Nancy DeMarco and Bonnie Milani, who suffered the first beta-read and still want to be my friends. Bonnie: That particular... uhm... you know what I mean, right?

Anne and Kay Steele, you loved The Devil's Grin and agreed to beta-read an annoying version of The Fall. Thank you for your helpful input!

Sabrina Flynn, you were a very critical reader of my first book and a great help at improving both, The Devil's Grin and The Fall. Thank you my dear! Also: You took on the troll and that was amazing!

Cian Goggin, for agreeing to beta-read and loving the almost-final version of it. Lawrence Burdick, Janet Taylor-Perry, and Patti Anne Hauge from TheNextBigWriter - thank you my dears for reading and reviewing those very raw chunks of text.

My parents who helped us restore our old house—thank you! I wouldn't have had the energy to write without your help.

Lee Jackson—thank you for providing so much wonderful information for us Victorian fans.

Many thanks to the lovely people who backed the fund raising campaign for the professional editing of this book: My German publisher Kiepenheuer & Witsch, Le Doktorente (I KNOW WHO YOU ARE DUDE!), Liz Shaw, Ludger Menke, David Pandolfe, Patti Anne Hauge, Anne Steele, Raquel Gabriel, Méloe Jadaud, Leah Guinn, David Graham, Laura Jeffersen, thefabflea, Kathy Enget, Heather Homann, Rita Singer, and several anonymous backers.

To the crowd of individuals and organisations who helped to spread the word for the fund raiser—I'm awed by your support: Sherlockology, The Baker Street Babes, Neil Gaiman, The Stormy Petrels, Crime Fiction Lover, A Simple Taste for Reading, Peter Kavanagh, Luke Benjamen Kuhns, Krimiblog, Deutsche Sherlock Holmes Gesellschaft, Better Holmes and Gardens, Le Boudoir de Méloe, A Scandal in Wordpress, Consulting Writer, Alistair Duncan from The Sherlock Holmes Society London, Dan Andriacco and Ulli Rische.

2nd Edition: Phyl Manning who worked through the 1st edition to eradicate 'em evil punctuation and grammar nits.

3rd Edition: My editors Lutz Dursthoff and Ante Röttgers for their helpful suggestions, and Janis McDermot for a final proof read.

This edition: Tom Welch, ever-patient proofreader of mine: Thank you :)

Made in the USA
San Bernardino, CA
14 February 2018